the UP SIDE OF DOWN

REBECCA TALLEY

the UPSIDE OF DOWN

BONNEVILLE BOOKS

SPRINGVILLE, UTAH

The views expressed within this work are the sole responsibility of the author and do not necessarily reflect the position of Cedar Fort, Inc., or any other entity.

This is a work of fiction. The characters, names, incidents, places, and dialogue are products of the author's imagination, and are not to be construed as real.

ISBN 13: 978-1-59955-454-9
Published by Bonneville Books, an imprint of Cedar Fort, Inc.,
2373 W. 700 S., Springville, UT 84663
Distributed by Cedar Fort, Inc., www.cedarfort.com

LIBRARY OF CONGRESS CATALOGING-IN-PUBLICATION DATA

Talley, Rebecca Cornish.
  The upside of Downs / Rebecca Cornish Talley.
    p. cm.
  ISBN 978-1-59955-454-9
  1. Motherhood--Fiction. 2. Down syndrome--Fiction. 3. Mormon
women--Fiction. I. Title.
  PS3620.A5374U6 2010
  813'.6--dc22

                        2010026019

Cover design by Danie Romrell
Cover design © 2011 by Lyle Mortimer
Edited and typeset by Melissa J. Caldwell

Printed in the United States of America
10 9 8 7 6 5 4 3 2 1

Printed on acid-free paper

To my wonderful and amazing children,
who gave me plenty of fodder for this story.

To my husband, Del,
who is steadfast and immovable in his faith
no matter what trials come our way.

To all of those valiant spirits,
who may struggle with mortal challenges,
but will ultimately gain eternal rewards,
and to those who see beyond the challenges
and realize that each person truly is a child of God.

To my magnificent son, Jared,
who has taught, and will continue to teach me,
far more than I will ever teach him.

SPECIAL THANKS TO

Melissa Caldwell, my editor, who got more than she bargained for with this book, the staff members at CFI who've helped make this book the best it can be, and Heather Moore who took the time to teach me with grace and patience.

Thanks to all of you who will read this book and share its message.

PROLOGUE

Natalie sat with her arms folded and head bowed on the green and gold upholstered chair they'd purchased from Deseret Industries a few weeks earlier. Her husband's hands rested atop her head, and she silently repeated his inspired words.

She focused on a sentence in the blessing: "Soon Heavenly Father will send you a spirit to begin your family, one of many." Spence concluded the blessing, and a soft reassurance wrapped itself around Natalie as the Spirit witnessed the truthfulness of the promised blessings. She drew in a breath and reveled in the peace that filled their one-bedroom apartment near Brigham Young University.

Spence leaned down and kissed her on the cheek. She stood and embraced him. "I feel better now. Thank you."

"We'll have children. We need to be a little more patient," he said in a tender voice. He pushed a wisp of her dark brown hair from her face.

She held the gaze of his pale blue eyes. "I know. I'm eager, that's all. I want to raise a bunch of kids and teach them the gospel. That's all I've ever wanted. Everyone in our ward either has a baby or they're expecting one . . . except us." She brushed a tear from her cheek.

"We don't know Heavenly Father's timetable or His reasons, so we need to have faith it will all work out. I'm confident we'll have the children Heavenly Father intends to send us when the time is right." He ran his fingers along her cheek.

She nodded. "I needed that blessing."

1

Spence smiled and it made her heart skip a beat, the same way it had the first time she had seen him on the dance floor at Ricks College. His reddish-blond hair, strong jaw line, and vibrant smile had caught her eye, and when he'd asked her to dance, she wasn't sure her legs would comply. From that moment, her attraction had grown into a deep and mature love.

Spence broke into her thoughts. "While I was pronouncing the blessing, I saw—"

Natalie cut in, almost afraid to mention what she'd seen. "A baby?"

Spence's eyes widened. "Yes. A girl."

"With big, round blue eyes?" The dazzling color and clarity of the child's eyes stood out in her mind.

Spence nodded. "And blonde hair."

Natalie's skin pricked while a tingling sensation traveled up her spine to the top of her head. "Our first baby?" Joy enveloped her as she imagined holding a baby in her long-empty arms.

"Maybe. I saw her so clearly."

"Did you see any others?"

Spence shook his head. "Only a baby girl."

Natalie's insides warmed at the thought of realizing her dream to be a mother. "She must be coming to our family." Anticipation wound itself around her heart.

That night Natalie lay in bed as other words and phrases from the blessing circled her mind. After two miscarriages and three long years of watching every woman around her give birth, it seemed as though the time was now right for her and the baby she'd seen would soon come to her home. She focused on remembering every detail of the child's face so she would recognize her. Excitement surged through her body. At long last, it would be her turn.

Though she'd recently graduated from BYU with a degree in psychology, she had no interest in pursuing it. She'd finished her degree to appease her parents, but her goal was to start a family. She wanted to raise a righteous brood, hold family home evening each week, have daily family prayer and scripture study, and attend church together—something she hadn't been able to do with her parents. An eternal family was her first, and only, priority.

Her eyelids became heavy. Euphoric images of children running through her home and laughter bouncing off the walls danced across the stage of her mind until she fell asleep.

Chapter
ONE

Natalie grabbed the hands of her two youngest children, five-year-old Mariah and three-year-old Bradley, and walked across the parking lot into the fast food restaurant. After a long morning at the doctor's office for immunizations, she was eager to eat lunch quickly and return home so she could prepare her Primary lesson. She wanted to get through the line without incident.

A young family stood in line ahead of Natalie. "I told you to stay next to your mother," demanded a man who looked only a few years older than Natalie's oldest child, Andrea. His gray eyes almost seared a hole into a little red-haired girl who stepped behind her young mother. Natalie noticed the young girl's physical features—slightly upward slanting eyes and a tongue that seemed too large for her small mouth—and concluded she had Down syndrome.

"Take your mother's hand, right now. I mean it," the man commanded again.

The girl reached up and slipped her hand into her mother's.

Natalie positioned herself between the family and her own children, hoping to shield them from the young man's harsh demeanor. In an attempt to divert her kids' attention, she turned back to Mariah and Bradley and said, "Look outside the window. Do you see that big truck across the street? Isn't it huge?"

"Where?" Mariah stood on her tiptoes to see out the window.

"Make sure she behaves and doesn't embarrass me," the man in front of Natalie said. His wife cast a glance to the floor, and she brushed at her flushed cheeks. A loose ponytail held her mousy brown hair back from her plain face.

"Over there in that parking lot. It's orange," Natalie said to Mariah.

The raw anger of the young man clamped around Natalie's throat. She bit at the nail on her right index finger and avoided looking in the family's direction.

While they waited to order their food, Bradley wrapped himself around Natalie's left leg and Mariah eyed the toys included with each meal. "I want that one," Mariah said, flipping her long dark braid and pointing to a small figure in the display case.

The sizzle of the french fries laced through the heavy air while the scent of cooking hamburger patties stung Natalie's nose. The soda machine hissed as an employee filled paper cups with soda pop. Natalie squinted her eyes to read the small print on the menu above the counter so she could order as soon as she stepped up to the register.

"Stop moving, right now. Do you hear me, or are you too stupid to understand a simple thing like that?" the man in line said to his daughter. Without meaning to, Natalie glanced at him and saw his bright red face.

The little girl froze in place. The mother whispered something to her husband. He countered, "Don't give me any lip. I know what I'm doing. You're as stupid as she is, anyway."

Natalie's heart beat furiously at hearing his cruel words. She pulled at her shoulder-length hair. The man didn't seem to care that he was verbally abusing his daughter. He stepped up to the counter to place his order. Natalie seized the opportunity to soften his callous words. She bent down and said, "You sure are pretty."

"Don't talk to my kid," he barked from the register.

Startled, Natalie stood quickly, fear strangling her voice.

"Leave her alone," he said, his eyes blazing.

"I'm sorry. She looks so frightened."

"Mind your own business. You don't know nothin'."

"But—"

He stepped toward her. "She's retarded. You got a retarded kid?"

Natalie wanted to put this bully in his place, but instead she pulled Mariah and Bradley closer to her, attempting to shelter them with her hands. Other customers in the dining room stopped talking, and she felt their gaze on her. The cashier took a few steps back, her eyes wide.

"Well, you got a retarded kid or not?"

In a barely audible voice, Natalie said, "No."

"Then shut up."

He whipped around and finished placing the order for his family. He instructed his wife where to sit in the dining room.

Natalie's cheeks throbbed. Rage-induced shaking overtook her body. His vicious words hung in the air, reminding her that she did not want to fight with him. Yet she desperately wanted to reach out to this innocent girl and her helpless mother.

"Next?" the cashier's voice rang out, but Natalie, still paralyzed by the confrontation, didn't move.

"Mommy?" Mariah tugged on Natalie's shirt.

Natalie stepped up to the counter.

The cashier, a teenage girl with large brown eyes and a nose piercing, said, "Can I take your order?"

Natalie tried to concentrate on the menu. "I . . . I," she stammered.

"He ain't no kind of dad talkin' like that," the cashier said. Her gaze darted to the table where the family sat.

Natalie cleared her throat. "No. He's not."

"Poor kid. She can't help it."

"I want a cheeseburger. And a toy," Mariah said.

"Toy," Bradley said, his blond curls bobbing up and down with his vigorous nodding.

"I guess we'll have two kids' meals. Cheeseburgers. With Sprite to drink."

"Anything else?"

"I've lost my appetite." Natalie gave a weak smile.

"I don't blame you. He should be ashamed of himself, actin' like that." The cashier rang up the order.

Natalie searched the dining room for an empty table and found one much too close to the young family. They sat down, and Mariah grabbed her cheeseburger. She took a bite and then slurped her soda while Bradley played with the action figure that came with his meal. Natalie was grateful they were both entertaining themselves.

"Eat your lunch," the man said to the little girl in a rough voice.

Then he turned to his wife, "What're you lookin' at?" He paused for a moment. "What? You think I'm proud to have a retard for a daughter? She can't even do nothin' but stare at me with those bug eyes. I'm tellin' you, we shoulda given her to them people when she was born. She ain't ever gonna do nothin'."

Natalie closed her eyes to stop the tears. She couldn't believe anyone could be so nasty about any child, let alone his own, especially one with a handicap. His words cut into her heart, and sadness settled heavily on her shoulders as she considered the little girl's home life.

She wanted to get involved, to protect the little girl and her mother from this raving maniac, but when she accidentally made eye contact with him, a tremor of fear raced down her back. She didn't want to put her own children at risk, so she remained quiet, uttering a silent prayer in the girl's behalf.

"He's mean," Mariah said.

"Shh." Natalie put her finger to her lips.

"But, Mommy, he has mean eyes."

Natalie placed her fingers on Mariah's lips to quiet her. "We'll talk about this later. Okay?" Natalie glanced up to make sure the man hadn't heard Mariah.

He yanked his daughter out of the chair and walked out of the restaurant while the mother followed them, staring at the ground. As the older model pickup truck left the parking lot, Natalie's stomach twisted.

During the twenty-minute drive home from Farmington, New Mexico, to rural La Plata, where they lived, the situation replayed itself in Natalie's mind. How could a father be so heartless? She said a prayer of gratitude that her own husband was a kind and devoted father and that none of her children had been afflicted with Down syndrome, or any other handicap, so they didn't have to encounter such repulsive behavior from others, especially family.

Mariah interrupted her thoughts. "I don't like that mean man."

Natalie nodded. "He wasn't very nice. That's not okay, is it?"

"Nope. He wasn't being like Jesus. He's a bad man."

Natalie paused, remembering her own judgment of the young man. "He's not a bad man, but he was doing something bad. Remember, we're all Heavenly Father's children, but sometimes we make bad choices that hurt other people." She needed to convince herself as much as Mariah. "You're a nice mom."

A tear rolled down Natalie's cheek. "Thank you."

After they arrived at their gray, Victorian-style, two-story house, set back from the highway, Natalie talked Mariah and Bradley into watching a Disney movie. Mariah agreed as long as she could have some popcorn. Natalie glanced at the clock on the wall. She had enough time to study her lesson before the school bus dropped off nine-year-old Justin and sixteen-year-old Laura. She mentally tracked Ryan, her eighth grader, who had soccer practice, and Andrea, a senior in high school, who was staying after school for her student council meeting.

She crept up the stairs to her bedroom and found her sanctuary— the master bathroom. It wasn't always a place of solitude, but she figured that Mariah and Bradley would keep themselves occupied long enough for her to think about her lesson and have a little quiet time. The situation at the restaurant still disturbed her, especially how the young father called his daughter stupid and retarded. *How cruel.*

As she perched on the toilet with her manual spread across her lap, the phone rang. "Let the machine get it," she yelled from the bathroom.

Another ring. "Don't answer the phone! I'm busy right now." She listened for the next ring but only heard a thundering silence. "Oh no," she said aloud.

Before she could do anything, she heard Mariah's voice. "It's okay. She's going potty. I'll get her because she takes a real long time in there. Nope, she won't mind. I'm almost there."

Natalie gulped. It obviously wasn't Spence on the phone. The door slid open slightly, and Mariah's petite hand appeared, grasping the handset. Natalie cleared her throat and grabbed the phone.

"Hello?" she eked out, still hoping for a familiar voice on the other end.

"Sister Drake?"

"Uh, yes?" Her cheeks flushed.

"This is Brother Lakes. Bishop Franken would like to schedule an interview with you and your husband for this evening, if possible."

"I'm sure that'd be fine." She tried not to think of how she'd face Brother Lakes after what Mariah had told him.

"Seven at the church?"

"We'll be there. Thank you."

Natalie hung up the phone, determined to give Mariah a stern lecture, again, about what was and was not appropriate information to share with people on the phone. "Going potty" definitely topped the not-to-be-shared list.

As her embarrassment abated, her thoughts turned to the purpose of the phone call. She'd been teaching the CTR 7 class for less than a year, and she loved being in Primary. She loved the kids' natural curiosity and their willingness to learn. They were like sponges, soaking up everything. Their small but sincere testimonies touched her, and she loved their energy, at least most of the time.

Spence had only been serving as the Scoutmaster for a few months. He was so comfortable with the young men and looked forward to an adventure-filled summer of campouts and hikes.

Maybe it wasn't a new calling for her or Spence after all. Maybe it was about Justin or Mariah acting up in Primary or Bradley's antics in Sunbeams. Perhaps the bishop wanted to visit about Laura's pathetic seminary attendance or Andrea's plans for this summer after graduation. Or maybe he wanted to call Ryan to serve in the teachers quorum presidency.

Natalie's head hurt trying to figure out why the bishop wanted to see them, so she decided to put it out of her mind and not think about it. She needed to concentrate on teaching her Primary class about the Word of Wisdom.

❧

Natalie unlocked the front door to let Spence into the house. He stepped into the entryway, his sandy hair windswept, and Natalie attempted to smooth it back into place. Spence pulled her into a hug and then gently kissed her.

"Daddy!" Mariah squealed. She and Bradley both rushed their father, pushing Natalie out of the way.

Spence embraced Mariah and then picked up a giggling Bradley. "How's my little man?"

Bradley let out a few more giggles. Spence set him down, and he ran off down the hallway.

"Hi, Dad," Justin said when he rounded the corner from the living room. He gave his dad a hug, his light brown hair peeking out from under his Arizona Diamondbacks baseball cap, reminding Natalie he was due for a haircut.

"Something sure smells good. What's for dinner?" Spence said as he and Natalie walked into the kitchen while Justin and Mariah trailed in behind them.

"Lasagna," Natalie said.

"My favorite," he said with the familiar sparkle in his pale blue eyes. He leaned against the beige-tiled countertop in the kitchen.

"Every dinner is your favorite, Daddy," Mariah said. She was wearing a pink tutu and a glittering crown.

"Are you a ballerina today?"

Mariah placed her hands on her hips. "No, Daddy, I'm a princess."

"Oh, I see."

She smiled and turned abruptly, her long braid whipping around her head as she ran off after Bradley.

"Has Ryan fed the animals?" Spence asked.

"He's not home from practice yet, but he should be here in a few minutes. The Kings picked him up tonight. Andrea called and said she'd be home soon too." Natalie opened the oven door to check the lasagna. The blast of hot, garlic-spiked air made her blink. She pulled the lasagna out and set it on top of the stove. "Dinner's almost ready. Time to set the table."

"I think I need another kiss." Spence swept Natalie into his arms and gave her a long kiss.

"Eewww. That's so disgusting," Laura said from the dining room table. "Do you have to do that? I'm trying to do my homework." She shook her head, and her dirty-blonde hair fell around her shoulders.

"You have one hot mama," Spence said. He gave Natalie another squeeze. She enjoyed his playful, romantic side. Even more, she enjoyed Laura's protests.

Laura overacted a dry-heaving motion. "You're so embarrassing. The kids at school don't even act like you two."

"Aren't you glad we love each other so much? You wouldn't be here otherwise." Natalie moved her eyebrows up and down.

"Okay, that's gross. No more details."

"What's gross?" Justin asked, sitting at the table.

Laura rolled her blue-green eyes. "Never mind." She gathered up her books and headed down the stairs to her bedroom.

"Dinner is in five minutes," Natalie called after her.

"How was your day?" Spence asked.

"The doctor's office was incredibly fun, as usual. We waited for a long time. Bradley rolled all over the floor, went through all the drawers, and then climbed up and jumped off the examining table. How such a cherubic-looking child can be so mischievous is beyond me."

"I'm sorry I couldn't help. I had one meeting after another and couldn't get away this morning."

"No worries. Both the kids got their immunizations." Natalie tossed the salad inside a large red bowl. "Why so many meetings?"

"Discussions about some new legislation and how it may impact the company." Spence reached over and grabbed a cookie from the cupboard.

"Should we worry about your job?"

"I don't think so." He snatched another cookie.

Natalie gave him a look. "You can't snack on cookies when dinner's ready. You're as bad as the kids." She turned to Justin, who was still sitting at the table, absorbed in playing his Nintendo DS, an extravagant gift from her mother. "Go wash up for dinner and tell the other kids it's ready."

"Huh?" Justin didn't look up from his game.

"Justin," she said in a loud voice.

"What?"

"I'm going to take that thing away." She took a few steps toward him, intent on taking the handheld device and disposing of it. She disliked Justin's obsession with it, and she was still angry with her mother for giving it to him against her wishes.

"Okay, okay, I'll turn it off." He slipped it into his pocket.

"I better not see it the rest of the night. Now, go wash your hands and tell the other kids that dinner's ready."

Justin scurried out of the room.

"How was the rest of your day?" Spence asked.

"I took Bradley and Mariah to lunch and witnessed a disturbing scene that hasn't left me. A young man treated his wife and his little daughter with such contempt. He was downright mean to them."

"What happened?"

Natalie grabbed some bottles of salad dressing from the refrigerator. "His little girl had Down syndrome, and he was calling her names. It broke my heart. His poor wife seemed so scared." She placed the bottles on the counter.

"Did you say anything?"

Natalie nodded. "He told me it was none of my business, among other things." Reliving the experience brought back the fear she'd experienced at the restaurant. "I can't seem to get it out of my head. I don't know why it's affected me so much."

"Because you're a compassionate and caring person. That's one of the reasons why I love you so much." Spence ran his finger along her cheek.

"Even after all these years? With all of my gray hairs?"

"What gray?"

"If I didn't pluck them all out, there'd be plenty."

"You're as beautiful today as you were twenty-three years ago."

Beautiful wasn't how she'd describe herself. Exhausted, bedraggled, wrinkly, frumpy—those were much more descriptive terms. "I think you need your eyes checked."

"You are. And I love you." He squeezed her around the waist.

"I love you too."

The front door opened, and Natalie's tall, lean son, Ryan, walked into the kitchen. He dropped his backpack with a thud. "Yes! I love lasagna."

"Hurry and wash your hands for dinner," Natalie said.

Ryan returned from the bathroom, and the rest of the kids filed into the dining room. After the usual argument of who would sit next to Natalie, Bradley said the blessing, as he did for nearly every meal. Everyone began eating.

"How was soccer today, Ryan?" Spence asked.

"Good. Coach says I'll probably be a starter for the next game." He piled lasagna on his plate and then reached for a piece of garlic bread.

"You'll need to feed the animals after dinner. Be sure to take the slop out to the pigs and check on the horses' water," Spence said.

The front door flew open. Andrea shouted from the entryway, "Sorry I'm late. I had to stay longer than I thought. Mmmm, smells de-lish."

Andrea found her seat at the table.

"How was school?" Natalie asked.

"Interesting," Andrea said.

"Must be about that guy," Laura said with a smirk that exposed her braces.

Andrea's blue-gray eyes lit up, and a smile appeared her face.

"What's this?" Natalie asked.

"His name is Tristan. He's Ali's cousin. He's living with them until he finds an apartment, and he's going to San Juan College," Andrea said.

"Ali who?"

"We're on student council together. I've talked about her before." Andrea flipped her long auburn hair behind her shoulder.

"What about this boy?" Spence asked.

"Dark, thick hair and green eyes. He's from Grants, and he's almost twenty-one. I wish he'd ask me out," Andrea said.

"Is he a member of the Church?" Natalie handed the bowl of salad to Justin.

"No, but there's no one to date from our ward. It'd only be for fun. Stop worrying. I'm sure he'll never ask me out, anyway."

After dinner, according to the job chart, Laura cleared the table, Justin unloaded and reloaded the dishwasher, and Ryan wiped down the table.

Natalie grabbed hold of Bradley. "I think you wore more of your dinner than anything. How about a bath?"

Natalie and Bradley ascended the stairs together, one step at a time. They walked into the bathroom, and Natalie laid Bradley on the dark green bathroom rug to remove his diaper. "Remember, potty in the diaper? No, no." Natalie shook her head. "Potty in the toilet? Yes, yes." She nodded. "Let's make a deal. I'll pay you one million dollars if you potty train. How does that sound?"

Bradley nodded, his blond waves bobbing. "Potty in toilet."

"That's right." Natalie finished filling the tub and was placing

Bradley in the mound of bubbles when the phone rang.

A few moments later, Laura stood in the doorway holding the handset. "Mom, it's for you."

Natalie whispered, "I'm a little busy right now." She pointed to Bradley, who was draped in suds. "Who is it?"

Laura shrugged. "It's a man."

"Fine." Natalie wiped her hands on her well-worn black sweats and grabbed the phone.

"Sister Drake?" Her stomach tightened.

"Bishop, I'm so sorry. I completely forgot. We're on our way, but it'll take us at least twenty-five minutes."

"I have another interview I can take care of. I'll see you in a bit," the bishop said.

Natalie hung up the phone. "Laura!" she yelled from the bathroom.

"Yeah?"

"Please finish bathing Bradley," Natalie said.

Laura stood in the doorway of the bathroom, a large textbook in hand. "I have a ton of homework."

"I need your help. I have to go to the church." Natalie mentally chastised herself for being so forgetful.

"Why?"

"I'm not exactly sure. But I'm late. Where's your dad?"

Laura shrugged. She placed her book on the floor, bent over the bathtub, and patted Bradley on the head. "I'll wash your hair, okay?"

Natalie raced down the hall. She peeked into each bedroom as she passed. "Spence?" No response.

She spotted Mariah in her bedroom. "Can you find Daddy and tell him I need him right away."

"Okay." Mariah ran away calling for Spence.

Natalie yanked a black skirt and bright pink blouse out of her closet. "I cannot believe I did this."

Spence entered the bedroom. "What's wrong?"

"We have an appointment with the bishop." Natalie glanced at the clock radio on the nightstand. "About twenty minutes ago."

"Huh?"

"Brother Lakes called earlier and made the appointment. I got so busy with dinner and bathing Bradley that it slipped my mind." Natalie's fingers fumbled as she tried to button her blouse. "Bishop Franken is waiting for us."

Spence stepped over to his closet and grabbed a white shirt. "Did he say what it's about?"

"I have no idea. I'm so embarrassed." She finished buttoning her blouse.

During the ride into Farmington, Natalie tossed the reasons through her mind of why they were meeting with the bishop. "Do you know anything?"

Spence shook his head. "I'd guess it's for a new calling."

"But both of us have only had our callings for a short time."

"What else could it be?"

"I don't know." Natalie applied some mascara and brushed her hair. "I can't believe I forgot about this appointment. I'm so spacey lately."

Spence gave a big smile. "Do I have anything in my teeth?"

"Nope. Perfect as usual. Though you still have some unruly hair in the back." She patted down a clump of his hair.

They pulled into the church parking lot. Natalie checked her hair one more time and fluffed it before exiting the car. She hoped the appointment would be short and simple so she could get back home and put the kids to bed.

Inside the foyer of the building, the bishop, a short man with round glasses, stood at the top of the stairs just outside his office.

Natalie gazed up at the bishop and said, "I'm so sorry we're late." The embarrassment rose to her cheeks.

"No problem. I finished my other interview and had a bit of paper work. Brother Drake, may I have a word with you first? Sister Drake, we'll only be a moment."

Natalie sat on the upholstered couch at the foot of the stairs. The soft fluorescent lighting bounced off the cream-colored walls. Plum-colored carpet lined the entryway and the stairs leading down to the family history library. Her Primary classroom was across the cultural hall. She tried to imagine the large three-level building as the stake center many years ago when the stake included wards in New Mexico and Colorado. Now it housed three wards in Farmington, New Mexico, one of which included her rural La Plata ward.

Natalie bit at her fingernail, a nasty habit she'd picked up as a kid. Who could blame her after growing up with *her* mother? She placed her hands on her lap and laced them together. What was the bishop discussing with Spence? A calling? For him? Her?

Time dragged on while she waited. She checked her watch. A queasy feeling tempted her to bite her nails again, but she resisted.

She checked her watch again. *How long could this take?* Finally, after a few more minutes that felt like hours, the door opened, and Bishop Franken invited Natalie into the office. Natalie sat in a chair opposite the bishop's desk. She glanced at Spence to see if she could read his expression. He gave her a reassuring smile.

"How are you doing this evening, Sister Drake?" the bishop asked, drawing her focus to him.

"A little frazzled, but okay." A nervous laugh fell out of her mouth while her heart thudded.

"I've spoken with your husband. I'd like to extend a call to you."

"Me?" *No wonder Spence was smiling.* She looked back at Bishop Franken. "But I've only been teaching my Primary class for a few months."

"I know," the bishop said, his eyes piercing. "But we, as a bishopric, have prayed, and the Lord would like you to serve as Relief Society president."

She stared at the bishop's dark brown eyes. "Come again?" *Relief Society president? He must be insane.*

"I'd like to extend a call to you to serve as the Relief Society president." He leaned forward, looking deeply into her eyes.

"Are you sure?" she whispered.

"Yes."

Natalie sat back against the chair, her hands damp. She let out a sigh and looked over at Spence. Her eyes pleaded with him to object, but his face radiated delight.

"I've never served in the Relief Society." She paused while both men stared at her. "I don't know what happens in there. I—I can't even remember the last time I attended. I've only served in Young Women and Primary since I got married." *Surely this would convince the bishop that he had the wrong woman.*

The bishop didn't retract the call. In a soft but firm voice he asked,

"Sister Drake, would you accept this calling from the Lord?"

Natalie drew in a long, deep breath. Relying on her desire to do the right thing, she said quietly, "If that's where the Lord would like me to serve, then . . . yes." Her eyes stung with emotion. "I will accept the calling." She could hardly believe the words as they escaped her mouth.

Spence's eyes glistened as he reached over and squeezed her hand.

"Thank you," the bishop said.

She gave a faint smile, feeling like her face might crumble. "You're absolutely sure?" Natalie asked, knowing the answer but still in a state of disbelief.

"Yes. We all had a strong witness that you should serve in this calling." He studied her for a moment. "The sisters in the ward need you."

Her eyes widened. "They need *me*?" Natalie repeated the words in her mind, clutching onto Spence's hand.

"Yes," the bishop said.

She raised her eyebrows, her throat suddenly thick. "I'll take your word for it."

Her mind spun in a thousand different directions, trying to absorb the implications of her new calling. "Your husband has agreed to support you. It will be busy and intense at times, but the Lord will bless you as you dedicate yourself to Him."

Spence nodded. Natalie reluctantly let go of Spence's hand when the bishop extended his hand to shake hers. He shook hands with Spence and then turned back to Natalie. "We'll set up some training for you. You'll need to pray about the sisters in the ward and submit names for your presidency. We'd like to sustain you a week from Sunday."

Natalie stood and numbly followed Spence out the door and into the late-winter evening, cold air licking at her cheeks. Sitting in the car, she stared ahead of her, lost in her thoughts. Her head pounded with so much pressure it felt like it might explode.

Chapter
TWO

Natalie listened to the purring engine as they left town and headed north on the La Plata Highway.

"What are you thinking?" Spence asked, his eyes full of concern. He reached for her hand.

"That Bishop Franken is crazy. I'm not at all Relief Society-ish. I'm Primary through and through. Maybe Young Women here and there, but definitely not Relief Society. I don't think I can do this."

"Why not?"

"Because," Natalie held up her hand and extended her index finger, "number one, I don't can. I never have. My mother, of course, didn't can. I didn't even know that you used jars to can until I moved out to La Plata. Number two, I can't grow a garden because I have the blackest thumb ever. If it weren't for you, there wouldn't be any garden produce at all."

"That's not true. You helped decide what to plant. That's an important job."

She shot him a look, and he gave her one of his teasing grins.

"Number three, and this is the most important prerequisite to serve as Relief Society president, I don't quilt. I've never, ever made a quilt. I thought when women talked about batting they were referring to baseball, not quilting. How on earth can I serve in an organization where the women have been quilting from birth?"

"I—"

"And, don't forget, I'm not very compassionate, either. You're the one who looks for things to do for other people. You're always doing service for our neighbors or members of the ward. Not me. I never think of anyone outside of you or the kids. I live in my own little world . . . and I like it that way."

"Now—"

"I don't see how I can do this calling. Bradley is constantly sucking the energy out of me and when he's done, Mariah is there for the leftovers. And trying to keep track of the other four kids is mind-boggling. How can I be a good mom and a good Relief Society president? I know lots of women can balance callings and raising a family, but I'm not one of them." She stopped to take a breath.

"Can I say something? Anything?" Spence patted Natalie's hand.

"I guess, but I'm not sure you can say anything that will change my mind. Bishop Franken probably hasn't thought it through."

"Think about what you're saying," Spence said.

"I'm saying I can't handle this calling and raising our kids too. Besides, I'm not fit to be a Relief Society president, especially compared to Sister Crocker. She's always out helping the sisters and making dinners. And she's so spiritual. I need to call the bishop when I get home and tell him I've reconsidered and I can't do it."

"Are you sure you want to do that?"

Natalie nodded, though her stomach tried to squeeze out her conviction.

"Do you believe in God?"

Natalie jerked her head up. "Of course, I do. I always have, even before I knew about the Church. What does that have to do with anything?"

"If you believe that Heavenly Father established His church through Joseph Smith, then you must believe this calling came from Him." Spence paused for a few seconds. "Do you?" He glanced at her.

Natalie contemplated Spence's penetrating question.

"Do you think the bishop makes these assignments as he pleases?"

"No." She dropped her gaze to her hands.

"If you believe in God and that He extends callings through the bishop, then wouldn't it make sense that you would be able to fulfill a calling from God?"

His words pricked her heart.

A few moments passed. "Do you believe that Heavenly Father is aware of each of His children?"

She gave a slight nod, her lips beginning to tremble.

"Would He call you to do something that you couldn't do?"

She tried to protest, but she knew he spoke the truth. Serenity encompassed her, immersing her in the sweetness of the Spirit.

"Heavenly Father knows our talents, our weaknesses, our strengths. He knows what we can handle. If He has called you to serve as Relief Society president it's because you are the one who can not only handle it, but also needs to serve for a specific reason."

A tear trickled down Natalie's cheek.

"Heavenly Father can magnify all of us in whatever He calls us to do if we put our trust and faith in Him." Spence reached over and brushed the back of his fingers along her jawline.

"You're so good at accepting things and moving forward without hesitation. I need explanations. I need to understand everything. It has to make sense to me because I'm a Laman. A Lemuel. You're a Nephi. You have so much more faith than I do." She cast a sideways glance at him.

He shook his head slightly. "Not true. You're a woman of great faith, and I know you can fulfill this calling."

Natalie took a deep breath. She grabbed a tissue from her purse and wiped her nose. "I feel so overwhelmed. How can I serve sisters who know so much more than I do?"

"Don't let Satan discourage you."

She closed her eyes. Her shortcomings and faults marched in full force across her mind, followed by a dark, hollow feeling. She brought her hands to her face. She felt so incapable, yet she knew Spence was right. She couldn't let Satan win. She had to push the doubts, and Satan, out of her head and focus on the Lord, on the light. With His help, she could overcome her weaknesses.

Seeming to sense her internal struggles, Spence squeezed her knee and asked, "Would you like a blessing when we get home?"

Relief and gratitude encircled her. She removed her hands from her face and turned to Spence. "Yes. That's exactly what I need."

Spence smiled and kept his hand on her knee the rest of the way home.

Natalie wanted to savor the peaceful feeling as she and Spence entered the kitchen from the garage. Immediately, Mariah and Bradley rushed past her, screeching, as they ran into the living room.

"You can't catch me!" Mariah shouted.

Natalie stepped farther into the kitchen. A layer of white powder covered the counters and floor, exposing little footprints. "What's this?" she said in a loud voice.

"Looks like flour," Spence said.

"Again? I swept up flour yesterday. How can these kids make such a mess?" Natalie gave a heavy sigh. "Where are Laura and Andrea? I asked them to watch Mariah and Bradley."

The two little kids made another pass, and flour floated through the air.

Natalie bent down and gathered up some small pieces of paper. "Mariah's been cutting things up again. I hope it wasn't Laura's homework this time." She pursed her lips, vowing to hide all scissors as soon as she found them.

"Get off, Laura. You've been on the computer all night," Ryan's voice carried from the family room into the kitchen.

"Stop bugging me. I'll get off when I'm done," Laura said.

"You're not even doing homework," Ryan said. "You're on Facebook."

"What I'm doing is none of your business," Laura said, her voice booming.

"I'm so tired of these kids arguing over the computer. I think we should get rid of it." Natalie started in the direction of the family room, determined to punish both kids.

Spence stepped in front of her. "I'll take care of it."

She glanced over at the clock. "It's bedtime, and we still need to read scriptures and have family prayers. Let's gather everyone, so we can get it over with."

Spence gave her a look.

"That's not what I meant."

Bradley ran into Natalie and grabbed her leg. His toxic scent hit her nose like a fist. "I can tell someone needs a new diaper." Natalie scooped him up.

Bradley nodded with a broad smile on his face.

"Mom, we're playing," Mariah said as she ran past.

"What happened here?" Natalie pointed to the white floor.

Mariah sucked in her lips, and her eyes grew wide.

"What did I say yesterday when you two spilled the flour?"

Mariah shrugged.

"Go find the dustpan. You get to help me clean it up this time."

After the usual bedtime routine, Natalie followed Justin, Mariah, and Bradley upstairs to make sure they brushed and flossed their teeth. She entered the bathroom to find an entire roll of toilet paper stuffed into the toilet.

"Who did this?" she said with a hand on her hip.

"Not me," Bradley said, his blue eyes full of mischief.

"Bradley did it. I told him no, but he did it anyway. And..." Mariah paused. She yanked a brush out of the drawer and began brushing her long, dark hair.

"What?" Natalie asked.

"He put his car in there too," Mariah said.

"Anything else?"

"Daddy's comb."

Natalie rubbed her eyes. "I can't believe you did all of this while I was gone." Aggravation crept up her back.

"Where did you go, Mom?" Justin asked.

"To the church."

"Why?"

"To talk to the bishop."

Justin placed his toothbrush in the holder and then ran his fingers through his light brown hair, spiking it in the front. "Can I wear my hair like this tomorrow?" He grinned, exposing the gaps between his front teeth.

Natalie shook her head. "Definitely time for a haircut."

"No. I like it long." He admired himself in the mirror.

Natalie reached down and pulled the soggy roll of paper from the toilet. She grabbed the car and the comb. "At least it wasn't used toilet water. Thank goodness for little blessings," Natalie whispered to herself.

She gave Justin and Mariah a kiss good night and then placed

Bradley, amid his shouts of protest, into the crib.

She walked into her bedroom. It resembled the aftermath of a tornado. Barbies, books, the pink tutu, and Mariah's makeup set littered the bed. Matchbox cars lined the floor while crumbs were scattered across the carpet. Spence's dirty clothes, the pile she'd asked him at least ten times to put in the hamper, were spread across the room. No doubt Mariah and Bradley had played dress-up with Daddy's clothes while she'd been gone. *Did she live with humans or pigs?*

She shook her head and pushed Mariah's junk onto the floor. She then fell, face first, onto the bed and lay there, paralyzed, for several minutes until Spence entered. "Andrea is finishing up some homework, and I talked to Laura and Ryan about following the rules with the computers. Except for homework, I grounded them both from the computer through the weekend."

Natalie rolled to her back and stared at the ceiling. "How can I possibly keep the women of the ward together when I'm already failing in my own home?"

"Mom," Mariah whined as she ran into the room, clutching her lavender fleece blanket.

Without looking at her, Natalie asked, "What is it?"

"I had a nightmare."

Natalie rolled to her side to face her imaginative daughter. "How could you have had a nightmare when you haven't even been asleep?"

Mariah tapped her mouth. Peering out under her dark lashes, she said, "I was almost asleep."

"Mariah, you need to get in your bed." Her voice was firm, resolute.

"Can I sleep in here? With you and Daddy? Please?" She kissed Natalie on the hand.

"Big girls sleep in their own beds."

Mariah paused. "I thought about it, and I don't want to be a big girl anymore."

Too tired to argue, Natalie said, "If you can be very quiet and go right to sleep you can lie on the chair. But you can't say a word."

Mariah's face lit up with a smile. She nodded but said nothing while she climbed up on the navy blue recliner by the bed.

Spence sat on the bed next to Natalie. He caressed her shoulder. "Would you like a blessing now?"

She glanced over at Mariah. "Can you be reverent while Daddy gives me a blessing?"

Mariah nodded. She folded her little arms and bowed her head.

Natalie sat up on the edge of the bed. She drew in a deep cleansing breath and then exhaled, letting go of her irritation with the kids. She concentrated on clearing her mind of any negative thoughts so she could be receptive to the Spirit. "Yes. I'm ready now."

Spence placed his hands on her head and offered a blessing of comfort. The warm reassurance of the Spirit washed over Natalie and testified, once again, that she was indeed called to this position by the Lord and that He would support and strengthen her. Spence also blessed her that through her trials she would find great strength if she would turn to the Lord.

After the blessing, Natalie stood and Spence embraced her. She melted into his arms, allowing the peace to surround them.

She pulled back and met Spence's tender gaze. "More trials? Sounds like I may need to schedule regular blessings."

Chapter

THREE

With Justin, Ryan, Laura, and Andrea on the school bus, Spence on his way to work, and Mariah and Bradley still sleeping, Natalie sat on her bed and quietly pondered the blessing from the night before. She opened the Book of Mormon and read 1 Nephi 3:7. The Lord commanded Nephi to do something difficult, and Nephi had faith that the Lord would give him the ability to do what he'd been asked to do. *Wouldn't He do the same for me?*

She closed her eyes, hoping to have some alone time to consider counselors.

"Mom?" Mariah said, catching Natalie off guard.

"You're up early this morning."

"What're you doing?" Mariah yawned and then climbed up on the bed.

"Thinking."

"About what?"

"Lots of stuff." Natalie gave Mariah a squeeze. "How about some breakfast?"

Natalie held Mariah's small hand as they descended the stairs to the kitchen. Natalie cooked scrambled eggs and toasted a bagel. She placed the plate in front of Mariah, who said the blessing. A few minutes later, Bradley wailed from his crib, so Natalie got him up, dressed him, brought him to the table, and scrambled an egg for him.

Bradley rubbed his eyes and yawned, his curls flattened on one side.

Natalie poured a tiny amount of orange juice into a cup and handed it to him. He slurped the juice and then poked his fork into the eggs. Natalie looked over at Mariah, who had a bit of egg perched on the corner of her mouth. "After breakfast, you can play for a bit, okay?"

"Do you have more thinking to do?" Mariah licked the egg into her mouth.

"I'm afraid so." Natalie's mind wandered back to the ominous task of finding counselors to serve with her. *Why don't the names pop into my head?*

Both kids finished their breakfast and roamed into the family room while Natalie loaded the dishwasher. While she was considering different sisters in the ward, the phone rang, jolting her out of her thoughts. She recognized the number on her caller ID.

"Hi, honey," Natalie said.

"Hey, Foxy Mama."

"Yep, that's me." She glanced down at her faded pink T-shirt and grubby sweats and ran her fingers through her unbrushed hair.

Mariah rushed into the room. "Mom. Mom. Mommy."

"Hang on. Mariah's having a meltdown." She took the phone from her ear. "What is it?"

"Bradley took my favorite Barbie, and he won't give it back. No matter what."

"Try to work it out with him. I'm on the phone with Daddy."

Mariah pouted and plodded away.

"I think she'll survive," Natalie said into the phone.

"Are you feeling a little better about your new calling?"

"Mom," came a screech from the family room.

"Hang on again." Natalie lowered the handset and said in a loud voice, "What's the problem, Bradley?"

"Mariah a meanie."

"Can the two of you find something quiet to do together? Please?" Natalie returned to the call. "The natives are restless this morning. They both woke earlier than usual. I think they knew I needed alone time to consider counselors, so they got up to torture me."

"But they're both so cute."

"Uh-huh."

"I hope you have a nice day and that you find some time to think about who should serve with you."

"Me too. I'm feeling a little sick, probably the same stomach flu that Laura and Justin had last week. I love it when we pass all the sicknesses around, especially when I get to participate. But I'm sure I'll find time to think about things *sometime* today."

"I love you. And I think you're a wonderful wife and mom. You'll do well in this calling. I'm sure of it."

"I'm glad someone is. At least Mariah and Bradley have stopped fighting. That's something."

"I'll be home at about 5:30 tonight. I love you."

"Love you too."

Natalie hung up and enjoyed the momentary quiet. She wanted the kids to play together without any problems so she could contemplate some names. They usually played well together, except, of course, when she was on the phone.

She poured a glass of water and drank it. She walked from the kitchen to the living room and froze. At her feet was a pile of dark brown hair. A few more steps and another pile of hair. Natalie's stomach churned, and a throbbing began in her temples.

"Mariah? Bradley? Where are you?"

No answer.

Natalie checked the bathroom downstairs and found no one. She took the steps two at a time and ran into her bedroom. "Are you two in my bathroom?" She heard a thud in the shower and rushed in, opening the shower door. She bit her lip and silently counted to ten.

Mariah and Bradley stood in the shower together with cut hair strewn about them. Mariah's hair was cut to her scalp in the front. One side had a chunk of hair missing a few inches from the top of her head, while the other side hung unevenly around her face.

"What have you done?"

"I showed Bradley how to give me a haircut, Mommy. We played beauty shop together, like you said."

"Turn around," she said through clenched teeth.

Natalie covered her mouth as she viewed a large piece of hair in the back of Mariah's head that was only an inch long. "I can't believe this." Natalie shook her head. "I don't even know what to do."

"Pretty," Bradley said.

"How did you get scissors?" Natalie asked.

"Laura's room."

Rubbing her chin, Natalie said, "I need chocolate."

"What's wrong, Mommy?" Mariah asked.

"Lots of chocolate."

"Why?"

"We finally grew out your hair and it was so nice, and now it's . . ."

"Pretty," Bradley said.

Natalie tapped her face with her fingers. "Let's go downstairs and see if we can fix this."

After her best effort in styling Mariah's hair, Natalie sent both children to their rooms to think about their actions.

Natalie entered the laundry room and opened the dryer. At least the wash would be uneventful. She pulled out a T-shirt with a strange green stain. "What's this?" She grabbed a towel with the same kind of stain. Article after article of clothing, she noticed the same green color until she found a pair of pants with the largest stain yet. She shut her eyes and said, "Crayon." She opened her eyes. "How can such a small thing cause so much damage?" She placed all of the ruined items into a plastic bag and set them aside until she could figure out a solution.

She opened the washer and carefully inspected each article to make sure it was crayon-free before placing it in the dryer. "I don't know what to do with these kids. They're out of control," she said to herself.

She sorted through the five laundry baskets to wash a load of whites. "The commandment in Genesis must also apply to laundry because it definitely multiplies and replenishes the earth, especially when my back is turned." She checked each pocket and looked in every possible place for other stowaway items.

On her way to the kitchen, she wished the cleaning fairies had visited. *No such luck.* She surveyed the counters littered with dishes. "How can there be so many dishes?" The sink was full of red-hued water from the lasagna she'd made the night before and had bits of cereal floating around the edges. She stuck her hand in the water and sunk her fingers into soggy bread. She covered her mouth with her other hand as she dry heaved. While she cleaned the sink, she tried to concentrate on the women in the ward, hoping a few names would pop into her mind.

A knock sounded. Natalie wiped her hands and walked to the front door. She could see flashing lights through the front windows.

Her heart raced. Fear squeezed her chest. Flashes of one of her children, or Spence, in some kind of accident, flooded her mind.

She opened the door to two sheriff's deputies with solemn looks. Her heartbeat thundered in her ears. "What's wrong?" she choked out.

"We're responding to the phone call from your landline," said one of the officers. He was tall and thin and had a sparse moustache.

"Excuse me?"

The other officer, with blond hair and rosy cheeks, said, "We received a 911 call from your residence, and we've been dispatched to help."

Natalie's face flushed. "A 911 call?"

"Is there an emergency, ma'am?" the first officer asked.

Natalie cleared her throat. "Uh, no." Confused, she added, "I don't know what's going on."

"Do you have small children, ma'am?" the second officer asked.

Those two have been way too quiet. "Yes, I do." Natalie turned and said in a loud voice, "Mariah? Bradley?" She turned back to the officers. "I'm so sorry. My kids must have called you. I don't know what to say."

Mariah and Bradley trotted into the entryway. "Hi, Mom," Mariah said.

"Have you been on the phone?" Natalie asked in a firm voice.

Mariah looked at Bradley and then at Natalie.

"Did you call someone, Mariah?" Natalie bent down to look her in the eye.

"I saw it on TV. A little girl called 911 to save her mom. I showed Bradley." Mariah grinned, pleased with herself.

With a stern look, the tall officer said to Mariah, "Look, 911 is only for emergencies. We drove all the way out here because we thought you were in trouble."

"There might be someone who's in real trouble, but we can't help because we had to come to your house," the officer with blond hair added.

"Oh." Mariah's smile disappeared.

"You need to apologize, Mariah. It was wrong for you to call 911 when there's not an emergency," Natalie said.

"Sorry," Mariah said.

"Sowwy," Bradley said.

"Please teach your children when it's proper to call 911, ma'am," the tall officer said.

"We'll have a long talk, believe me. Again, I'm sorry." A cloak of embarrassment covered her.

The officers returned to their vehicle, and Natalie closed the door. "I cannot believe you did this, Mariah. I've told you not to play on my cell phone or the house phone."

"But the girl saved her mommy."

"Am I hurt?" Embarrassment gave way to anger.

Mariah shook her head.

"You should never call 911 unless someone is hurt or trying to hurt you. Do you understand?"

"Uh-huh."

"I'm going to take you to your room, and this time I want you to stay there for a long time. No more phone calls. When Daddy gets home, we'll have a talk."

Natalie inspected Mariah's bedroom and found the handset under the bed. She grabbed it and left Mariah sitting on her bed. She escorted Bradley to his room and placed him in his crib. "I want you to sit here for a time out. You did a bad thing. No phone," she said in a serious voice.

Bradley's bottom lip pooched out, and his eyes filled with tears. Natalie refused to let it affect her. She closed his door. His whimpers turned into full-fledged crying before she reached her bedroom door.

She entered her bedroom and collapsed on the bed. She lay there for a few minutes with thoughts of renegade children, the ever-growing mountain of laundry, and a house that never seemed clean tumbling inside her head. How would she ever attend to the needs of the sisters in the ward, when she felt so overwhelmed with her own life?

Unable to even find time to pray without interruption, she was certain she'd never discover the names of who should serve with her in the midst of her chaotic life. She rolled to her side, searching for the reasons that she'd been called to serve in Relief Society when there were so many other much more capable women.

The phone rang. The day couldn't get any worse, could it? She glanced at the caller ID.

Yep, it could get worse.

Chapter
FOUR

"Hi, Mom." Natalie massaged her forehead, attempting to prevent the headache that usually followed her mother's phone calls, especially when it involved her mother's favorite pastime—criticizing her.

"You sound winded. Is something wrong? Are those kids running you ragged again? You need to teach them to be better behaved. You let them walk all over you," Carma said in her standard disapproving tone.

Natalie clenched her jaw. "Nothing is wrong. How are you?" She tried to keep her defenses at bay. She absently brought her index finger to her mouth and started chewing the tip of her fingernail.

"I have some fabulous news." The sound of her mother's voice always frayed her nerves.

"You do?" Whatever the news was, she hoped it had nothing to do with her. She loved her mom, but every conversation or encounter took so much energy. It exhausted her.

"Yes. It's very exciting."

"Okay, what is it?" Natalie laid her head back and stared at the ceiling, bracing herself since she and her mom rarely agreed on anything, even what constituted good news.

"I've sold the house."

Natalie snapped her head up, sure she'd heard her mom wrong because selling their family home, the one she'd grown up in, could never pass as *fabulous* news. "You've what?"

"Isn't it unbelievable, especially with this economy?" Her mom sounded gleeful.

A sickly sensation tickled Natalie's stomach, and she fought the tears forming behind her eyes.

"You know, ever since your father passed, I've been trying to figure out what to do. This house reminds me so much of him, and it's too large for only one person."

"But I grew up there. I don't even know what to say." Sadness welled up at the thought of losing the memories of her dad in that house—the times they'd worked on school projects together, when they painted the fence together, and when they'd camped out in the backyard, under the stars, together.

"I've been toying with the idea for some time."

"You have?" The thought had never occurred to Natalie. "Why didn't you say anything before?"

Carma hesitated. "I didn't want to upset you."

"Upset me?" *Devastate* was a far better word.

"I think this is the best thing. I only had the house listed for a week, and a buyer offered my full asking price. The housing market in Mesa isn't doing well, but my house sold." She could hear the excitement in her mom's words.

"I—I can't believe you sold our house. *Our* house." The words skittered around her tongue.

"I haven't told you the best part."

The best part? Natalie shook her head, searching for anything that could be termed as *good* about this decision, but nothing came to mind. She eyed her ring finger, ready to chew another nail. "What?"

"I've decided to move to Farmington."

"Farmington?" Natalie's mouth dropped open, and her head started pounding, signaling another mother-induced migraine.

"Yes."

"Why?" She tried to collect her thoughts amid the potpourri of emotions that raged inside her. Shock, anger, resentment, and fear all whirled around her head.

In a patronizing tone, her mother said, "To be closer to you, of course. You are my only child."

"I know, but—"

"Though you have far too many children, they are my grandchildren, and I'd like to be closer to them." Her mother never failed to seize an opportunity to condemn her family size.

"You would?"

"Don't be so critical, Natalie. I want to spend more time with my grandchildren. Is that so bad?" The condescension oozed through the phone.

Natalie blinked her eyes, astonishment still fluttering through her mind. "No. You've never wanted to before, that's all."

"A lot has changed."

Natalie pulled the handset from her ear and stared at it. *It has?*

"Hello? Natalie, are you there?"

"Still here." *Barely. Wasn't her mom too old to have a midlife crisis?*

"Why aren't you saying anything?"

"I don't know what to say. You've sold our family home and are moving to Farmington. It's a lot to take in, Mom." *Make that a thousand times a lot.*

"I thought it'd be fun to go house hunting next weekend."

"Okay," Natalie said with trepidation. Not only did she not want to leave her family and spend time in town looking at houses, she couldn't imagine spending that much time with her mother without starting World War III.

"I'll fly up, and we can spend the weekend together looking at houses." She paused for a moment. "Sunday is the best day for open houses."

She could always count on her mom casting aspersions on her lifestyle. "You know we go to church on Sunday."

"I know, dear, but not all day. You attend church in Farmington, right?"

"Yes." Natalie knew where her mother was headed.

"Mom." Mariah's voice carried into the bedroom. "Mommy, come here."

She heard Bradley banging his crib against the wall.

Unable to deal with Mariah or Bradley, Natalie shut her bedroom door so she could finish the conversation with her mother in private.

"We can go to the open houses after you get done with church. Oh, and invite Andrea and Laura as well. We can go out to lunch, stop at the mall, and make it a real girls' day." Even after twenty-four years, her mother refused to accept Natalie's choice to live the gospel.

"Mom, I've explained over and over and over again what we do on Sundays. House hunting, going out to lunch, and shopping at the mall are not things we do." Her mother knew better, but she still needled Natalie about her beliefs every chance she got.

"Don't be so narrow-minded." Her mom clucked her tongue. "Certainly you can take time off from being a Mormon long enough to help your mother find a house."

Natalie swallowed back the angry words forming in her throat. "You do this to me all the time."

"I don't know what you're talking about."

Carma always acted so innocent, as if her words weren't carefully designed weapons meant to penetrate Natalie's armor. "Try to make me feel guilty about the Church."

"Oh, Natalie." Her mom sighed. "You're so dramatic. I've come to terms with the fact that you want to spend your life with a cult. I don't like it, never have, but I've learned to live with it. But it doesn't have to ruin our fun, does it?"

Natalie pursed her lips. She drew in a long breath through her nose and silently counted to ten while she exhaled. "We can look for houses on Saturday."

"That won't be enough time. I'll take Andrea and Laura with me on Sunday if you refuse to go."

Shaking her head, Natalie said, "I'm sorry, Mom, but they won't be able to do that." She brought her hand to her forehead.

"I suppose you're raising all of your children to think the same way you do?" A familiar barb.

"I'm not having this argument again." She ate any harsh words before they could escape her lips.

"In any case, I'll fly up Friday afternoon and return home on Monday morning. It is okay for me to stay with you, isn't it?" Her mom was a master at wrapping pleasantness around condescension.

"Yes, Mom, that will be fine."

"I'll rent a car at the airport. How far is Farmington from your little farm?"

Natalie silently screamed. "About twenty miles or so."

"That's perfect. I'm sure I can find a nice, smaller home in Farmington, and then we can spend more time together."

"Sounds great." Natalie hoped her sarcasm wasn't obvious.

"I'll see you next weekend then. Bye."

Natalie hung up the phone and tossed the handset on the bed. She reached up and pulled at her hair. It wasn't enough that Mariah and Bradley had exhausted her and she had the impending choice of counselors hanging over her head, but now her mother would be staying the next weekend. She beat her head against the mattress, adding to the throbbing pain already present.

"Mom?" Mariah yelled from her room. "I'm ready to be sorry now."

"Me too," Bradley echoed.

"I'm the one that's feeling sorry . . . for myself," Natalie whispered as she traipsed down the hallway.

Chapter
FIVE

Natalie carried dirty dishes from the dining room into the kitchen. She washed the chunks of unappetizing food into the sink and down the disposal, trying to hide her irritation that dinner was cold because she'd waited—again—for Spence to come home from work. One of these days, she'd learn to serve dinner when it was hot instead of waiting for Spence.

"I'll finish up the dishes and make sure all the kids get to bed." Spence stepped up behind her. "Why don't you go upstairs to the bedroom, and I'll be up in a bit," he said as he began loading the dishes.

"You shouldn't have to do the dishes," she said as evenly as possible so they wouldn't have to discuss Spence's inability to come home on time.

"I'm sorry I was late. I'm guessing you've had a hard day." He smiled. "I like Mariah's new hairdo."

Natalie nodded, struggling to hold back the tears of fatigue and stress.

"I'll be up in a few minutes, and we can talk." Spence kissed her on the cheek.

"Mom?" Andrea said, her auburn hair pulled up in a messy ponytail.

"Yes?" Natalie turned to face Andrea.

"Laura is on the computer, and I have to write an essay. You said we'd work out some kind of time thing, but I can't do that tonight."

"Mom is going upstairs. Try to work it out with Laura," Spence said with firmness.

"Are you kidding, Dad? She's completely unreasonable. She's always crabby this time of the month." She glanced over at Natalie, her gray-blue eyes pleading. Natalie resisted the urge to get involved.

Their conversation trailed off as Natalie ascended the stairs. She reached the bedroom and shut the door, hoping to avoid interruptions so she could pray about counselors and enjoy a small respite from her hectic life. Though she was tired, she knelt beside her bed. She needed to ask for some inspiration as to who should serve with her. She also needed to ask for strength in dealing with the kids and, now, her mother. Since she was still fighting an intermittent stomach bug, she desperately wanted to snuggle up in the covers and sleep for a few days, but she had far too many things to think about. Worrying about her mother would have to wait until she resolved the issue of counselors.

She began an earnest prayer, begging Heavenly Father to help her know who He wanted to serve with her. Her mind searched through the faces of the women she'd come to know while living in the rural ward for the last fourteen years. She recalled sisters she'd served with in Primary and Young Women. No one in particular came to mind, so she prayed for inspiration.

The door flung open, and Natalie quickly ended her prayer.

"Mommy?"

"Yes, Mariah?"

"Ryan said the *s*-word."

"He did?"

"Yep." Mariah placed her hands on her hips. With a shake of her head, she said, "He said I was the *stu*-word."

"Hmmm."

"He said I was *stupid*." Mariah's eyes grew large.

Natalie ran her fingers through Mariah's now short hair. "Ryan knows we don't use that word. Name calling isn't okay, right?"

Mariah stared at the ground.

"Did you call him a name?" Natalie tugged up on Mariah's chin.

Mariah shrugged.

"What have we said about name calling?"

"Not to."

Natalie leaned in closer to Mariah's face. "You need to apologize to Ryan."

Mariah marched out of the room. Natalie rested her head in her hands and let out a long sigh. Inspiration seemed out of her reach. Constant interruptions had already prevented her from sincerely praying earlier in the day.

She entered the bathroom, washed her face, and brushed her teeth. A feeling of nausea overcame her, so she lay down while she waited for Spence. Her eyelids felt heavy, and since she struggled to keep them open, she decided to close them for a moment.

"Honey?" Spence said.

Natalie, a bit groggy from nodding off, sat up in bed. She swiped at her mouth.

"I'm sorry. I didn't mean to wake you."

She cleared her throat. "It's okay."

Spence closed the door and sat next to her. "Tell me about your day," he said, stroking her hair.

After Natalie shared most of the day's events, she drew in a deep breath and said, "I haven't told you the worst part." She sat back to gaze at him, pausing to give him the full effect of the news. "My mother sold the house and she's moving . . . ." She couldn't finish her sentence.

"She sold the house?" The shock was evident in his voice.

"Yep." Natalie still struggled to believe it.

"Where's she moving?"

Natalie laced her fingers together and rested her head on them, trying to convince herself to utter the answer.

"Nat?"

"Farmington . . . to be closer to us." Defeat settled on her shoulders as she considered the long-term implications of her mother's move. "I can't even fathom the idea of my mom moving to Farmington—it's way too overwhelming. I'll have to think about it later because right now my main concern is finding counselors."

"No luck?"

Natalie peered into Spence's eyes. "I've thought about every woman in the ward, but I haven't had any lightning bolts about who should serve with me."

"It doesn't usually happen that way."

"How did you figure out who should serve with you when you were elders quorum president?"

"I thought about different men in the ward and prayed for inspiration. The more I thought about it, the more a few names seemed to stand out. When I prayed about those names, I felt at peace." He brought his hand to his chest. "No thunder, no lightning, no heavenly messengers, only a peaceful, calm feeling."

"I wish I knew who He wanted to serve with me. What if I submit names and they say no?" She finally voiced her biggest fear. "What if I'm not in tune enough to be inspired?"

Spence reached over and cupped her chin in his hand. "You will be. I have no doubt you'll know who should serve with you."

"I need to be patient."

"Exactly." His clear blue eyes sparkled.

An hour or so later, Natalie listened to the rhythm of Spence's breathing as she thought about their conversation. Again, she considered various women in the ward. She pictured Sister Cantwell, who always wore a big smile and found something positive to say about everyone. Sister Pringle knew all the gossip and always prefaced her comments with, "You didn't hear it from me, but . . ." Then there was Sister Manning who was married to a non-member but traveled to the Albuquerque temple every other Wednesday to do temple work. She thought about the young mothers in the ward, including Sister Applebay who was expecting her third child in as many years, and Sister Kastning, who seemed to struggle every week at church with her twin babies.

She slipped into a deep sleep.

Chapter SIX

Natalie unbuckled Bradley and Mariah from their car seats. Friday was her appointed grocery-shopping day. She found a cart and strapped Bradley and Mariah into the kids' seat attached to the front.

"Can we have a treat?" Mariah asked.

"We'll see how well you behave while I get the groceries." Natalie heaved a breath as she pushed the cart uphill toward the store.

Bradley reached over and pulled Mariah's hair. Mariah screamed.

"No treats if we pull hair, Bradley. Tell Mariah you're sorry, please."

Bradley shook his head and yanked Mariah's hair again.

"Why did you pull her hair?" Natalie struggled to keep her breathing under control. She was so out of shape, it was pathetic. *Definitely time to start an exercise program so pushing a cart won't induce a heart attack.*

"She meanie."

"Is it too much to ask that we get the shopping done without fighting or other problems?"

Natalie pushed the cart into the grocery store. Inside the doors, she pulled out her list and started the ominous task before her.

"Can we have gum?" Mariah asked.

"No gum." Visions of the last gum and hair escapade played in her head.

"Why?" Mariah whined.

"I told you the last time I had to cut gum out of your hair that we wouldn't get any more. Ever."

"But my hair is short."

"Don't remind me."

She stopped in the cracker aisle to compare prices between Ritz crackers and saltines. When she settled on the Ritz, she noticed several boxes of other snack crackers in the cart. "Stop grabbing things off the shelves."

"We want them," Mariah said.

Natalie shook her head. She restacked the other crackers and then proceeded to the next aisle. It took almost as much time to remove unwanted items from her basket as it did to fill it with what she did want to buy. She piled cereal boxes on top of the canned goods, orange juice, and bags of frozen chicken.

"Hi, Sister Drake," Natalie heard as she examined some cake mixes.

Natalie glanced up to see Janice Keller, a short, round member of the ward. "Hi. How are you?"

"Fine. Looks like you're having fun." Sister Keller adjusted her bifocal glasses.

"Torture would be a better word." Natalie wiped the perspiration from her forehead.

"I'm still not used to cooking for one," Sister Keller said in a wistful tone, eyeing Natalie's cart. "I love it when my grandkids come to visit so I can cook more. I wish they visited more often."

"If you ever want a few kids on loan, I can probably accommodate you." Natalie patted Mariah on the head.

Mariah grabbed a toy out of Bradley's hand. Bradley screamed.

"What are you doing?" Natalie asked.

"He's stealing this toy," Mariah said indignantly.

"No, he's not."

"Yeah-huh. That's not our toy." She pointed her finger at Bradley.

"Yes, it is," Natalie said. "Andrea brought it home for him last week."

"No, she didn't." Mariah narrowed her eyes.

"Yes, she did." *Arguing with a five-year-old? Really?*

"Do you need some help? I'd be happy to entertain your kids while you finish shopping." Sister Keller smiled at Bradley, who promptly gave her a big grin.

"Thank you, but I think we'll be okay." Natalie shot Mariah a look.

"Have a nice day, then." Sister Keller gave a sincere smile.

"You too."

As Sister Keller pushed her cart away, Natalie contemplated s,
ing with her in Relief Society. A calm feeling encompassed her. W.
this an answer to her plea for counselors? A tingle traveled up her spine.

"Mom?" Mariah intruded into her thoughts.

Natalie blinked. "Yes?"

"Bradley is getting out of his seat."

Natalie checked the strap and fastened Bradley securely into
the cart. Chasing an escapee through the aisles wasn't something she
wanted to do today.

Halfway through her shopping trip, Mariah started whining again.
Natalie rubbed her eyes. "What is it?"

"I have to go potty."

"Of course you do. Can't you wait until we're done?"

"Nope."

"Are you sure? The bathroom is so far away. Besides, public rest-
rooms are nasty." She made a please-don't-make-me-take-you-to-the-
bathroom face, but Mariah didn't notice.

"I gotta go." In a louder voice, Mariah said, "Right now."

Mariah's face reddened while she rocked back and forth in her seat.
The countdown had begun. Natalie quickly unstrapped both kids and
rushed, with one child tucked under each arm, to the front of the store
to find the restroom. She set them down inside the bathroom.

Mariah dropped her pants before they were fully inside the stall,
and Natalie hurried her in, with no time to spare.

"Bradley?" Natalie peeked around the stall door. "Come in here,
please."

Bradley crawled under the stall wall.

"Bradley," Natalie shrieked, trying not to freak out. She yanked
him off the floor and stood him next to her. "We need to wash your
hands because the floor is yucky."

He gave her a smile, pulled down his pants, and began removing
his diaper.

"Not here, Bradley."

"Potty in toilet, yes, yes." He clapped his hands.

"You want to use a public toilet but not the one at home? I don't
think so."

Natalie reaffixed his diaper and pulled up his pants. She turned ound to see the enormous amount of toilet paper Mariah had shoved nto the toilet. "Don't flush—"

The toilet gurgled. Natalie whisked Bradley up into her arms and grabbed Mariah by the hand before the toilet overflowed.

"You clogged the toilet."

"Sorry, Mommy," Mariah said.

Natalie scanned the bathroom for a plunger and was grateful she couldn't find one. She quickly washed everyone's hands and exited the bathroom to let an employee know what lay in wait.

Natalie said to herself, "I can do this. I can finish shopping. I can."

"Where are we going?" Mariah asked.

"Crazy. Want to drive?"

"Huh?" Mariah gave Natalie a quizzical look.

"We need another cart. Might as well get it now since we're at the front of the store."

Natalie pushed the second cart back to the one that she'd left behind. After placing Bradley and Mariah back into the seats, she proceeded to pull the loaded cart and push the second one. She filled the second cart with fresh produce and some frozen items. She also placed bread and tortillas in the cart. "I better get a few bags of chocolate. I have a hunch I'll need a lot."

Grateful the shopping trip was almost over, Natalie pushed and pulled the carts to a check stand and waited in line. A tall woman with manicured nails and polished makeup pushed a cart in line behind hers. "Looks like you've done your shopping for the month," she said in a pleasant voice.

"Oh no. This is my weekly shopping." Natalie fanned herself with her hand, glad the kids were still strapped into their seats because she was sure she'd never catch them if they escaped.

With an arched eyebrow, the woman studied Natalie's baskets. "Do you own a restaurant or something?"

"No. This is for my family."

The woman chuckled. "How many people are in your family?"

"I have six children."

"Six?" The woman's eyes widened.

"Yes." Natalie mentally prepared herself for another battle against a nosy stranger who would undoubtedly share her unwelcome opinion of large families.

"You have six children?" the woman said, emphasizing each word.

"Yes." Maybe the woman had a hearing problem. *Not likely.*

"You must've adopted some of them." She eyed Natalie up and down.

"Nope. I gave birth to all six of them." With her medical history of miscarriages and difficulty in conceiving, she was grateful the Lord had seen fit to bless her with six wonderful children.

"Humph. That's an outrage." *Can't the sneering woman at least say something original?*

"Excuse me?" Natalie said, trying to stay calm and not let this woman's lack of conversational etiquette ruffle her.

"Aren't you aware that the world is overpopulated? How can you be so selfish by having that many children?"

"Selfish?" *That was a new one.*

"Don't you believe in birth control? Is it fair to have so many children in this world?" With a wagging finger, she added, "What's wrong with you?"

In a controlled voice, Natalie said, "My husband and I are blessed to have our children. We love each one of them and are thankful every day to have them."

The woman looked down her nose and said, "Having so many kids, you must be crazy."

"Most days, but I love them anyway." She smiled at the woman and then proceeded through the checkout line.

Natalie wheeled the baskets out to the parking lot. She stood for a moment, looking for where she'd parked. Finally, she spotted her blue twelve-passenger van and made her way over to it. She packed the bags into the van and reviewed her reply to the woman in the store. She was surprised at her reaction. In the past, she would've let the woman have it by telling her to keep her big, pointy nose out of Natalie's business. She'd often had the opportunity because people somehow felt compelled to lecture her on overpopulation and her irresponsibility in mothering so many kids. Today, though, it was different. Perhaps Heavenly Father was blessing her with added compassion because of her new calling.

Chapter
SEVEN

Natalie turned off the highway and followed the quarter-mile lane to her home. A few patches of snow still remained from the last storm. She looked forward to spring and its warmer weather and longer days.

After unloading the kids from the van, she handed a few lighter bags to Mariah to bring into the house. She made several trips carrying the multitude of grocery bags from the van into the kitchen and stacked them on the counter.

"Can I paint?" Mariah asked.

"Not right now. I need to put the groceries away. Can you play with Bradley since it's too late for his nap?"

Mariah shrugged. "Come on, Bradley. Let's play Barbies." They both ran off into another room.

Natalie squeezed the cans into the pantry and shoved the ten-pound bag of potatoes under the counter next to the twenty-five-pound bag of beans. She pulled out the leftovers from last week to make room for the eight gallons of milk. She balanced on her tiptoes to load the cereal boxes on the top of the refrigerator and stacked the apples in the bowl on the dining room table.

With Justin and Ryan home from school and Spence supposedly on his way home from work, Natalie consulted her menu and grabbed the ingredients for tacos. Though the kids alleged they ate tacos at least three times a week, quite a stretch of the truth, they all liked them, and it was an easy dinner after battling the grocery store.

Natalie had just finished the preparations for dinner when Andrea and Laura flung the door open. "Hi, Mom," Andrea said, a wide smile dancing across her lips.

"You seem happy today."

"I am," she sang out, her eyes alight.

"Any particular reason?" Natalie scooped the still-sizzling hamburger into a glass-serving bowl and placed the grated cheese on the counter.

Andrea shrugged. She gave Natalie an even bigger smile, motioned to Laura, and ran downstairs.

"I wish someone would tell me what's going on with Andrea," Natalie said.

Laura gave a shrug and followed her older sister downstairs.

"I can't keep up with the estrogen pendulum in this house," Natalie said. She eyed the job chart and called for Justin to set the table. She picked up an envelope that had come in the mail for Andrea and headed down to the basement.

Andrea's door was ajar. Natalie stopped just short of the door to give a knock, but before she could, she heard Andrea and Laura deep in conversation.

"Tristan is so hot, but even better, he's so nice. He wants me to go out with him," Andrea said, her voice filled with eagerness.

"Mom and Dad won't let you. He isn't a member," Laura said. "Why is it that the hottest guys are nonmembers?"

"I'm not going to marry him—I only want to go out and have fun. He's the first interesting guy I've met in a long time," Andrea said. "Besides, Mom and Dad don't have to know everything."

"That's not exactly honest."

"He wants me to go to dinner sometime. It's not like we're going to elope or anything. It'll be a friendly dinner. No big deal."

Andrea's nonchalant attitude knocked the breath out of Natalie. Her shoulders drooped as she replayed Andrea's words. She rapped on the door.

"Mom." Andrea sat back against the headboard. An apprehensive expression flashed across her face.

Natalie handed Andrea the envelope. "Here's a letter from BYU."

Andrea took the letter from her mother's hand but didn't meet her gaze. "Thanks."

"Aren't you going to open it?" Natalie prodded.

"Sure. I guess." Andrea opened the envelope and pulled out the letter. She read it silently.

"What does it say?" Natalie stepped closer to Andrea, excitement tingling through her.

With little enthusiasm, Andrea said, "I've been accepted."

"Cool," Laura said. "Think about all those gorgeous RMs up there."

"That's great news," Natalie said. She wanted Andrea to go to BYU for educational as well as social reasons.

"Thanks."

"You don't seem very excited," Natalie commented, perplexed by Andrea's emotionless reaction.

"I'm not sure I want to go to BYU." Andrea picked up a copy of *Seventeen* and started thumbing through it.

Natalie stepped back. "Why not?"

"I don't think BYU is the place for me." She didn't look up.

"When did you decide this?" Natalie tried to keep her tone even.

Andrea shrugged.

Baffled, Natalie said, "I don't get it."

Andrea closed the magazine. She bit at her lip and then said, "I don't want to go to BYU. I only filled out the application because you and Dad kept bugging me about it."

Disappointment settled on Natalie. "Where do you want to go to college?"

"I don't know. I need more time to think about it." Andrea finally made eye contact but looked away quickly.

"I see," Natalie said. Obviously, they'd had a communication breakdown. Somewhere along the line, Andrea had changed her mind about BYU, and Natalie had to consider that perhaps she'd changed her mind about more important matters. Her stomach soured. *What if—*

"Are you and Dad going on a date tonight?" Laura's question broke into Natalie's thoughts.

Natalie glanced at Laura. She cleared her throat and said, "We'll probably go to Red Lobster for dinner." She then turned to Andrea and in a controlled voice asked, "Are you still going to Nicole's?"

Andrea briefly looked up. "Yeah."

"Tell me again what you'll be doing," Natalie said, trying not to overreact to Andrea's change in plans.

"We're going to watch some movies and then sleep over."

"Will her parents be there?" Natalie said.

"Mom, I'm a senior in high school, and I'm eighteen." She ran her fingers through her hair and then scrunched it up on the sides.

Again, Natalie asked, "Will her parents be there?"

"Yes, Mom. I promise. And we won't watch any R-rated movies or do anything wild or crazy." Andrea crossed her heart with her finger.

"No boys, right?" Natalie said.

"Are you kidding? We're going to eat ourselves sick and watch chick flicks. Definitely no boys allowed." Andrea grabbed a bottle and sprayed some of her citrus-scented perfume on her wrist.

"You need to be home by ten tomorrow morning to do your chores and laundry."

"Okay."

"And I'll be babysitting. What a fun Friday night for me." Laura moaned, falling dramatically back on the bed.

"Maybe Jake Collins will call," Andrea said with a giggle.

"Jake? The new priest in our ward?" Natalie asked.

Laura sat up and scowled at Andrea, who, in turn, made a face at her. "Don't listen to her, Mom. Have a good time tonight."

Natalie left the room and closed the door behind her. She stood in the hallway and attempted to digest what she'd heard. She was shocked that Andrea didn't want to attend BYU, but even more alarming was her interest in dating a nonmember. Maybe Andrea saw it only as friendly dating, but Natalie knew the risk it presented, especially if the young man had different dating standards. Not to mention the threat of serious dating, falling in love, and then marriage outside of the temple. Natalie placed her right hand on her forehead and dragged it down her face.

She set her hand on the doorknob, ready to open the door to talk to Andrea when the phone rang. Justin yelled, "Mom!" She ascended the stairs, and Justin handed her the handset when she entered the kitchen.

"Sister Drake?" she recognized the deep voice.

"Hi, Bishop."

"Is this a bad time?" he asked.

Her thoughts flitted back to Andrea, but she forced herself to focus on the phone call. "No. It's fine." She hoped he had good news about the names she'd submitted.

"I wanted to let you know that Sister Keller, Sister Cantwell, and Sister Richins all accepted."

She smiled while warm rays of peace showered her. "That's great news."

"We'll sustain you on Sunday and then set you apart after the meetings."

"Thank you." She ended the call and gazed out the kitchen window, her heart full of gratitude for answered prayers and willing sisters.

"You look nice tonight," Spence said. He opened the car door for her.

"Thank you." Natalie smiled. "I'm looking forward to our date. It's been a wild day, and I need a relaxing evening."

Natalie admired her still-attractive husband as he walked around the front of the car. He looked even more handsome after losing fifteen pounds. His jeans snugged up in the right places, and his belly didn't overhang his pants anymore. Spence entered the car, his blue shirt accentuating his eyes, and started the engine. The yellow moon rose slowly over the bluffs as they drove south along the two-lane highway toward Farmington.

"The bishop called and said all of the sisters accepted," she said with a deeper understanding of how the Lord had worked through her.

Spence beamed. "I'm glad." He reached over and brushed her cheek.

"I don't know Sister Richins very well, but I know the Lord wants her to serve with me. I feel calm and peaceful about my presidency." She paused for a moment, staring out the front windshield. "Wish I felt that way about . . ." She chewed on her thumbnail.

Spence placed his warm hand on her knee. "Your mom's visit?"

"Uh-huh."

"What time will she be here?"

"Her flight leaves at eight thirty, so she should get to Farmington about ten and to our house before eleven in the morning."

Spence smiled.

"Wipe that grin off your face. It's going to be horrible having her live here."

"I don't think it'll be that bad," he said. At times, his cheerful attitude annoyed her.

"We'll see what you think when she starts in on you. You haven't had to endure her assaults." Memories of previous conversations swirled around her head.

"Your mom isn't assaulting you."

"Yes, she is. She's constantly on the prowl to find a way to make me feel bad about myself."

"I admit she can be a little rough sometimes." He passed the beat-up farm truck ahead of them.

Natalie shot Spence a pained look and said, "Sometimes?"

"I'm sure she'll mellow out when she moves."

Natalie rolled her eyes. "I don't think I can take her reaction when she finds out I have a new calling that will take a lot of time. You know how much she hates the Church." Thinking about having to defend the Church on a regular basis, face-to-face, overwhelmed her.

"Maybe this will be a good opportunity for her to see the Church in a different light."

"And maybe pigs will fly." She envisioned the absurdity of their 800-pound mama sow flying around the pen.

"Give her a chance." He smiled the same hopeful smile he always wore when they discussed her mother because, for some reason, he was still optimistic about her mother's attitude. She knew better.

"I've been giving her a chance ever since I was baptized. And twenty-four years later, she's still mad I joined the Church. She thinks you made me have all these kids. At least we're done having kids. I can't begin to imagine her reaction if we were going to have any more."

"You never know—we might have another baby."

Natalie gave him a sideways glance. "Honey, I'm old. Besides, after Bradley, the doctor said it was more likely that you'd conceive a child than me. I'm sure Heavenly Father is done sending us kids, and I'm okay with that. Six kids is a lot to handle."

"Especially at your advanced age." Spence laughed.

Natalie slugged him in the arm. "Funny."

They arrived at the restaurant. Spence opened the car door and walked with Natalie, hand-in-hand, to the waiting area inside the restaurant. Plaques of stuffed fish adorned the walls. They stood next to a large tank of live lobsters with their pincers taped shut. Natalie watched the poor animals and wondered if they felt anything when the cooks immersed them in boiling water. She vowed not to eat lobster for dinner. Spence stepped close to her, sneaking a kiss on her cheek. He grabbed her hand and caressed her fingers while they waited.

After a few minutes, a waiter escorted them to the dining area. Spence pulled out the chair and seated Natalie at the table.

The usually delicious seafood-scented air seemed to have an adverse effect on her stomach.

"I appreciate that you still treat me so well," Natalie said, thankful to have some time alone with Spence.

Natalie surveyed the menu, but none of her favorite entrees appealed to her. She finally chose soup and salad. After they ordered, Natalie said, "I think we have a serious problem brewing."

"What's that?" Spence focused on her.

"Andrea's been accepted to BYU."

Spence's face registered his confusion. "How is that a problem?"

"She doesn't want to go." Natalie unrolled her napkin and removed the silverware, still disappointed in Andrea's reaction to her acceptance letter.

"Why not?" Spence furrowed his brows.

"She didn't give me a good answer." Natalie considered possible reasons such as not wanting to leave home, being afraid to live on her own, or lacking interest in BYU itself, but none of them made sense.

"I thought she was all set to go if she was accepted." He sipped his water.

"Me too, but something has changed."

"What do you mean?"

"I don't know." She shrugged. "I can't quite put my finger on it, but she seems different somehow. I overheard her telling Laura that she wants to date this kid, Tristan, even though he isn't LDS." Natalie worried that the lack of interest in BYU and obvious attraction to Tristan might mean Andrea was drifting away from the Church. She pushed that thought aside.

Spence shifted his weight in his chair, concern flickering in his eyes. "The boy she was talking about the other night?"

"Yes. He's asked her to go to dinner."

The waitress set their salads and cheese biscuits on the table. Spence took a cheese biscuit and broke it in half. "When is this dinner date?"

"Not a specific night yet, but she wants to date him, which is what bothers me." She looked into Spence's eyes. "He may be a nice kid, but I'm sure he has different morals. She has no idea how dangerous that could be, especially if she falls for him."

"We need to counsel her not to date him. But, in the end, it has to be her decision." His voice betrayed his apprehension.

"We can forbid her to date him." The idea sounded good.

He shook his head. "No, I think that would push her into it. She's an adult now." He took a bite of the biscuit.

"But she's still in high school, and she lives with us, so she needs to follow the rules about dating." Natalie attempted to eat her salad, but it turned her stomach so she pushed it aside.

"I think we're about to enter a difficult parenting time. Up to this point, we've been able to exert some control over Andrea, but now we have to let her make her decisions and live with the consequences."

"She's at such a vulnerable age, especially when it comes to dating." Natalie took a sip of her water, hoping it might settle her stomach. She cringed at the idea of Andrea dating someone who may not respect her standards and might pressure her into breaking the law of chastity.

"Let's talk to her and see if we can help her make the right choice." He held Natalie's gaze with hopeful eyes.

The waitress delivered their meals. Natalie's soup wasn't any more appealing than her salad. She chocked it up to being upset about Andrea. Spence began eating his meal when his cell phone rang.

"Hello?" He glanced at Natalie and mouthed, "It's Laura."

Natalie worried the call might mean someone was hurt.

Spence said, "Turn off the water. . . . It's right behind the toilet. . . . Turn it to the right. . . . Don't be silly; it's only water. . . . It won't kill you. . . . If you don't turn it off . . . yes, you can . . . right now. . . . Get some towels and start mopping it up . . . okay." He closed his cell phone.

"What's going on?"

"Apparently, the upstairs toilet is overflowing, and the water is dripping down the walls in the dining room."

Natalie covered her mouth, imagining the soggy mess.

"Laura doesn't want to step on the water because it's toilet water."

Natalie rolled her eyes. "Of course she doesn't."

"I told her to turn it off, but—"

"If she doesn't, the water's going to keep flooding the floor and running down the walls until we get home." Frustration with Laura's germaphobic personality began to build.

"I told her to start wiping it up. I hope she takes care of it." He raised his eyebrows.

"She's so paranoid about germs. It's ridiculous. It'll take us almost half an hour to get home." Frustration turned to anger.

"We need to hurry. Sorry about our date ending so fast." His face communicated his irritation.

Natalie shook her head. "I can't believe the toilet is overflowing the night before my mother arrives."

Anger turned to utter panic.

Chapter
EIGHT

Natalie and Spence rushed into the house to find a bulging ceiling and Laura with a distressed expression, wiping her hands with a towel. Justin, Mariah, and Bradley crowded around, watching the swollen ceiling.

"Laura, did you turn off the water?" Spence asked.

"I think so," she answered with a glum expression.

"When?"

"A little while ago." She gazed at the floor.

Spence shook his head. "I'll go check." He ran upstairs.

"How did this happen?" Natalie asked, glancing from one child to the next.

"I heard a weird sound so I went upstairs and saw water all over the floor. I ran to get Laura," Justin said, his eyes wide.

Ryan walked through the front door with his soccer ball under one arm and his backpack under the other. He dropped both as he approached the dining room. "Whoa, what happened to the ceiling?"

"Toilet overflowed," Natalie said through clenched teeth.

"Who did it?" Ryan looked at his mom.

"Mariah or Bradley," Justin said.

"Not me." Mariah scowled at Justin.

Spence returned to the dining room and said, "It's off." He gazed up at the ceiling. "The latex paint is acting like a balloon and holding all the water."

"I'm sorry. I didn't know what to do," Laura said with emotion.

"Turning off the water right away would've been a good option." Anger colored Natalie's cheeks.

"Eewww! It's gross toilet water. I didn't want it to touch me." Laura scrunched up her face.

"This is better?" Natalie fanned her arm to indicate the water on the floor and the walls and the swelling above their heads.

"I said I was sorry." Laura wiped at her eyes. "You're acting like it's my fault. I didn't make it overflow."

"But you refused to turn it off right away. If you would have watched the kids better—"

"Let's focus on solving the problem instead of arguing about it," Spence said in a stern voice.

Trying to shelf her anger for the moment, Natalie eyed the ceiling and said, "What can we do?"

"We need to relieve the pressure. I'll poke a hole and let the water out," Spence said.

"Excuse me?" Natalie envisioned her mother walking into the house and immediately detecting evidence of toilet water.

"That's so disgusting," Laura said.

"Any other ideas?" Spence asked.

"Ryan, get a big bowl," Natalie said, pointing to the cupboard by the stove. "Justin, find more towels."

Spence took a knife from the drawer and inserted it into the ceiling in a few places. Water gushed out and filled the bowl. Bradley played in the water that sloshed over the sides of the bowl.

"No, no, Bradley." Natalie picked him up and handed him to Justin. "Please, take Mariah and Bradley into the family room so we can clean this mess."

Natalie mopped up the floor, and Ryan wiped down the walls.

"The smell is awful," Laura said and covered her nose.

"Next time this happens, turn off the water immediately, and we can avoid such a big mess." Natalie's voice betrayed her frustration.

"You're acting like I did this on purpose. Like I planned it. This isn't my fault. You always blame me for everything." Laura stomped out of the room.

Natalie blew out a breath. "I've got to clean this so my mom doesn't have one more thing to criticize. I'll get some air deodorizer. How can we fix the holes and hide the water damage?"

"We can't yet. We'll have to let the sheetrock dry out before we can do anything. Otherwise it'll mold," Spence said.

Natalie's shoulder muscles tensed. She knew she'd spend all night, if necessary, working to hide the evidence from her mom's critical eyes.

Chapter NINE

Natalie wiped beads of sweat from her hairline. She surveyed the kitchen, noting the dishes in the sink, the dust layer on the oven hood, the bits of food spread across the island, and the spots on the floor. She noticed the cans and boxes in the pantry and reminded herself to organize them before her mother's arrival. She glanced at the clock on the face of the microwave. Less than an hour to finish all the work. She shook her head. "I'll never get this house clean enough."

"I'm sure Grandma won't mind," Ryan said. "You're way too stressed out."

"I doubt Grandma will notice a tiny speck of dirt here and there," Laura said.

Holding a duster in her hand, Andrea said, "Our house is cleaner than anyone else's I know."

"I don't care what other people's houses look like. And I think I know your grandmother better than you do. She's going to inspect every detail of the house," Natalie said. She caught sight of the top of the refrigerator and picked up a rag to wipe it down. "Please keep cleaning. She'll be here soon."

"Mom, I have a soccer meeting in a couple of hours," Ryan said.

Natalie felt faint, so she steadied herself against the refrigerator. "When did that come up?"

"Yesterday, but I went over to Dan's, and I guess I forgot to call and tell you," Ryan said.

"Your grandmother wants to go house hunting. I'll have to see if I can drop you off. Maybe you can go with the Kings."

"I'll call," Ryan said, backing out of the kitchen.

"After you finish your jobs."

"But, Mom . . ."

Natalie pointed at him. "Don't start with me. I have to get this cleaning done, and I still need to get in the shower and put on my makeup. My mother does not like it when I'm not put together."

Spence walked into the kitchen. "Okay, I've tidied the yard and fixed the gate. Justin is sweeping the front porch. I fed and watered the animals, and Mariah and Bradley are in the backyard."

Natalie shook her head. "I don't think we'll be ready for her." She drew in a breath, desperation setting in. "Are we ever?"

"Honey, stop worrying so much," Spence said.

"Do other people feel like this about their mothers? I love her, but it's so stressful when she comes. I feel like a teenager all over again. Most of the time, I feel like I should go to my room."

"Your mother can only have as much power over you as you give her," Spence said.

Like Satan. She knew her mom wasn't actually Satan, but the comparison made her smile. "I know." Natalie wiped down the kitchen counters again. She grabbed the broom and swept the floor while the vacuum roared in the background.

"I see Grandma," Mariah bellowed.

With shaking fingers, Natalie fiddled with her hair. She checked her teeth, smoothed her blouse, and turned to study her backside in the mirror. "Why are these pants so tight? Great, I'm fat and she'll tell me all about it. I think I'm going to have a nervous breakdown," she mumbled to herself. She checked her makeup one last time.

"Mom, Grandma's here," Laura's voice carried up the stairs.

Natalie pursed her lips and trudged out of her room. She saw her mother in the entryway. "Hello, Mother," she said as she descended the stairs, walking toward her.

Carma gave Natalie a slight hug and kissed at the air. "Hello, Natalie."

"How was your flight?"

"All these safety regulations are simply ridiculous. I told them as much."

"I'm sure," Natalie said.

Her mom gasped, and Natalie braced herself. "What on earth happened to Mariah's beautiful long hair?"

"New haircut." She didn't elaborate so her mother wouldn't lecture her on allowing the kids to play with scissors.

Carma gazed up at the ceiling. "Hmmm. What's this? It looks as though the ceiling is about to fall down."

"It's nothing," Natalie said, trying to downplay the damage.

"It doesn't look like nothing." Her mom gazed around the room. "Is the house falling apart?"

"No, Mother," Natalie said, wishing the house would fall down and bury her.

"It *is* quite an old home," Carma said over the top of her nose.

Natalie grabbed the small suitcase and said, "We'll have you sleep in the basement."

"How is the ceiling down there?" She glanced in Spence's direction. "Hello, Spencer."

"Hi. We're happy you're here," Spence said in his typical upbeat tone.

Carma eyed him up and down. "I'm hoping to find a new home this weekend. I may need Natalie to house hunt tomorrow as well."

"Mother." Natalie gazed at her. "I told you that we have church tomorrow and I won't be able to go to the open houses."

"Surely Spencer can spare you for the afternoon to help your mother find a house. Right, Spencer?" She gave Spence the familiar I-dare-you-to-disagree-with-me expression.

"Let's take your bag down to the girls' room. You can freshen up before we leave for town." Natalie hoped to divert her mother's attention.

"For the life of me, I cannot understand why you enjoy living so far from everything. You're in the middle of nowhere. I never pictured you living like this," Carma said.

"I know. We've had this conversation so many times I've lost count. I've told you that I like it out here and I'm happy."

Natalie placed her mother's bag next to Andrea's bed. She was relieved that the room was decent. A few things were out of place, but it was clean.

Carma swiped her hand across the top of the dresser. She studied her fingers and then pulled out a tissue to wipe them off. "Natalie, you need to teach your daughters the importance of cleanliness."

Natalie tightened her jaw while her heart raced. *Nothing was ever good enough.*

"I'll need a few moments and then we can drive to Farmington. I've contacted a real estate agent, and we can meet with her first." Carma fluffed her short, professionally styled brown hair and adjusted her glasses. "I don't want to look like a wreck when I meet the agent. You could use some freshening up too."

Natalie gave a weak smile and made her way up to the dining room where she found Spence. The hammering in her head sent her in search of ibuprofen.

"Your mom seems to be doing well," Spence said.

"So far, she's tried to stop me from going to church, she's blasted me for living out here, and she thinks our daughters are pigs." She fumbled with the top of the bottle of ibuprofen. Finally, she opened it and plopped two pills out on the palm of her hand. "Just an ordinary visit from my mother." Natalie gave a fake smile, brought her hand to her face, and popped the pills into her mouth.

Spence handed her a glass of water.

She took a sip and laid her head back for a moment. "I hope we can find a house as far away from us as possible. She's so exasperating."

Natalie followed Carma and the tall, wide-waisted real estate agent into a home with a flat roof, beige stucco, and a two-car garage. It was the tenth home, at least, that they'd toured so far. She wanted her mother to make a choice.

Inside the terra-cotta-tiled entry, a hall led to the master bedroom. "We can view the master suite and adjoining bathroom first," the real estate agent said as she directed them to the bedroom.

"I do like this room. It has a lot of natural light and it feels spacious," Carma said.

"You'll love the bathroom," the agent said, tugging on her blonde-from-a-bottle hair.

"That's what you said about the last four homes you showed me. You obviously do not understand what I will and will not love." Carma brushed past the agent and inspected the bathroom. "For example, see there," she pointed to the corner of the vanity, "the tile is chipped. That won't do at all."

The agent glanced at Natalie, who shrugged her shoulders and half-smiled. Memories of her mother's sharp tongue suddenly made her feel like she was a five-year-old again.

After a thorough assessment of the house, Carma suggested they take a break and meet up a bit later. The agent seemed relieved as she left Natalie and Carma in the driveway.

"You're giving me a look," Carma said.

"No, I'm not." Natalie didn't want to have a scene with her mother.

"I know when you're giving me a look." She emphasized the last word.

"It's nothing."

"Obviously, it's something."

The words teetered on the edge of her tongue, begging to be released.

"Natalie, I demand you tell me." Carma planted her feet and folded her arms.

"Fine." Natalie looked directly at her mother. "I think you were rude to that poor agent. She's been working hard to show you homes."

"Oh, please. That's her job," Carma said with an attitude.

Unable to keep the words inside, Natalie blurted out, "You're so picky. About everything. No one can ever please you." The words caught in her throat for a moment before she pushed them out. "I certainly can't."

Carma straightened. "I cannot believe you said that to me."

Chiding herself for saying anything, Natalie said, "I'm sorry." She checked her watch. "It's almost two. Let's not discuss this anymore. We need to get some lunch."

The silent drive to the restaurant seemed longer than the ten minutes it took. The tension was as thick as oatmeal as Natalie pulled into Applebee's full parking lot. She wished she were home enjoying time with her family instead of trying to attempt the impossible task of finding a home that would please her persnickety mother.

Without a word, the women exited the car and proceeded to walk toward the restaurant. Inside, the twenty-something-year-old hostess with multiple earrings asked for Natalie's name, wrote it on a list, and then directed them to wait until a table was ready.

Carma wore a fastidious expression while she scrutinized the restaurant. She pulled a tissue out from her purse and stepped over to the waiting area. She studied the bench for a moment before taking the tissue and wiping down the seat. She stiffly sat on the edge of the bench.

Natalie let out a breath, hoping her mother would keep her opinion of the restaurant to herself so they could get through lunch. If she was lucky, it might even be a quiet—as in silent—lunch. She stood next to a wall covered in sports photos to avoid a conversation. She examined the photos and a framed football jersey, trying to ignore her mother's obvious body language.

After several minutes, a curvaceous waitress with thick black eyeliner called Natalie's name and escorted them to a booth by a window. Carma used her tissue to wipe down her seat. The waitress watched her and then glanced at Natalie, who shook her head, wishing she could evaporate when her mother did such things.

Carma settled into her seat. She inspected the table before flipping through the menu. Without looking up, she said, "Honestly, Natalie, I don't know what you expect from me."

Here it comes. Natalie kept her gaze on her menu.

"Well?" Carma said.

Natalie could feel her mother's frosty stare, so she placed the menu flat on the table. She sucked in a breath and said, "Nothing. I expect nothing from you, Mom." She knew she wouldn't be lucky enough to have a nonverbal lunch.

"Perhaps this isn't such a good idea."

"Lunch?" Natalie played with the edges of her menu.

"No." Carma paused. "Moving here to be close to you and your family. Maybe it's a mistake."

Natalie considered the idea of agreeing with her since that was the best thing she'd heard all day but resisted the temptation to be brutally honest. "I'm sure it will be fine." She looked at her mother.

"Fine?" Carma gave a shake of her head. "I don't want *fine*."

"What is it that you want, Mom?" Natalie couldn't begin to guess what to say to placate her mother.

"Is it too much to ask that my only daughter treat me with some respect and show some speck of enthusiasm that I'm moving here?"

"You're right." Natalie took a breath. "We're all very excited to have you close and look forward to spending time with you." *Sounded sincere.*

Carma clicked her tongue. "I don't appreciate the sarcasm. You've always been a sarcastic child."

Natalie gritted her teeth. She couldn't win. Why was she surprised? "We're happy to have you move here."

The waitress served them both a glass of water and took their order.

Carma studied Natalie for a few moments. "You look peaked. Are you getting enough rest?"

"Yes, Mother. A lot has been going on, that's all." She placed a straw in her water and took a sip.

"Like what?"

Natalie argued internally. She knew far too well how her mother would react to the news of her calling as Relief Society president.

"Well?" Her mother tapped the table with her painted fingernails.

Natalie cleared her throat. "I have a new assignment at church."

"What is it this time?"

"I'm going to serve the women. Tomorrow, at church, they'll sustain me."

"The women?" She could hear her mother's disapproval.

"Yes." She fingered her napkin. "I'll be tending to their spiritual, physical, and temporal needs."

Carma pursed her lips for a second. "You aren't qualified to do that. You might have graduated in psychology, but you have done nothing with your degree." She raised her eyebrows. "You had your whole career ahead of you but you gave it all up and wasted your education on raising children."

Natalie's insides roiled. "I don't want to argue about my choice to stay home and raise my kids." Natalie drew in a deep breath. "Besides, the Lord will help me in my calling."

With a haughty expression, her mom said, "You believe that?"

"Yes, I do." She struggled to keep her voice even, but conviction backed her words.

Carma shook her head. "For goodness' sake, Natalie, aren't you busy enough with all of your children?"

"I—"

"You don't have time to do more. Look at you—you're exhausted. Why doesn't Spencer step in and tell that church how busy you are?"

"Mother—"

The waitress delivered their meals, but Natalie had since lost her appetite. Again. She wondered if her upset stomach were here to stay forever or for as long as her mother lived near her.

Carma leaned in. "Why you spend all that time volunteering for your church is beyond me. Charity work has its place and it's nice to help people now and again, but you have so many responsibilities. I should have done more when you told us you wanted to be baptized so many years ago."

Natalie wanted to beat her head against the table.

"I had no idea what that baptism would mean to your father and me." She sat back, a hard expression on her face.

"I didn't join the Church to hurt you."

"Excluding us from your wedding didn't hurt us? Our only daughter." She pointed at Natalie. "I'd been planning your wedding since you were born and then I wasn't even allowed to attend. What kind of church separates families like that?" Her voice broke.

Feeling frustrated and defensive, Natalie said, "I've been trying to explain this to you for over twenty years, but you won't hear me." The usual exasperation rolled down her back.

"I've heard all I need to." Carma placed a bite of her chef salad into her mouth.

After a few minutes of uncomfortable silence, the waitress stopped at their table. "Are you ready for dessert?"

"I think we're both full." Natalie had barely touched her lunch.

"I'm full up to here." Carma tapped the top of her forehead with the side of her index finger. Natalie noticed the double meaning.

"I'll bring you the check." The waitress glanced awkwardly between Natalie and her mother.

"Thank you," Natalie said, embarrassed.

When the waitress came back, Natalie prepared to pay.

"I'm paying for lunch today." Carma pulled out her wallet and removed her credit card. She handed it to the waitress.

"Mom, you don't have to buy lunch."

"It's the least I can do since you're house hunting against your will." Carma gave her a quick glance.

Natalie wanted to jump up and run out of the restaurant, as far away from her manipulative mother as possible, but instead she said, "That's not true."

The waitress returned with the credit card slip. Carma filled it out and said, "I'm not giving you a tip. You don't deserve one. You should find a job in another field because you aren't a good waitress."

"Mother—"

"I'm only trying to help her," Carma said matter-of-factly. She handed the slip to the waitress.

Humiliation rose in Natalie's cheeks, and she couldn't wait to leave the restaurant.

On the way over to the next house, Natalie thought about the conversation with her mother about her calling as Relief Society president. Maybe her mom had a point. Maybe Natalie wasn't qualified to serve in this new position. Carma knew Natalie well and never failed to remind her of all of her weaknesses, but maybe this time Carma spoke the truth.

Chapter
TEN

Natalie trailed her family as they rushed into the ward building. She wiped the moisture from the back of her neck. No matter how she tried, it was next to impossible to get to church on time. Today, with her about to be sustained, she'd hoped to arrive a little early. But, as was the norm, Mariah couldn't find her other black shoe, Bradley's socks had mysteriously disappeared, and sleepy teenagers moved like turtles on Sunday mornings, the most stressful day of the week.

Natalie made a quick pass of the congregation as she sat down and saw all of the women to be called to the presidency in attendance. Natalie grabbed the hymnbook and joined in singing the opening hymn. Her heart thumped as she waited for the announcement.

After the prayer, Bishop Franken stepped to the pulpit. "Brothers and sisters, we have a bit of ward business to conduct this morning." He proceeded to release the current presidency with a vote of thanks and then asked for a sustaining vote for Natalie and her new presidency.

Natalie feared someone might oppose her as the new president, so she kept her gaze fixed on the bishop.

"Thank you. Sisters, we will set you apart after the block meeting today."

Laura reached over and jiggled the back of Natalie's right arm. "You do have Relief Society arms," she whispered.

"You're hilarious." Natalie jerked her arm away from Laura.

Spence reached his hand around Laura and rested it on Natalie's shoulder.

After sacrament meeting, an older woman with bluish hair and a pinched face approached Natalie. "Sister Crocker was an awfully good president. She's such a dear and so attentive to everyone's needs. You have large shoes to fill."

"Yes, I know, but I'll do my best." Natalie gave a sincere smile.

"I don't know—"

"I promise to work hard, Sister Allen. I hope you'll show me how to be the best Relief Society president I can be."

"Well, I—I will." Sister Allen didn't seem to have anything else to say, so she stepped away.

"What was that?" Spence held a flailing Bradley in his arms.

"My first disgruntled sister." Natalie hoped she said the right thing to Sister Allen.

"You'll do fine, honey."

"If I can handle my mother, I guess I can handle anyone." *Right?*

Natalie and her presidency, along with their families, sat in the Relief Society room. A sweet spirit filled the room as the bishopric set apart each of the sisters. Sister Cantwell's optimism would keep the presidency focused on the good that all of the sisters in the ward brought to Relief Society and would buoy them up when they encountered hard times. Natalie admired Sister Keller's faith and knew it would help them all serve with more commitment, even through trials. Peace radiated from Sister Richins, and Natalie looked forward to getting to know her better. Again, the Spirit witnessed to her Heavenly Father's desire that they serve together.

After Natalie expressed gratitude and gave each sister a hug, the Drake family made its way home. On the porch, Carma waited for them. Natalie hoped her mother's presence wouldn't interfere with, or worse, prevent her from, meeting with her presidency later in the afternoon.

"Hi, Grandma," Ryan said. He loosened his striped blue tie.

"You look nice in your shirt and tie. You remind me of your grandfather." She ruffled his light brown hair.

"Thanks." Ryan attempted to put his hair back in its proper place.

"Grandma, I want you to read me a book about butterflies. It's my favorite." Mariah pulled Carma by the hand into the house.

"I've been waiting for your mother to get home so we can—"

"I need to make lunch, and then I have a meeting this afternoon," Natalie said. She walked into the house, her nerves on edge.

"What about house hunting?"

"I said I wouldn't do that today." Natalie removed her high heels and bent down to grab them.

"I'm only here until tomorrow evening, and I must find a house." Carma set her purse on the counter in the kitchen. "You can make an exception to your rule. Personally, I don't know how you live by so many rules all the time. It must be exhausting keeping up with all the things you can't do."

"Mom—"

"Andrea, Laura, would you like to go to some open houses this afternoon?" Carma turned in their direction as they walked into the kitchen. "It'll be fun. We can go out to lunch."

"Mother—"

"I need some help. I don't know my way around Farmington, and I don't want to drive around town with that realtor. She's a ninny." Carma held up her hand. "I promise I won't corrupt them."

"It's not that," Natalie said. Somehow, her mother always made her out to be the villain.

In a sharp tone, Carma said, "Oh, please. I'm not asking for much. Simply that my granddaughters accompany me to town today. You're acting as though I'm committing a crime, for goodness' sake."

Spence entered the house with Bradley in his arms.

"Spencer, I've tried to convince Natalie to help me find a house, but she won't. I'd like to take the girls with me this afternoon. Would that be acceptable to you?" Carma pulled a mirror out of her purse and glanced at herself. She applied some lipstick.

"We're about to have lunch," Spence said. He set Bradley on the floor, and he promptly ran off.

"I can treat them to lunch in town."

"Generally on Sundays, we spend the day with the family." Spence had a knack for explaining things in the most nonoffensive way possible.

"I am family," Carma said.

"Yes, you are. And we'd love to have you spend the afternoon with us here at home," Spence said. He took off his suit coat.

"I must find a house, and I need help." She gazed around the room. "Doesn't anyone care about helping me?"

Natalie rubbed her temples. Her mother had such a dramatic flair.

"We'd be happy to help you look on any other day but today," Spence said. "I'll even take the day off tomorrow to help you find a home."

Natalie pinched him in the back.

"Natalie and I can both help you find a house tomorrow. We can make a day of it." Natalie wanted to remove Spence's sincere smile from his face. She pinched him again.

"Perhaps, I do need a rest. I am a bit tired," Carma said. "A day with the family does sound nice."

Spence had worked his magic again. If only Natalie could soothe the raging mother-beast the way he could.

"Great. We'll get lunch started," Spence said.

"But Natalie said she has to leave for a meeting."

"I have to meet with my presidency." Natalie refused to give in to her mother.

"I thought you said today was a *family* day," Carma said with raised eyebrows and a tilt of her head.

Natalie stood in silence, marveling at her mother's manipulation skills. "When will you be leaving?"

Carma took a few steps back. "You sound like you're trying to get rid of me."

"Not at all." She tried to sound sincere.

"Actually, I'm considering changing my flight and staying until I find a house."

Dread socked Natalie in the stomach. "I thought you had to get back to Mesa for your house appraisal."

"No, no." Carma waved her hand. "That was moved to next week."

Natalie nodded, accepting defeat. "Fine. I'll call the sisters and reschedule." She ignored her mother's smirk.

Natalie sat on the bed next to Spence. "I do *not* want to go house hunting with her again."

Spence rested his hand on her knee. Natalie laid her head on his shoulder. "You know she completely manipulated the situation. She stopped me from having my meeting, and she's trying to control me, just like when I was a kid."

"Maybe she's simply trying to find a house."

Natalie rolled her eyes. "You know she only wants to move here to make my life miserable."

"You don't actually believe that, do you?"

"All I know is that she makes me crazy. She has no respect for me or my life." She straightened.

"I think she does." Spence gazed at her.

"Are we talking about the same Carma James? Average height, dyed brown hair, snobby, and completely oblivious of anyone around her?" *Perfect description.*

Spence placed his arm around Natalie. "Your mother loves you. She may show it in a different way than some mothers—"

"Some? Try *all* other mothers." Natalie raised her eyebrows.

"But she loves you. Maybe this move will be a good thing for her. And for you."

"How can having my mother drive me totally insane be a good thing for me? I'm too exhausted for this." Natalie gave a heavy sigh, memories of her mother's past demands and criticisms hanging over her. She shuddered to think how that would multiply now that her mother would live nearby. She wondered if there was such a condition as momophobia—fear of your mother living too close to you.

"Maybe she'll find a house tomorrow and then you can meet with your presidency on Tuesday." Spence always saw the silver lining.

"I'm not sure a house exists that meets my mother's expectations. Nothing ever meets her approval."

Spence massaged her neck. "I'm happy to take the day off tomorrow if you need me."

"It's okay. I'm sure we can manage." She tried to conjure up some optimism. "I'll have to drag Mariah and Bradley along, but that's why she's buying a house near us, right? She wants more contact with the kids. Of course, after a day with those two, she might change her mind.

Hey . . ." Natalie gave a half-smile.

"Maybe I could stay home and watch the kids, so you can be free to concentrate on your mother."

Natalie gave him a no-way-was-she-going-to-spend-another-day-alone-with-her-mother-looking-for-houses look. "I think I'll need the kids as comic relief. We could meet you for lunch, though."

He gave her a kiss. "It's a date."

Chapter
ELEVEN

Carma, Natalie, and the kids entered the restaurant. Though it was a challenge when he went limp, Natalie kept hold of Bradley's hand. Mariah pointed to a large sculpture hanging above their heads. "That's a super big cucumber." She craned her neck to view it from the backside.

Natalie laughed. "That's not a cucumber, silly. It's a chili."

"Why is it up there?" Mariah stared at it.

"Because that's the name of this restaurant."

Mariah scrunched up her nose. "Do we have to eat chilies?"

"No, you can get a hamburger."

Mariah smiled. "I like hamburgers."

Bradley wriggled his hand out of Natalie's and started down an aisle. Natalie looked over to see Spence motioning them to a table in the middle of the restaurant. A strong onion scent filtered through the room.

"How are the house hunters?" Spence said while he helped Bradley sit in a high chair.

Natalie gave a pained smile. She hoped lunch would go better than their search for an impossibly perfect house.

"You'd think I could find a decent house in this town," Carma said as she wiped down her seat with a tissue.

They sat at the table. Mariah grabbed a glass filled with ice water. It slipped and spilled all over Carma, who shrieked.

Natalie silently chastised herself for even thinking they could have a peaceful lunch.

"Sorry, Grandma," Mariah said, her eyes wide.

"Let me help." Spence handed Carma a few extra napkins. He wiped at the water pooled on the table while Natalie mopped up the floor.

"Can I get you some more water?" their pregnant waitress asked.

"Thank you, I think we've had quite enough," Carma said.

"Are you ready to order?" She pulled a pen out from behind her ear.

They all proceeded to order, and Natalie ordered a hamburger for the children to split.

"Tell me about the houses you saw," Spence said with enthusiasm.

"I might consider one or two, but the rest were a waste of time. I was very specific with my agent, and she ignored me and took us to homes that will not meet my needs."

"I thought the house with the blue trim was nice," Natalie said, trying to find something positive about the experience.

"In that neighborhood?" Carma crinkled her nose.

"What about the house over by the mall?" Natalie asked.

"Too much work with that yard."

"The one on the hill? The yard was landscaped with rocks and wouldn't need much maintenance." She mentally dared her mother to find something wrong with that house.

"But the layout was all wrong." Carma shook her head. "I don't want my kitchen at the front of the house."

With exasperation Natalie said, "What about the one with the small pool?"

"What would I do with a pool?" Carma pointed at herself.

"The kids love to swim," Natalie offered.

"A pool? Swimming is my favorite, especially after working outside on a hot summer day," Spence said.

"The price was too high on that house, and the kitchen cabinets were outdated," Carma said.

The waitress delivered their orders. "Can I get you anything else?"

"I think we're fine. Thank you," Spence said.

Bradley snatched the ketchup and squeezed it all over his fries. Some of it spilled on the table. He leaned over and licked it up.

"Bradley, where are your manners? We don't lick tables," Carma said.

Bradley smiled with ketchup outlining his lips. He wiped at his mouth and smeared it worse. Before Natalie could stop him, he slimed his grandmother. Natalie's stomach lurched at the sight of ketchup all over her mother's sleeve.

"You've ruined my beautiful blouse. How could you?" Carma frowned at Bradley.

"He's only three, Mom. He didn't mean to do it." Natalie turned to Bradley, "Tell Grandma you're sorry, please."

"Sowwy." He gave her a ketchup grin, his blue eyes twinkling.

"Sorry isn't going to take ketchup out of this blouse." Carma wiped at her sleeve.

Not wanting to focus on Bradley's faux pas, she tried to call her mother's attention back to the housing situation. "Mom, what exactly do you want? We've seen over a dozen houses. Probably more like twenty. You've found something wrong with each house. It's like you're looking for an excuse to hate them." Trying to control the anger bubbling up inside, she added, "And you don't even enjoy being with the kids."

"That's not true. I do like being with my grandchildren. You need to train them better, that's all. When you were a child, you were a little lady. I took you everywhere with me and you never uttered a peep." She looked at Bradley. "You kept your hands, and face, to yourself."

Of course, it was *her* fault. It always was. A scene at the restaurant wouldn't be appropriate, but Natalie wanted to strangle her mother. She took a deep, cleansing breath, hoping to calmly discuss the house hunting and not have the usual debate about her lackluster parenting skills that always seemed to be connected to her membership in the Church. "About the houses—" Natalie started.

"I want a home that fits me, that's all." With a sullen expression, Carma added, "Is that so hard for you to understand?"

"We could always put a mobile home on our property or even build a house," Spence said.

"She would never enjoy living out by us." Natalie enlarged her eyes and stared at Spence.

"Out in the middle of nowhere? I should say not. I need the action of the city, even if it is Farmington." She wagged her finger. "No, no. I'm sure I can find a house in town."

"Maybe you'd be happier staying in Mesa," Natalie said.

Carma scowled. "What are you trying to say?"

"You can't seem to find a house you like. Maybe it's because you don't want to leave Mesa." *Sounded reasonable.*

"Maybe you don't want me to move here because you don't have time for me." Her mom played the pity card like an expert. If Natalie didn't know better, she would have felt sorry for her.

"Mom, you're reading way too much into what I said." *Really.*

Spence said, "Of course we have time for you. I think Natalie is only trying to point out that you have lots of choices. You want to make the best choice for yourself." *Always the diplomat.*

"Yes, that's it. You have a much more level head than Natalie," Carma said. She patted Spence on the arm.

"And I'm so gosh darn good-looking too," Spence said with a laugh.

His sense of humor cut through the tension that seemed to build when Natalie spent more than a few hours with her mother, especially when it ended in a disaster like this lunch.

⁂

"I don't know about this tile. And the second bathroom seems a bit small," Carma said with a wave of her hand. "I don't like the carpet in the master bedroom, either."

"But you like it?" Natalie said, afraid to anticipate an affirmative answer.

Carma gave a slight nod.

"We can write up an offer if you're interested, and we can include some conditions," the real estate agent said with a look of hope and gratitude.

"Hmmm. I'm not sure." Carma ran her fingers along the counter-top.

"Would you like some time to think about it?" the agent said.

No, no, no. Don't give her an option. Natalie sent a mental message to the agent. *Hog tie her to that stool and force her to sign the contract right now.*

"What do you think, Natalie?" Carma said, interrupting Natalie's fantasy of her mother bound and gagged with a pen in hand.

She cleared her throat. "I think it's a beautiful house. The neighborhood is in a good area, and the other homes are well-maintained. It's close to the mall and to restaurants. I think you should buy it." As if her mom would take her advice.

"Where do I sign?" Carma said.

A wave of shock almost knocked Natalie over.

"I think you'll be happy with that house, Mom," Natalie said the next morning while they sat at the dining room table. She placed a glass of orange juice in front of her mother, secretly hoping the deal would fall through and her mom would go back to Mesa where she belonged.

Carma sipped her juice. "It is a pretty house. I'll need a new sofa and possibly a new bedroom set."

The phone interrupted their conversation.

"Hello?" Natalie said, not recognizing the number on the caller ID.

"Sister Drake?"

"Yes?"

"This is Julie Davis. I have a big favor to ask."

"Okay."

"I have to go to work in a little while, and my babysitter won't be able to watch my little boy, Cody. I know this is last minute, but I don't have anyone else." She paused for a moment. "Could you watch him today? My sitter will be able to watch him again tomorrow. I'm sorry it's such late notice." Natalie could hear the desperation in Julie's voice.

Natalie quickly recalled the planned activities for the day, including her mother's highly anticipated departure and her presidency meeting. "Sure. Bring him by whenever you need to."

Julie let out a sigh. "Thank you so much. I appreciate it. I'll see you in about thirty minutes."

Natalie hung up the phone.

"Who was that?" her mother asked.

Feeling happy that she could render some service, she answered, "A young woman from church."

Carma peered at her. "What did she want?"

"She needs someone to babysit her son today while she goes to work."

"And you agreed?" Her mom clucked her tongue.

"Yes."

"Don't you know how to say no? You're far too busy to watch another child." She shook her finger at Natalie.

Natalie pursed her lips so angry words wouldn't escape. She fought the nausea floating around the edges of her stomach. Her mother's presence made so many emotions churn inside her.

Carma checked her watch. "I need to get the rental car back and check in at the airport."

Natalie cleared her throat. "What can we do to help you move?"

"I'm going to hire movers to pack everything up and drive it here to Farmington." Carma reached into her purse and pulled her sunglasses from their case.

"We could make a trip—"

"Nonsense. You have more than your fair share to handle here. I'm certainly not going to add to it." She arched her eyebrow. "One of these days, I hope you wise up."

Natalie carried her mother's bag out to the car, gave her a hug, and watched her drive down the driveway and turn onto the highway. Relief soaked deep into her bones.

She rushed back into the house and began loading the dishwasher when the doorbell rang. Bradley skipped to the door and flung it open. Natalie was right behind him.

On the porch stood a tall twenty-something-year-old woman with short, dark hair, holding a pudgy toddler in her arms. "Hi, Julie. Come in."

"Thank you so much for watching Cody. I'm sorry about the late notice." Julie set Cody on the floor.

"No worries. I'm sure we won't have any problems at all, right, Cody?" Natalie reached down and tousled his dark waves.

"Here's a bag with his diapers and wipes. I'll be done with work about 5:00. I hope everything will be okay." Julie turned to leave.

"We'll see you after 5:00." Natalie said, sure Cody wouldn't be any trouble at all.

Cody followed Mariah and Bradley into the family room where they found some toys.

Natalie fed the kids some lunch. She changed diapers and took Cody upstairs to Bradley's room to lay him down for a nap in the crib while Bradley watched from the doorway.

After a relatively easy time putting Cody to bed, Natalie took Bradley by the hand and walked down the hallway. "Wouldn't you like to take a nap too, Bradley?" she asked, knowing the answer, but hoping she might convince him to lay down somewhere else.

Bradley shook his head violently.

"Do you want to watch a DVD in my room with Mariah?"

Bradley rushed to Natalie's room, opened the door, and disappeared inside. Natalie picked up some toys in the hallway, gathered up a blanket and pillow, snatched some dirty clothes that had been tossed into the hallway, folded some towels, placed them in the linen closet, and then grabbed the trash can in the bathroom, intending to empty it into the larger garbage container in the garage. *How can this house become so messy in such a short time?*

Downstairs, she wiped the kitchen counters. A queasy feeling began to overtake her, but she pushed it aside. She couldn't deal with the stomach flu right now because she had far too much to do. Besides, the laws of the universe dictated that moms couldn't afford the luxury of being sick.

She had just finished sweeping the kitchen when the doorbell rang. Hoping the house was clean enough, she smoothed her hair and opened the door to welcome the sisters into the house. She directed them into the living room. Thankfully, the living room was still decent.

After the opening prayer, Natalie handed an agenda to each of the sisters. Sister Cantwell's bright smile made her feel at ease.

She glanced at Sister Richins, her black hair cut in a short bob, and said, "We'll need to replace our pianist now that Sister Richins is serving in the presidency."

Sister Richins smiled and then looked down at her hands.

They began discussing sisters who could play the piano.

Natalie excused herself for a moment to check on Mariah and Bradley and was pleasantly surprised to find them engrossed in *Dora the Explorer.*

She returned to the sisters and said, "Everything seems to be fine with my kids." She crossed her fingers. "We need to discuss helping Sister Jackson."

"I visited her the other day, and she seems to be healing well," Sister Richins offered.

They proceeded to talk about how to help her as well as other pressing needs in the ward. Natalie excused herself a few more times to check on Mariah and Bradley. She stopped at Bradley's door each time to listen for Cody but heard nothing.

She returned to finish her meeting. Sister Keller offered the closing prayer and thanked Heavenly Father for the opportunity to serve in Relief Society.

"Thank you for coming," Natalie said as she stood.

"You will be a wonderful president. I can feel it." Sister Cantwell took Natalie's hand in hers and smiled.

"Thank you," Natalie said.

Sister Cantwell patted Natalie's hand and then stepped outside.

"I'll check to see what else Sister Jackson needs and get back to you," Sister Richins said as she walked out of the door.

Sister Keller held her binder to her chest. She grinned. "I'm going to organize these notes so we can go over them at our next meeting. Organization is very important."

"Thank you," Natalie said. She watched the sisters leave and then ascended the stairs. A strong scent stung her nose, and she followed it to Bradley's room. She opened the door and stood there, stunned.

Cody chattered to himself at the head of the crib. Brown marks decorated the white walls, the sheets, and the blanket. Cody still had what Natalie determined was the contents of his diaper all over his hands, and he proceeded to paint his face. Natalie gasped and covered her mouth. The urge to vomit overpowered her, and she ran to the bathroom to throw up.

With her head hanging over the toilet, she summoned all of her strength to face Cody's finger painting.

She stood in the doorway. "What have you been doing?"

Cody giggled.

Bradley and Mariah appeared next to Natalie. "Mommy, what's on that wall?" Mariah asked. "And on the curtains? It smells like Bradley's poopy diaper." Mariah covered her nose and mouth.

Natalie uttered a prayer and asked for strength to face Cody's mess. She hesitated before walking in to face it. Cody turned to her with a grin swiped across his face. He giggled and wiped his hands on the wall once more.

"No, Cody. That's yucky." The putrid smell hung over the room.

Natalie grabbed Cody under the arms. She hurried to the bathroom, her stomach gurgling. She placed him in the tub and proceeded to remove his diaper. "I cannot believe you painted my walls with poop. This has got to be the most disgusting thing ever."

Cody giggled again.

Natalie struggled to clean Cody. The stench attacked her, and she had to stop a few times to convince herself not to vomit again. Changing the diapers of her own children didn't bother her, but she'd never had the stomach to change other kids' diapers. She didn't want to fail at her first service opportunity, but this poopy masterpiece was almost her limit.

After wiping him down, Natalie ran a bubble bath to soften the smell. She washed his soiled hair and even checked under his fingernails. She cringed when she realized she'd have to use tooth floss to remove bits between his teeth. *He actually ate . . .* She couldn't finish her thought.

Mariah and Bradley stood off to the side of the tub. "Why did he smear that on our wall?" Mariah said.

"I don't know. This is a definite no-no, Bradley."

"No, no," Cody mimicked.

Natalie snatched a towel and dried Cody. She dressed him in one of Bradley's T-shirts and took Cody, his clothes, and the sheet, blankets, and curtains to the laundry room to do a rush wash job before Julie returned. She left Cody in the family room and asked Mariah to keep an eye on him and Bradley while she returned to the bedroom. She held her nose and wiped down the walls and crib. Surely, nothing else would happen this afternoon.

She walked back into the family room to check on the kids. She spied

Mariah, Cody, and Bradley playing quietly with some toys. The front door squeaked open, so she stepped toward the entryway to greet Justin.

"How was your day at school?" Natalie asked.

Justin shrugged. He didn't look at her.

Natalie moved closer to him and studied his face. "Did something happen?"

Again, Justin shrugged, still avoiding eye contact.

"Did you get in trouble today?"

He peeked at her from under his eyebrows.

"Justin?"

He reached into his backpack and begrudgingly handed her an envelope.

Natalie removed the letter and read it. "Where's the handset? I can never find it when I need it." She rummaged through a pile on the counter and then checked behind the pillows on the couch in the family room. "Has anyone seen the phone?"

Mariah searched the toy box. "Here it is, Mommy."

"Who put it in the toy box?"

Mariah shrugged. Bradley followed suit. Cody giggled.

Natalie dialed the number from memory. "Hi, is Mr. Graves still at school? This is Natalie Drake." She waited a few moments.

"Mrs. Drake, how are you today?" Mr. Graves said in his deep voice.

"Fine, thanks. I received your note. What happened?" She reached up and twirled a section of her hair while she waited for the principal's response.

"Apparently, Justin has been telling some of the younger children that I'm an alien and when anyone is sent to my office, I suck their brains out."

She shook her head. "He's been reading a book about an alien principal."

"I would like you to convince him that I am not an alien." He gave a slight laugh.

"I'm sorry. I'll speak with him this afternoon and make sure he doesn't say anything else." If she throttled Justin, that'd solve the problem.

"I've had a few phone calls from parents of younger children." Natalie ended the call.

"I'll take care of it. Again, I apologize."

She set the handset on the counter. "Justin!" she yelled.

Justin appeared from around the corner.

"Why are you telling kids that Mr. Graves is an alien?" She rested her hand on his shoulder.

"He looks like one. He's like the principal in the book." Justin sounded confident.

"A book is not real life." She cupped his face in her hand. "Mr. Graves is not an alien."

"He sucks the brains out of kids, though. That's for sure." Conviction filled his light blue eyes, and his voice took on an excited tone. "It's true. This one kid went into his office, and he never came back to school. Chance Taylor said it's because Mr. Graves has to eat brains to stay alive."

Natalie tapped her forehead with her fingers. "Stop telling stories like that."

"But, Mom."

"I mean it. Please, go out and feed the pigs. And do the rest of your chores. No more stories about aliens." Her tone was harsher than she intended.

Natalie shook her head and thought about Justin's claim. Though Mr. Graves was odd-looking with his bulging eyes and long, skinny hooknose, she didn't want her son making up stories about him eating kids' brains, even if the thought elicited a smile. Justin certainly had an active imagination; if only he'd use it in a more productive manner.

She began dinner preparations, trying to recover from the day's events. She began thawing the chicken and then turned her attention to boiling the water for the rice.

The house phone rang, and she found it under a dish towel. "Hello?"

"Hi, hon. How was your meeting?"

"I think it went well. We got a lot accomplished." She looked forward to serving with these sisters.

"How about the rest of your day?" he asked with genuine interest.

Natalie recounted the day's events in her mind. "Better not go there."

"What happened?"

"I'll tell you about everything when you get home."

"That's why I was calling. I'm going to be late. I have a project I need to finish," he said in an apologetic tone.

"What about dinner?" She glanced over at the microwave, watching the bowl of chicken as it circled inside during the thawing process.

"Save some for me."

"How late will you be?"

"I hope I'm home before bedtime."

Natalie said good-bye and hung up the phone. She continued preparing dinner trying to squelch her disappointment. Mariah, Bradley, and Cody played in the family room.

"You're right—he's hot," Laura said as she and Andrea walked through the entryway and into the kitchen. They both giggled. "What's for dinner?" Laura placed her books on the dining room table.

"Chicken," Natalie said. "Who's hot?"

"Mom, you can't use that word. You're too old," Andrea said.

"Thanks a lot."

"Tristan," Laura said. "Andrea can't stop talking about him."

"We're just friends. That's all." Andrea tried to conceal a smile.

"What about this weekend?" Laura said.

Natalie glanced over at Andrea, who was glaring at her younger sister. "Don't have heart failure, Mom. A group of us is going bowling and then getting pizza. No big deal. It's not a date or anything."

With all that had happened over the past weekend, Natalie hadn't found time to talk to Andrea about Tristan. Seizing the opportunity to voice her concern, she said, "Isn't he a little old to be going with all of you?"

"He's Ali's cousin, remember? She invited him. Stop stressing, Mom." Andrea opened the refrigerator and grabbed a jug of milk.

Justin rushed into the house. "Mom?"

"In here, fixing dinner."

Between breaths he said, "The pigs are out."

"Are you serious?" Aggravation slapped her, hard.

"They've scattered. Can you help me?"

"Why does this always happen when your dad isn't home?" She turned to Laura. "Keep an eye on the little kids, especially Cody. He likes to paint."

"Huh?" Laura said.

"Never mind. His mom must be running late, but should be here soon. Andrea, please work on dinner."

"Mom, I was going to call Ali." Andrea's whiny voice sounded like fingernails on a chalkboard.

Annoyed, Natalie said, "You can call Ali later."

Natalie grabbed a jacket and headed outside toward the pens. It didn't take long for her to spot some of the piglets. They were nosing up the shrubs in the front yard.

"Get out of my bushes," she screeched while waving her arms in the air.

The piglets shot out in three different directions, squealing.

"I hate chasing pigs. Why do they always get out when Spence and Ryan are gone? I have had it with these things," Natalie whispered to herself. "Justin," she called out, "head off the black piglet before he gets through the other fence."

Justin ran, but the piglet was faster and pushed against the wire fencing.

Natalie caught sight of the sow, knocking over the trash cans by the shed. "Let's get in Mama Cass before she spreads trash all over the place." She motioned to Justin.

Natalie approached Mama Cass, their eight-hundred-pound, two-year-old sow. "Come on, Mama, back to your pen."

Mama didn't move. She kept nosing through the trash she'd knocked over. Natalie clapped her hands and shouted at the pig, but the infuriating animal didn't move.

"I really don't enjoy this. In fact, I'd be more than happy to cook you over a barbecue pit. Now, come on. Back to the pen."

Suddenly, Mama bolted and ran to a temporary corral. She smashed into the green panels that housed a chestnut mare and her colt. Mama placed her nose under a panel and lifted it in the air. The mare whinnied and the colt paced back and forth.

"You're upsetting Nutmeg and Socks." Natalie's heart pumped fiercely and her face grew red. "I mean it, you big, fat pig, back to your pen before I make you bacon right here on the spot." Perspiration dripped down her back.

"Mom," Justin said with a look of dismay.

"Sorry. I'm frustrated. We have to get her back in and then maybe the piglets will follow."

"Let me try the grain," Justin said.

"I'll take care of her." Natalie slowly approached Mama. She pushed on her, but Mama wouldn't budge. "Get going."

Mama dug in and refused to move. Natalie pushed harder. Mama stood her ground.

"Mama doesn't like that," Justin said.

Natalie heaved in a huge breath and used all of her strength to push the pig. Without warning, Mama took a few steps forward and Natalie lost her balance. She fell into a mud puddle. Mud oozed between her legs and flooded her shoes while Natalie's anger boiled and threatened to explode like a volcano. She shut her eyes tight and pictured a nice ham roast sitting on her dining room table. "That's it. I've had it."

Justin hurried over with a bucket in his hands. "I have some grain. Let me try to get her in."

"Fine." Natalie stood and wiped at her face. Her mouth fell open as she watched Justin gently lead Mama back into the pen. Her piglets followed, and Justin shut the gate behind them.

Natalie stomped over to the pen. "How did they get out this time?"

"I didn't latch the gate when I went in to water them, and they got past me."

"Obviously, you didn't need my help. They came right in for you." Frustration poked her like the sticker bush by the fence.

"I said a prayer."

Natalie did a double take. "What?"

"I asked Heavenly Father to help us because you were getting pretty mad."

Natalie studied her nine-year-old son. Her heart immediately softened, and the guilt over her behavior humbled her. "How did you become so wise so fast?"

Justin gave her a smile. "Sorry about the gate."

"It's okay. Thank you for getting the pigs in and for reminding me."

"About what?"

"Just reminding me, that's all." Natalie surveyed her clothing and shook her head. She noticed a car turn down her long driveway and made her way over to the house in time to meet Julie.

"Sister Drake?" Her face registered surprise at Natalie's appearance.

"Hi, Julie. Our pigs were out. Don't worry—Cody doesn't look like me. He's inside the house with my daughter, Laura."

"I'm sorry I'm late. Things got hectic at the store. I sure appreciate this. I didn't know what to do because I couldn't miss work today."

They walked into the house. "I'm glad I could help."

"Did Cody cause any problems?"

"He was a perfect little boy all day." *No need to share his expert painting skills.*

After Julie and Cody left, Natalie retired upstairs for a few moments to shower. She stood in the shower with the steam draping around her. *What a wild day. Calmer days will follow, right?* The hot water filtered through her hair and slid down her back.

While the day hadn't turned out the way she'd planned, at least it was over.

Chapter

THIRTEEN

The next morning Natalie was pouring herself a glass of water when Spence walked into the kitchen. "Aren't you going to be late for work?"

"Since I worked so late last night and you have your doctor's appointment this morning, I thought I'd help with the kids," Spence said.

"Really? I wasn't sure what to do with them while I had my physical since the sitter didn't work out." She rarely used a sitter because it was so hard to find one during the day and by the time her kids got home from school to babysit, it was too late to schedule any appointments.

"I already told my boss I wasn't coming in this morning so I could help you."

She was relieved for Spence's offer. "Thank you." She smiled at him lovingly. "I love the annual exam. Of course, after birthing six kids, it's not like I have any dignity left anyway."

"I'll take them to the park to play while you're there."

Natalie entered the doctor's office and noticed a few people sitting on the upholstered chairs. She walked over to check in, hoping for a quick appointment, figuring it'd be uneventful since Spence had Mariah and Bradley. Picking up a magazine and sifting through its pages, she was surprised when the nurse called her back after only a few minutes.

"We need to weigh you," the Hispanic nurse said. She pointed to the scale that Natalie recognized as her enemy.

"Hmmm. That's my favorite." She averted her gaze so she didn't have to face the numbers on the screen.

The nurse took her blood pressure and temperature and entered the information into her laptop. She then showed Natalie into a small room and instructed her to remove her clothing.

While waiting for the doctor, Natalie read a few articles on health issues for women over forty since she'd passed that benchmark over two years ago. She shuddered at the thought of another routine mammogram and decided it was much like lying on the cold, hard garage floor and letting a car drive over her chest.

The same nurse entered the room and drew some blood. "We'll test your cholesterol level and check for diabetes and any other blood abnormality."

"Thanks." *Nothing like being poked and prodded.*

"The doctor will be in shortly."

Natalie returned to her magazine. An article on menopause caught her attention.

The door opened and a tall, slender man with graying hair stepped inside. "Hi, Natalie. How are you?"

She closed the magazine. "Hi, Dr. Thomas. I'm fine. Here for my annual check. Yippee." She oversmiled.

"How are the kids?" He'd delivered most of them so he always asked about them.

"Keeping me plenty busy. And they keep sharing the stomach flu with me. Seems like I've been nauseous for weeks."

The doctor looked into her ears, checked her throat, and examined her neck and shoulders. He listened to her heart and asked her to take several deep breaths.

"Go ahead and lie back. I'll call the nurse so I can give you a pelvic exam and do a pap smear," he said in a calm, reassuring voice.

The nurse entered the room for the exam. Natalie lay back on the table, placed her feet in the stirrups, and counted the tiles on the ceiling. "You know, you'd think I was used to this, but it's still embarrassing."

The doctor proceeded to examine her. "Hmmm."

Natalie wrinkled her forehead, almost afraid to ask, and said,

"What does that mean?"

"You do know you're pregnant, right?"

Her breath caught in her throat. "Excuse me?"

"You're pregnant."

Her heartbeat thundered in her ears. "I'm what?" Natalie rose up on her elbows.

"From the feel of things, I'd say about sixteen to eighteen weeks."

"Pregnant?" She repeated the word, but it didn't sink in. Her cheeks burned and her chest constricted.

"I take it you're surprised."

"Surprised? How about completely shocked." Natalie lay back down, staring at the ceiling. "How did this happen?"

"Well—"

"No, I know how it happens, but I thought you had said it would be more likely for my husband to conceive than me." The doctor had even told her she didn't need to use birth control because it was so unlikely she'd conceive again.

"With your history of irregular cycles, uterine fibroids, and miscarriages, it's a miracle you've had any children, let alone six. But I'm certain you're expecting another one."

"I'm going to have a baby?" The words tripped on her tongue.

"Yes." He nodded with a smile.

"That explains some things." The vomiting, unusual exhaustion, and intense feelings of being overwhelmed at even the smallest things suddenly made sense. "It never occurred to me that I might be pregnant." Disbelief encompassed her.

"Congratulations. I'll give you a prescription for some pre-natal vitamins and we'll need to schedule an ultrasound right away, especially since you're well into your second trimester and past the time we do our screenings. We'll also be able to pinpoint your due date." She could hear his words, but they didn't seem to penetrate her bewildered mind.

The doctor concluded his examination and left the room. The nurse congratulated her and left as well, leaving Natalie to dress. She wasn't sure if she should laugh or cry hysterically. What timing. *A baby?* On top of her new calling, her mom moving to town, and being as old as dirt, according to what the kids wrote in her last birthday card—a baby.

Natalie drove to the park in a stupor. Thoughts ping-ponged inside her head. She sat inside the car, repeating the doctor's words aloud, thinking that would somehow make it less astounding. After a few minutes, she exited the car and, in a daze, walked toward Spence. He kept his gaze on her until she reached him.

"What happened at the doctor's office? You look—"

"Stunned?"

Spence squinted his eyes. "What's wrong?"

Natalie said nothing as she tried to digest the news. She stepped over to a bench and sat down. Spence followed. "Looks like the kids are having fun," she said.

"Hi, Mom. Watch me," Mariah yelled. She ran across the playground and climbed the steps to a circular tube slide. Natalie waved at her.

With a trace of fear lacing his voice, Spence asked, "Honey, what happened with the doctor?"

"I—I . . ."

"Are you sick?"

"Not exactly."

"What?" Spence stared at her.

Natalie placed her hands on his. "We're going to have a baby."

"A baby?"

"Yes." She nodded slowly still stunned by the news.

"Are you sure?" A smile edged across his face.

"The doctor is quite sure. I'm sixteen to eighteen weeks along." The idea still seemed surreal.

"I thought we couldn't have any more."

"Apparently, that's not true." She took a breath. "So much for medical opinions."

Spence blinked. "Wow, I didn't expect that news."

"I about fell off the table when he told me. I wasn't sure if I should start laughing or sobbing. I think I'm still in shock."

Spence hugged her. "What a wonderful, happy surprise."

"You're sure?"

"Yes." Spence hugged her again. "I'm thrilled that we'll have another baby. What about you?"

Natalie was silent for a few moments. "I love having babies. Newborns are addictive. But I thought we were done. We have so much going on right now. I don't have a clue how we'll do it."

"It'll work out." He grabbed both her hands in his. "This baby will be so lucky to have you as a mother."

Natalie buried her face in Spence's neck, trying to absorb his optimism.

Chapter
FOURTEEN

Natalie glanced at the clock on the microwave. *Why was it that seven in the morning always seemed to come so fast on school days?*

She stepped over to the refrigerator and pulled out some lunch meat and sliced cheese to prepare sandwiches for Spence and the kids. She grabbed the loaf of bread and placed slices on the countertop. She knew the drill so well she could do it in her sleep.

It had been two days since she'd learned that she was expecting again. Though Spence had been supportive and reassuring, she still struggled to wrap her head around it. Natalie wanted enough time to process the bombshell before she shared it with the other kids. Pregnancy definitely wasn't on her list of things to accomplish this year.

Of course, she believed Heavenly Father had a plan for her, it just wasn't agreeing with the plan she *thought* He had for her, and she disliked change.

Pregnancy? Now?

Andrea bounded up the stairs, interrupting Natalie's thoughts.

"What are your plans tonight?" Natalie asked, trying to focus on Andrea.

"Bowling and pizza, remember?"

"Oh, yes."

"What's with you, Mom? You seem way out there." Andrea gave a puzzled look.

"Nothing. I'm fine." She finished making the sandwiches and

packed lunches for Andrea, Laura, Ryan, Justin, and Spence.

Andrea found a glass and poured some orange juice into it

"What about this Tristan kid?" she asked as evenly as possible.

"I'm going over to Ali's after school, and then we'll meet everyone else. He'll be there, but we'll all be together in a group, I promise." She crisscrossed her chest with her index finger.

Natalie set Spence's lunch box next to Andrea's lunch. "Take Dad his lunch. He's out in the car already. Hurry, the bus will be here any minute, and you guys are going to miss it." She walked to the stairs and said in a loud whisper, hoping not to wake Mariah or Bradley, "Ryan, Justin it's time to go." She turned to Andrea, "Where's Laura?"

"She's coming. She had to change her outfit. Again." Andrea picked up a textbook from the counter.

Andrea gulped down her orange juice and grabbed a granola bar. "Thanks, Mom. Please don't worry about tonight. I'll be home before curfew. Promise."

"Don't forget the lunches." She handed them to Andrea, sure that Andrea would forget her own head if it wasn't attached.

"Oh, yeah." Andrea gave a laugh and walked out of the kitchen.

Laura rushed into the room. "I guess breakfast is out of the question. Is Dad in the car?"

"Yes. I hope you don't miss the bus."

Laura ran out, heading toward the garage door. Ryan raced through the room.

"Did you brush your teeth?"

"I've got gum," Ryan said.

Justin followed Ryan. He gave his mother a kiss good-bye, grabbed his backpack, and headed out the door. At least he and Ryan had been up early enough to have breakfast.

Natalie sighed. It was always a relief to get the kids off to school. She returned to the family room, sat on the oversized sofa, and gazed out the window. The sunrise painted the cirrus clouds in differing pink hues. The sagebrush, purple against the new sky, softened the lines of the horizon. Brown earth peeked between the bushes while birds joined in a rousing chorus. A new day, a new beginning.

Natalie rubbed her stomach. A baby. At her age and with her medical history, she'd been sure Bradley would be the baby of the family.

But a new life was growing inside her. For whatever reason, Heavenly Father wanted to send her another child.

She cringed when she thought about how her mother would react to her pregnancy. She didn't want to tell her. Unfortunately, time would betray her and she'd have to confess, eventually. Besides, once the kids knew, everyone else would too, including her mother.

Thoughts of Andrea worried her. Dating a nonmember was so dangerous. When love strikes, it's impossible to control or reason with it. And Andrea was far too young to get seriously involved with anyone, especially someone who had different standards and goals.

She patted her tummy. One life blossoming and another about to embark on her own. She hoped Andrea would still go to college even if it wasn't BYU. Parenting a newborn and attending to its needs were simple compared to guiding, teaching, and praying for a teenager to make the right choices.

She closed her eyes and bowed her head. In her prayer, she asked Heavenly Father to bless Andrea to make the right choices about dating. She also asked Him to bless her to adjust to this new twist in life and to bless this baby with health and strength. An image of the young girl at the fast food restaurant popped into her mind, so she specifically asked Him that this baby not have Down syndrome, spina bifida, cerebral palsy, or any other birth defect that might prohibit a normal, ordinary life. She also included a request to help her serve the best she could in her new calling. She then thanked Him for her many blessings.

The phone rang. Natalie made her way to the kitchen to pick it up, eyeing the caller ID.

"Hi, Mom." Natalie absently brought her hand to her temple and began massaging it.

"How are you?"

"Fine." It wasn't true, but she didn't want to engage in a long conversation with her mother.

"You seem a little, well, I don't know. Are you sure you're okay?"

"Yes." She searched her mind for a reason, any reason, to cut the conversation short.

"I wanted to let you know everything is on track. I've scheduled the movers in six weeks. I think both closing dates will work, and I'll soon be in Farmington." Her mom's voice was full of excitement.

"We're looking forward to it." She tried to sound as convincing as possible.

"I need to go through some of my things. I cannot believe how much your father saved. He was such a pack rat. But on with life, right? On to a new place. I better get going. I have a hair appointment in a bit. I'll need to find a new stylist. What's the name of yours?"

"Stylist? Hmm, don't have one of those." She ran her fingers through her messy hair.

"You don't? You do live in the backwoods, dear. We'll have to find you a stylist to fix your hair. You need a new style. Then the two of us can spend time together having our hair done. Won't that be fun?"

Fun wasn't the word that shot to Natalie's mind. In fact, chewing on cactus was more appealing than going to a salon with her mother. "We'll see, Mom."

"Better go. Give my love to the kids. Good-bye."

Yes, the timing was . . . interesting. Heavenly Father certainly had a sense of humor.

Chapter FIFTEEN

Natalie turned on the computer in the family room. After her meeting with her presidency, she realized that she needed to consider each visiting teaching companionship to see which ones needed reorganization. She pored over the current list hoping for inspiration. She heard some movement upstairs but wanted to finish evaluating the list, so she ignored it and focused on the names in front of her.

Mariah ran into the room, disturbing Natalie's concentration. "Mommy, Bradley took off his diaper. The rug in the bathroom is all wet," Mariah said between breaths.

Natalie rushed upstairs. "I thought you two were still sleeping," she said over her shoulder.

"Nope. Bradley woke me up, and I helped him out of his bed."

"Remember, I told you not to do that," she said with exasperation.

Natalie spied Bradley in the bathroom, stark naked. His soiled diaper was tossed to the side and he'd slimed the toilet seat, the floor, and the carpet with dark brown skid marks. "Bradley, what are you doing?"

"Potty in toilet. Yes, yes," Bradley sang. He clapped his hands and grinned.

"That's right." Natalie patted him on the head. "Of course, my idea was that you actually use the toilet."

Bradley giggled. "I get toy."

"You get to pick out a toy when you say bye-bye to your diapers forever and ever." Natalie closed her eyes and concentrated on controlling her burbling nausea. At least now she knew the source of her sickness and could try to deal with it.

"Okay." Bradley raced out of the bathroom.

"Wait. Come back here so I can clean you up."

"He's running down the hall," Mariah said.

Natalie hurried to catch Bradley. She scooped him up and brought him back into the bathroom. "Stay still so I can clean you."

After she washed Bradley, affixed a new diaper, and dressed him in clothes for the day, she cleaned the bathroom, fighting the urge to gag.

Natalie led Bradley downstairs. "How about some breakfast?" She planned to get the kids fed and settled down so she could tackle the visiting teaching list.

"Yeah," Bradley said.

"Can we have waffles?" Mariah said.

"Cereal," Bradley said.

"Eggs," Mariah said.

Bradley and Mariah giggled.

"I'll make some oatmeal, and we can top it with brown sugar. Yummy, huh?" Natalie smacked her lips, though her stomach didn't agree.

The kids nodded.

A few minutes later, Natalie spooned the oatmeal into bowls and placed them on the table.

"I say prayer," Bradley said.

"No, it's my turn."

"My turn."

"Bradley always says it," Mariah said with hands on her hips.

"My turn, my turn." Bradley jumped up and down on his chair.

Mariah reached over and slapped him on the back. Bradley screamed.

"You can't hit your brother, especially when you're fighting about the prayer. Tell Bradley you're sorry."

"Sorry," Mariah said through big lips.

Natalie shot a look to both kids and then said a short blessing. "Fighting over the prayer doesn't make me or Heavenly Father happy."

She put a spoon in Bradley's hand. "I need to work on the computer for a little while."

Natalie returned to the visiting teaching list. She said several silent prayers as she considered the name of each sister in the ward.

Mariah chased Bradley into the family room. "Riah get me," Bradley said.

"Did you finish your breakfast?" Natalie glanced at both kids.

"Yep," Mariah said.

Bradley nodded, wearing a grin.

"How about watching *Sesame Street?*"

"Yay!" Mariah and Bradley said together.

Natalie turned on the television. She found a couple of big pillows for Mariah and Bradley to use. She returned to the computer and compiled a list of changes.

When *Sesame Street* ended, both kids began running through the room. Not having the strength to combat their energy, she said, "I think it's time for reading some books. Why don't you go pick some out from the bookshelf in the living room and we'll read?"

The kids hurried out of the room. Natalie decided to take a short break and headed for the restroom. After a few minutes, she walked back into the family room to find Bradley playing at the computer. Her heart seized.

"What are you doing?"

"Watch me," Bradley said.

Natalie rushed to the computer. "What have you done? The screen is blank. Where's my list?" Natalie searched the document hoping he'd hit the return key multiple times—nothing. She clicked the undo key—didn't work. She tried to retrieve an autosaved copy—no luck. Hitting her forehead with her hand, she yelled, "Mariah?"

Mariah stepped meekly into the room.

"Do you know what Bradley did to my list?" she asked, trying to control her anger.

Mariah bit her lip. She gave a slight nod.

"Well?" Natalie balled her fists.

"I showed him on there." Mariah pointed to the keyboard.

"Showed him what?"

Mariah pointed to a key.

"The delete key?" Irate voices yelled inside her head.

"It makes all the letters disappear like magic." Mariah grinned.

Natalie chewed her fingernail.

"Then he did this." Mariah hit a bunch of keys at once.

Natalie grabbed at her hands. "Don't do that."

"Sorry, Mommy." Mariah blinked.

"All that work, gone. I should've saved it. I know better. Why were you playing on the computer?" She didn't expect a reasonable answer.

"I Mommy," Bradley said, moving toward the computer again.

Natalie stepped in front of him. She gritted her teeth and said, "Mommy is not happy. Both of you get time-outs." Counting to ten wouldn't do it this time, so Natalie counted to one hundred.

Chapter

SIXTEEN

That night Natalie sat on the worn sofa in the family room while waiting for Andrea to come home. Stretched out in the recliner, Spence made snoring sounds indicating he'd fallen into a deep sleep. The house was relatively tranquil. Mariah slept on the floor next to the sofa.

Twenty minutes past midnight, Natalie heard a vehicle in the driveway. She stood and stepped over to the living room window to peek out. She didn't recognize the dark-colored truck.

She wanted to find out about Andrea's evening, especially if it included time alone with Tristan, so she walked over to the entryway and waited in the darkness for Andrea to come in. A minute later, the front door opened softly. Andrea stepped lightly into the house and started to tiptoe across the tile floor.

"Curfew was at midnight," Natalie said from the darkness.

Andrea jumped. "You scared me."

"And you're late." Natalie flipped on the light and folded her arms across her chest.

"Only a few minutes, Mom. I'm a senior in high school and pretty soon I'll be living on my own—"

"Until then, you need to respect curfew. Besides, you promised you'd be home on time."

"Fine." A defiant look crossed her face.

Hoping to break through Andrea's attitude and find out what

happened, Natalie said in a softer voice, "Did you have a good time?"

"Sure." Andrea wouldn't look up.

"How many people were there?"

"A lot."

"Did you see Tristan?"

Andrea gave a slight nod, her mouth in a hard line.

"Tell me about it," she said impartially, wanting to get as much information about the evening as she could.

"I'm too tired. I want to go to bed." Andrea turned away from Natalie.

Natalie could tell that Andrea had no desire to open up. "Okay. See you in the morning."

Andrea rushed to the stairs and descended them to the basement.

Natalie returned to the family room feeling deflated. She plopped on the couch, convinced of Andrea's intention to date Tristan and even more afraid of where it might lead.

Two days later, Natalie walked tentatively over to the Relief Society room after Sunday School. With her heart pounding, she concentrated on what to say when she conducted her first meeting as president. She didn't want to say the wrong thing or do anything out of order, so once she was inside the room, she consulted her notebook. She listened to the prelude music hoping it would calm her fluttering nerves. She was grateful Sister Richins had agreed to continue playing the piano until the bishop called a new pianist.

She glanced at the clock on the wall and knew it was time to begin the meeting. Her knees knocking against each other, Natalie stood, cleared her throat, and said, "I'd like to welcome you all to Primary this morning. We're glad you're here." She felt a tug on her skirt, so she looked back at Sister Keller, who mouthed, "Relief Society."

Natalie's face warmed when she realized what she'd said. "Uh, I mean Relief Society. Welcome to Relief Society." She drew in a breath and added, "I guess you can take the girl out of Primary, but you can't take Primary out of the girl." A few sisters chuckled, which made Natalie feel a bit more relaxed.

After Relief Society, an older, plump sister with graying hair approached her. "Sister Drake, may I have a word?"

"What can I do for you, Sister Handey?"

"I need to speak to you about visiting teaching," she said in a rough tone.

"Ah, yes. I'm working on a new list. Bradley gave me a little help on it—"

"I simply can't visit Lorraine Jergens."

"Huh?" Sister Jergens was a kind woman who constantly served her neighbors and made the most delicious wheat bread.

"I tried to explain this to our last president when she gave us our new assignments a few months ago, but she wouldn't listen." She narrowed her eyes.

"I'm not sure I—"

"Her mother said nasty things about my mother all while they were teenagers."

Surprised at Sister Handey's complaint, Natalie said, "Wasn't that a long time ago?"

Sister Handey glowered at her. "We've never been friends. We've lived in the same ward but never associated with one another. It isn't fitting after the things her mother said."

Natalie took a deep breath. "Maybe you could learn to be friends?"

She pointed her finger at Natalie. "Are you listening to me? I said we're not friends and never will be."

"Well—"

"You're still new to the area."

New? "I've lived here fourteen years—"

"You don't understand the relationships. Neither did Sister Crocker or she would never have assigned me to visit teach Lorraine. Now, I'll thank you to see that it's changed." She jerked her chin up.

"I . . . I," Natalie stammered.

"I've said my piece. I'll expect a change in my visiting teaching this month. Thank you." She turned and ambled away.

Natalie replayed their conversation. Was she serious? A grudge that's lasted all these years. *Ridiculous.* She wagered that Sister Handey didn't even know what had transpired so many years earlier.

Laura walked up to her. "Can we go home?"

Natalie shook off her daze and said, "Yes, I think we can leave now."

Back at home, Natalie changed into some sweats and lay down on her bed.

"How are you feeling?" Spence sat on the bed and rested his hand on her shoulder.

"Tired, nauseous, appalled." She wanted to sleep for a month or so and let Spence take care of the house and kids.

"I'm sorry." He rubbed her shoulder.

"I don't understand how anyone can hold a grudge for so long. Oh, wait. My mother can do that." Thoughts of her mother overshadowed Sister Handey's bitter words.

"Still worried about her moving here?"

"Yep."

"Maybe—"

"She'll lose it when she finds out we're having another baby. I can already hear the lecture." Her neck muscles tensed.

Spence clasped his hands together. "I'm excited we're having a baby," he said with enthusiasm.

Natalie sat up. "I'd come to terms with the idea we wouldn't have any more babies. I didn't like it, but I'd accepted it and moved on. Now, everything has changed."

Spence's smile erupted. "When can we tell the kids?"

"I don't know. Maybe in a few days when I've acclimated to the whole thing. I'm thrilled I'll have a snuggly newborn again, but I'm still shocked. With everything else going on . . . "

"Heavenly Father will provide a way."

Natalie nodded and threw her arms around Spence's neck, wishing she had the same unshakable faith Spence had.

"This probably isn't the best time to tell you," he said, "but I have to go on a business trip."

Trying to be upbeat, Natalie asked, "When?"

"A week from Monday."

She gazed at him. "How long?" So much for sleeping and abdicating all of her household and childrearing responsibilities to Spence—nice fantasy while it lasted.

"Five days. I'll fly back to Farmington on Saturday. The last meeting is too late for me to come home on Friday. I hoped to avoid it but looks like I can't." He touched her face. "I'm sorry."

"It's not your fault." She put her hand on his. "We'll be okay. We can tell the kids about the baby when you get back." She mentally computed all she'd have to do in his absence and tried not to let it overwhelm her.

Spence gave her a hug. "Thanks for being understanding. I wish I didn't have to go."

Chapter
SEVENTEEN

Spence had been gone for three days, and Natalie felt his tangible absence. She surveyed the dinner table and kitchen counters littered with dishes. "Let's clean up. Ryan, it's your turn to clear, and Andrea, you're on dishes," Natalie said. Though it was a school night, she promised the kids a family movie if they did their chores without complaint. She looked forward to winding down.

"Mom, I can't," Andrea said.

Confused, Natalie said, "Why not?"

"I'm going to town." Her gaze darted between Natalie and the floor.

"What are you talking about?" Natalie couldn't figure out why Andrea needed to go back to town.

Andrea hesitated. Finally, she said, "I'm going to hang out."

"Not tonight."

"Why not?" Andrea said with a hard voice.

Natalie stood firm and said, "It's a school night."

Andrea placed one hand on her hip. "I'm an adult. I should be able to go hang out with friends whenever I want." Natalie could hear the rebellion in her voice.

With restraint Natalie said, "You still live here, Andrea, and you know we have rules about going out on school nights."

"But—"

"Not tonight. You can either watch a family movie with us or go downstairs to your room. It's up to you."

"He's already on his way," Andrea blurted out.

"Who?" By the look on Andrea's face, Natalie already knew the answer.

"Tristan."

Natalie's jaw tightened. "Better call him and tell him not to drive out here because you're not going out tonight." Natalie was taken aback by Andrea's audacity.

"Mom!"

"I'm serious. This is a school night." She refused to give in, especially since she didn't want Andrea to spend time with Tristan, school night or otherwise.

"But—"

"I thought you and Tristan were only friends. Has something changed?" Natalie concluded by the smile that poked around the corners of Andrea's mouth that they'd surpassed friendship. "Well?"

"Don't lecture me, Mom. We like hanging out, that's all. Don't stress about it," Andrea said, attempting to brush it off.

Natalie argued with herself. She didn't want to exacerbate the situation, but she couldn't remain silent. Her heartbeat pounded in her cheeks. "I'm stressed. Very stressed. You have no idea how dangerous—"

"We're only hanging out, Mom." Andrea shook her head. "No big deal."

With as much control as she could muster, Natalie said, "Not tonight."

Andrea narrowed her eyes. "Fine."

"You better call him, so he doesn't show up here." Natalie's cheeks burned.

"I will." Andrea stormed off, and Natalie heard her door slam shut.

Natalie exhaled, feeling like one of the horses had kicked her.

"Are you okay, Mommy?" Mariah stroked Natalie's arm.

Natalie took a breath, hoping to calm down. She gazed down at Mariah. "Yes, honey. Why don't you go play with Bradley until we start the movie?"

"Okay." Mariah trotted out of the kitchen.

"You're overreacting," Laura said from the dining room table.

"No, I'm not."

"They're just hanging out." Laura flipped her dirty blonde hair behind her shoulders.

Natalie raised her eyebrows. "I don't care what you call it. Andrea is playing with fire, and she's going to get burned if she isn't careful." Worry crawled up her back.

"It's not like that." Laura shrugged.

"Obviously, she likes him. What if she falls in love with him?" Considering that possibility brought her to the verge of tears.

"Mom, she's only eighteen." Laura popped a cookie into her mouth.

"You can't plan love. That's why it's so important to date, or hang out with, only young men that are worthy to take you to the temple." *Andrea knew this.*

"Andrea isn't interested in falling in love or getting married. You need to lighten up and stop harassing her about Tristan."

"If she wants to get married in the temple—"

"She does. I promise she won't marry Tristan. She only wants to hang out with him until she leaves for college in August. It's nothing serious." Laura leaned back in her chair.

"I hope you're right," Natalie said with disbelief.

Natalie handed some plates to Ryan.

"Mom?"

"Yes?" She turned to focus on Ryan.

"Coach wants me to play in the tournaments. He wants me on the tournament team." Ryan stacked plates next to the sink.

"We already discussed this after the parent meeting."

"I know, but I really want to play." His eyes pleaded with her.

"The tournaments are on Sunday." She opened the dishwasher and started unloading dishes since she was sure Andrea wouldn't return voluntarily to do the job and she didn't have the energy to fight with her about it.

"But next year I'll be in high school, and playing in the tournaments will help me make the team. The Scorpions have a great team."

"I don't think you have to play in tournaments on Sunday. You're a great player. I'm sure you'll make the team next year." She set some bowls in the cupboard wondering why she now had to stand her ground with another child. *Who forgot to notify her that it was National Push*

Your Mother to the Limit Day?

Ryan's voice was filled with emotion. "Mom, this is important to me."

"I know it is." She gazed directly into Ryan's eyes. "But keeping the Sabbath day holy is more important, don't you think?"

Ryan cast his glance downward and mumbled, "I guess."

"Don't you think that if you keep the commandments, Heavenly Father will bless you?" She placed some silverware in the drawer.

Ryan shrugged.

"Ryan?" She could tell by his expression that he didn't agree with her.

"I want to play as much as I can." He shrugged again. "I don't see why it'd be so bad to play a few times this spring. There aren't that many tournaments."

"You've never played in tournaments before." She couldn't understand his sudden desire.

"Yeah, but I wanted to. All the guys think I'm lame because I don't play in the tournaments." His voice quieted. "They're all better than me because they've had extra game time. I don't understand why—"

"I'm not going to discuss this with you anymore tonight." Irritation edged up the back of her neck.

"But, Mom—"

"No more." She threw some silverware into the drawer. "Finish clearing the table." Natalie wanted to pull her hair out.

After watching *Ice Age*, Natalie stepped over bits of popcorn and navigated her way around cups and bowls. She sent Justin, Ryan, and Laura to bed, and roused a sleeping Mariah to lead her to bed. She'd already placed Bradley in his crib an hour earlier after he'd fallen asleep on the couch. Andrea had chosen to stay in her room all night. Natalie was making her way to her bedroom when her cell phone rang, and she recognized the familiar ringtone assigned to Spence.

"Hi, honey," she said into her phone.

"How's my sweetheart?" came his soothing voice.

"Okay."

"What happened?"

"Why do you think something happened?" Spence could always tell when things were amiss.

"By the tone of your voice," he said in his usual gentle way.

She told him what had happened with Andrea and Ryan.

"I'm sorry the kids are being hard," he said with sincerity.

A tear snaked down her cheek. "It's been a long week without you."

"I'll be home soon to help." His concern flowed through the phone.

"I love you and miss you." Natalie couldn't wait for him to return home because she needed his strength and support.

"I love you and miss you too. Good night."

Natalie closed her phone. She lay down and drifted off to sleep. A flapping sound echoed in her dreams. Then she felt the displacement of air above her head. She opened her eyes, taking a few moments to adjust to the darkness. She could feel something flit across the room.

Her arms erupted with goose bumps.

She jumped to her feet and turned on the light. On the wall above her bed hung a bat. A creepy, crawly bug sensation traveled up her back and across her limbs.

A bat? In my bedroom?

She stood there, paralyzed, trying to decide what to do. Afraid to leave her bedroom and let the bat escape into other parts of the house, she called out for Ryan. After he didn't respond, she called out for Laura and then Andrea, realizing they probably wouldn't hear her but not knowing who else to call.

She kept her eyes fixed on the intruder with its beady eyes and shaggy body. She once again shouted for Ryan, Laura, and Andrea. She ignored her revulsion and focused on removing the flying rat.

Laura stumbled into her bedroom. "I was using the bathroom when I heard you yelling up here. What's wrong?"

"Go get a broom," Natalie shrieked.

Laura rubbed her eyes and asked, "Why?"

"There's a bat on the wall."

Laura caught sight of the creature and gasped. "Why do you need a broom?"

"So I can smash it."

"I'm going to be sick," Laura said, covering her mouth.

"Do you have a better idea?" Thoughts of a bat nesting in her hair sent shivers through her.

"Anything's better than having smashed bat guts on the wall."

The bat suddenly flew across the room and landed on the opposite wall. Natalie and Laura screamed.

Another idea emerged. "Hurry, get a sheet." Natalie kept her gaze on the winged creature.

"Huh?" Laura wrinkled her nose in confusion.

"I'll throw it over the bat, catch it, and take it outside," Natalie said as she pantomimed the actions.

Laura rushed to the linen closet. She handed her mother a light blue sheet.

Natalie tiptoed toward the bat. She rocked back and forth a few times, took a deep breath, and tossed the sheet over the creature. "I got him," she yelled, her arms and legs quaking.

"Now what?" Laura jumped on the bed.

"Grab the sheet."

"I'm not touching that sheet. No way." She held up her hands in defiance.

"Fine. I'll get it." Natalie reached down, a prickling sensation niggling at the back of her neck, and gathered the sheet into a ball. She ran through the hall, down the stairs, and across the entryway, and then thrust open the front door. She tossed the sheet out on the front lawn. She slammed the door and leaned against it, adrenaline shooting through her veins.

"Is it going to get stuck in the sheet?" Laura said as she ran up to Natalie.

"I don't care. It's out of the house. That's all that matters." Natalie tried to calm her rapid breathing.

Natalie rushed into the kitchen, found a glass, and filled it with cold water. She gulped it down, and her breathing relaxed.

"I won't be able to sleep now," Laura said.

"Check your room and then keep the door shut."

"So disgusting." Laura made a face and ran down to her room.

Natalie climbed the stairs back to her bedroom, sure she'd have nightmares about bats living in her hair.

As she lay in bed, flat on her back, she felt a fluttering sensation and placed her hand on her stomach. *The baby.* Suddenly overcome with love and gratitude for this new life, she let her tears flow freely. The baby was real, and it was time to tell the kids.

Then she'd have to tell her mother.

Chapter

EIGHTEEN

The following night, the kids were asleep, so Natalie decided to answer some emails. The front door opened, startling her, and Spence stepped inside. Natalie rushed to him and clutched him to her as tight as she could. She pulled back and looked at him. "I thought you weren't coming home until tomorrow."

"My meeting ended early, so I hurried over to the airport for the last flight. I wanted to surprise you." He smiled, and his blue eyes twinkled.

She hugged him again, reveling in his embrace and inhaling his familiar scent. "I love surprises like this. I missed you."

"Me too." He laid his warm lips across hers. His kisses still tugged at her heart.

After a few kisses, she said, "I felt the baby move." The joyful anticipation draped around her.

"You did?" He rested his hand on her stomach.

"You won't be able to feel it yet, but I think it's time to tell the kids."

He nodded and picked up his small suitcase, and together they ascended the stairs to their bedroom.

The next morning at breakfast, the whole family sat around the table.

"Mom and I have something to tell you," Spence said.

"Are we going to Disneyland?" Justin asked, a wide grin on his face.

"No, it's not Disneyland."

"You're getting me a car?" Laura said with enthusiasm.

Spence shook his head. "No, not a car."

"We're getting a PlayStation," Justin yelled out.

Spence held up his hands. "No more guesses." He smiled and said, "We're going to have a baby."

"A baby? Aren't you too old for that?" Andrea said with a sideways glance.

After a few moments of heavy silence, Natalie said defensively, "Apparently not."

"Is it a baby sister or a baby brother?" Mariah asked.

"Yes," Spencer answered.

"Which one?" Ryan asked.

"We don't know yet. We'll have the baby in about 4 months or so." Spence grabbed Natalie's hand.

"Yay, a baby!" Mariah clapped her hands.

Natalie leaned over to Bradley and said, "Mommy has a baby in her tummy."

Bradley made a face. "You ate it?"

Everyone laughed, and Bradley joined in, his bright eyes dancing.

"No, no. I didn't eat a baby." Natalie ruffled his hair.

"How did it get there?" Mariah asked amid giggles from the older kids.

"Let's talk about that later." Natalie patted Mariah on the head, glancing at her other children. She asked, "Aren't you excited?"

"I thought the doctor said you wouldn't have any more babies," Laura said.

"I guess he was wrong," Natalie said, wishing for more enthusiasm from her older kids.

"Does this mean no Disneyland?" Justin asked.

Natalie gave him a look.

"I'm sure it means no car," Laura sat back in her chair, sulking.

"I thought you'd be excited," Natalie said with disappointment.

"I am. A new baby sister." Mariah grinned. "She can sleep with me, and I'll take good care of her."

Natalie reached over and gave Mariah a hug.

❧

While Spence and Natalie cleaned the kitchen after breakfast,

Natalie said, "That didn't go as well as I'd hoped."

"Mariah and Bradley are excited," Spence offered.

"Blowing bubbles excites them."

"I think the other kids are in shock, that's all. We thought we wouldn't have any more children." Spence loaded the dishwasher.

"They could've at least shown *some* enthusiasm." She leaned against the counter, her feelings still hurt.

"They'll get excited when they're used to the idea," he said, his eyes filled with optimism.

Natalie held Spence's gaze. "Do you think . . . ?"

"What?"

She looked down for a moment, considering if she should mention what was on her mind.

"What?" Spence prodded.

"The baby we saw so long ago." A vivid image of the child with brilliant blue eyes appeared in her mind.

"During the blessing back in our first apartment?"

Natalie gave a nod.

Spence's expression turned pensive.

"When we had Andrea, I was sure she was the baby, but when I studied her I could see that her eyes and the shape of her face weren't what I'd seen during the blessing." Natalie recalled Andrea as a newborn, and a mixture of happiness and concern settled on her.

Spence shook his head. "No, it wasn't Andrea. Or Laura. Or Mariah with all that dark hair she had at birth." He closed his eyes. "I can still see that baby so clear, as though I'd seen her yesterday."

Natalie remembered her vision of the baby girl. "Large, round eyes, small heart-shaped lips, full cheeks, and blonde hair."

Spence opened his eyes and nodded. "A distinctive chin. And chubby."

Natalie smiled. "Yes, chubby."

"Since I thought we were done having kids, I figured it must be a granddaughter," Spence said.

"Maybe—maybe she's finally coming to our home." A tingle rushed down her back.

The ringing of the phone interrupted their conversation. Natalie checked the caller ID. Her nerves twitched. "Hi, Mom."

Chapter
NINETEEN

"I haven't heard from you lately." Her mom's disguised accusation jumped through the phone.

"I talked to you a few days ago." Natalie chewed on her bottom lip, determined not to tell her mother about her pregnancy yet. She eyed her thumbnail.

"A lot can happen in a few days."

"How are you?" It sounded less sincere than she intended.

"I've got the movers scheduled in two weeks. I may need to stay with you if my house isn't ready."

"Okay." Natalie hoped that wouldn't be the case because both of them in the same space for more than a few hours always seemed to end in disaster.

"You'll help me get settled, right?"

"As long as . . ." A slip of the tongue she knew she'd regret.

"What?"

"Nothing." She pursed her lips and shook her head.

"What are you keeping from me, Natalie?"

Natalie didn't respond.

"What is it? Tell me. Now," her mother demanded.

Natalie gazed up at the ceiling. Her mother would notice soon enough, so it was useless to put it off. Besides, at least she couldn't see her mother's reaction over the phone, which offered some solace. She squared her shoulders, prepared for the onslaught, and said, "I'm pregnant." Then she added, "But I'll do all I can to help you move."

"Very funny."

"I'm serious." After her kids' less than stellar reaction, she hoped her mom could at least muster a congratulations, especially since she claimed she wanted to be more involved with the family.

"You're going to have a baby?" Her mother said it as though Natalie were a young, unwed teenager.

"Yes. I'm due in about four months," she said, her voice beginning to tremble.

"You've got to be kidding." In reality, she didn't have to see her mother to envision the disapproving look on her face.

Sadness edged up Natalie's throat. "No, I'm not."

"You planned this?" She clucked her tongue. "Are you crazy?"

"Mom, I don't want to argue about it." She rubbed the back of her neck, certain that other mothers would be happy about a new grandchild, and certain her mom would never be one of those.

"At your age and with the size of your family, well, what are you thinking?"

Though she was still a bit overwhelmed by the idea, and struggling with how she'd manage a new baby, Natalie said, "That I'll hold my sweet newborn and do my best to raise it to be happy." She could almost feel the baby in her arms and smell its captivating scent, a vision she clung to despite her mother's lack of support.

"I don't know what to say. I thought you were done having children." Carma's condescending tone made Natalie feel as if she should stand in the corner for doing something wrong.

"I thought I was, too, but obviously Heavenly Father wanted to send another spirit to my family." She visualized the expression on her mom's face.

"Oh, please."

She could hold her tongue no longer and knew her shaking voice would betray her emotions, but she didn't care. "Wouldn't it be nice if you could be happy about this? How about, 'Congratulations, Natalie. What wonderful news'? Is that too much to ask from my own mother?" She swallowed through the thickness in her throat.

Her mother remained silent.

"You should be supportive. This is happy news for our family, and we're all excited about it." The edges around her eyes burned.

"It's not that I'm unhappy as much as I'm concerned about your health. And I don't see how you'll care for another child." Her patronizing tone made Natalie want to throw the phone across the room.

"We'll make it work." She found a tissue and dabbed at her eyes.

"How?"

"Through faith." She knew her faith would sustain her, even if most of the world, including her own mother, scorned her.

"Oh, Natalie. That sounds so childish."

Natalie cupped her hand around her eyes. She reminded herself that this was her mother, and she shouldn't call her names or hang up on her, but Carma made it so easy to want to. "You can be happy about it or not. I'll call you later."

"Natalie—"

"I need to go now." She hung up and then pushed the handset across the counter. Spence caught the phone before it plummeted to the floor. Most conversations with her mother were difficult, but this one had been even worse.

"Nice talk?"

"It's so aggravating." She raised her hands in the air. "Just once I'd love to have her support something I do."

"Not thrilled about our news?"

"She informed me that I'm too old and have too many kids. That woman—"

"Loves you in her own way." He ran his hand along the back of her arm until he found her hand, and then he squeezed it.

"I'm not so sure. And she'll be here, permanently, at the end of the month. I honestly don't know if I'll survive it." She wondered if the beds were comfortable in the loony bin.

༄༅༄

Two weeks later, Natalie glanced at the clock hanging on the wall in the dining room, knowing her mother would arrive soon. She tapped her fingers on the table, nervous waves rushing through her while she waited for the impending visit.

Natalie's mind wandered back to her calling as she tabulated some tasks that required attention. She needed to call the hospital to check on Sister Kine, a young mother who'd had an emergency appendectomy the day before. She also needed to fill out a food request for Sister Paddington, who'd recently been through a nasty divorce and struggled to support her three children. And she needed to pray about a new teacher.

Natalie sipped some lemon water and took deep breaths, trying to calm her mother-induced anxiety. At least Mariah and Bradley were engrossed in coloring on papers at the dining room table, so she didn't have to worry about them creating a disaster before her mother arrived.

It was just her luck that the new house wasn't quite ready and Carma had to stay overnight. She cringed at the thought of a longer stay, certain she'd lose her mind, especially since this would be the first time seeing her mom since she'd told her about the baby.

Unable to sit any longer, but knowing she had little time before her mother arrived, Natalie decided to start a load of wash, so she walked into the laundry room and rummaged through pockets before throwing pants into the washer. She pulled out a business card from a pair of Andrea's black jeans and stared at it, realizing it was a card from Zales jewelers in the Animas Valley Mall. A rush of fear ran through her bones while a barrage of thoughts assaulted her. Clutching the card, she walked slowly into the family room. Before she could digest the implications of the business card, she saw her mother's vehicle through the window.

She stepped inside the bathroom to check her appearance so she didn't give her mom any extra ammunition. Natalie hoped the visit wouldn't send her plunging over the edge and they'd be able to get her mom moved in tomorrow.

Natalie opened the door.

Carma examined Natalie. "Oh, yes. I can certainly tell you're pregnant. You've gained quite a bit of weight, haven't you?"

"Hello to you too."

Carma entered the house. "Where are the kids?"

"The older kids aren't home from school yet. Justin is playing at a friend's house—"

"Grandma," Mariah said as she ran into the entryway.

Bradley was right behind her. Natalie's nose tingled. "Have you been into my perfume?"

"Bradley did it. He poured it on your bed," Mariah said.

Natalie drew in a breath. "I thought you were still coloring at the table."

"Apparently, you need to keep a better eye on your children, Natalie."

"Thank you, Mom." Smiling on the outside, she silently screamed on the inside.

Mariah and Bradley hugged Carma, who then reached into her purse. She pulled out two candy bars. "Here's a treat for both of you."

"Thanks, Grandma," Mariah said.

Bradley tore into his before Natalie could stop him. He shoved a bite into his mouth and then grinned, chocolate drool dripping down his chin.

"Fantastic," Natalie muttered.

"Is there a problem?" Carma asked.

Natalie raised her eyebrows. "No problem."

"Can Grandma sleep in my bed?" Mariah jumped up and down.

Natalie silently chuckled to herself imagining Carma sleeping with Mariah wrapped around her. "Sure, honey, if that's okay with Grandma."

Mariah giggled and looked at Carma with a big smile.

Carma patted Mariah on the head and stepped around a chocolate-covered Bradley. "Maybe some other time, dear."

"You can sleep in Andrea's room, like usual." Andrea's name brought back the sinking feeling that something was secretly going on with her and Tristan, and Natalie needed to know what.

They went down to the basement, Natalie enduring biting comments about her poor housekeeping skills. Natalie teetered on the edge of her sanity and desperately needed her mother to move into her own home as soon as possible.

"Will the house be ready tomorrow?"

"I can move in after eleven in the morning. The final inspection should be completed by then. Will you come with me?"

Natalie searched the caverns of her mind for an excuse, any excuse. "I . . . well . . ."

"Unless you're too busy to go with me. Or are you too tired from being pregnant and chasing these two active children around the house?" *Typical guilt tactics.*

"It should be fine."

Natalie left her mother in Andrea's room. She gave herself a pep talk as she ascended the stairs, remembering that it was only for one night. She could tolerate one night. *Right?*

After making a phone call to the hospital and filling out the food order in the family room, Natalie noticed it was time to start dinner preparations. She walked into the kitchen and stared at the refrigerator, sure her mother wouldn't like the dinner she'd planned. Of course, her mom never liked any meals that Natalie prepared, so it didn't actually matter.

She pulled out some tomatoes and started chopping them on the kitchen counter when she heard Andrea come through the front door. Andrea had made herself scarce since their last argument about going out on a school night, and Natalie had left it alone, hoping things would cool down between them. But now that she'd found the card from Zales, a talk was in order.

"Andrea?"

"Yeah?" She could already hear the attitude in Andrea's voice, but she needed to find out what was going on with her and Tristan, and, hopefully, avoid an argument at the same time.

"Can you come in here for a minute?" She tried to keep her tone as pleasant and calm as possible.

Andrea walked into the kitchen and leaned against the wall with an I-dare-you-to-say-anything-to-me-about-Tristan look tattooed on her face.

Attempting to keep it light, she asked, "How is everything?"

"Fine."

"Anything going on?" She hoped Andrea would volunteer some information.

"Nope." Andrea blew a bubble with her gum and then popped it.

"What are your plans tonight?"

Andrea shrugged.

Since Andrea wasn't giving out any information, Natalie decided on the direct approach. "Will you be seeing Tristan?" Saying it aloud made her stomach tighten.

Andrea gave a slight nod, though she kept her gaze on the floor.

Unable to stop herself, Natalie blurted out, "What's going on with the two of you?"

Andrea's head popped up, and she looked at her mother. "I don't want to discuss it."

"Why not?"

"Because you'll freak out." Andrea jutted her chin out.

"Is that why you're so secretive about him?" Natalie looked at her. "Doesn't that say something?" *Obviously, she knows she shouldn't be dating him.*

"Why would I want to talk to you about him when I already know what you'll say?" Her voice cracked.

"That you're making a mistake dating someone who doesn't share your same values or goals?" *Why couldn't Andrea see the danger?*

Andrea rolled her eyes and sighed.

"Come on, Andrea. Your dad and I have always stressed the importance of dating boys who are focused on going to the temple. We've discussed it with the family, and with you privately." Natalie shook her head, trying to hold onto her emotions. "I don't understand why you'd put yourself, and the temple, at risk."

"Mom, you're getting all upset about nothing."

Natalie reached into her pocket and pulled out the business card. She tossed it across the counter toward Andrea.

Andrea grabbed it. "Where'd you get this?"

"Does it matter?"

Andrea narrowed her eyes. "Have you been snooping in my room?"

"Actually, I was going through pockets getting the laundry ready."

Andrea turned away.

"Why were you at Zales?" Natalie tried to keep her voice even.

Andrea said nothing.

"I asked you a question, and I want an answer." Her voice reflected her frustration and fear that Andrea's relationship with Tristan was becoming serious.

"It was a joke. We went to the mall for fun, that's all." Andrea shrugged, trying to play it off as casual, but her face communicated something else.

Natalie studied Andrea, searching for the right thing to say.

"Mom, stop worrying about it. I know what I'm doing."

Natalie hesitated for a moment. "If you're not going to BYU, are you still planning to go away to college?"

"Yes." The answer sounded good, but Andrea's eyes didn't agree with her mouth, and it made Natalie's heart race.

"I hope so."

"You're worried about nothing."

"Am I?" She desperately wanted Andrea to put her mind at ease and convince her that she wasn't interested in pursuing a more serious relationship with Tristan, but she suspected Andrea couldn't.

Andrea shook her head. "I am so done talking about this." She stormed off to her bedroom before Natalie could remind her that Carma was down there.

Natalie closed her eyes. How had she failed as a mother? All the mother-daughter talks, family home evening lessons, discussions after scripture reading—had Andrea not listened to any of them?

Natalie's eyelids flew open when she heard someone enter the kitchen.

"What on earth is wrong with Andrea? She didn't even say hello. She saw me and then disappeared into another room. What's going on?" Carma asked.

The last thing she needed was her mother taking Andrea's side.

"She seems very upset," Carma continued with the familiar disapproving sound in her voice.

"We'll work it out."

"Does it have something to do with a boy?"

The front door opened. "Mom?"

"In the kitchen."

Justin walked into the kitchen. "Hi, Grandma." He hugged her.

"How was your day? Did you have fun at Joey's?" Natalie shifted her focus to Justin.

"Yeah."

She placed her arm around him. "What did you do?"

"Looked for more frogs down at the creek." His face showed excitement.

"Frogs?" Carma said with a pinched expression.

Justin nodded and his eyes lit up. "Joey gave me his old terrarium, and Mom let me put it up in my room. Want to come see it, Grandma?"

"Not particularly." She stepped away from him, the corners of her mouth turned down.

"Be sure to feed them today." Natalie placed the sliced cucumbers in the salad.

"I cannot believe you have frogs in the house," Carma said with disdain.

"And lizards. And a snake," Justin said with a toothy grin.

"Oh, goodness. I could never have raised a boy."

"Don't worry. They're all safe and secure in Justin's room."

"I sure hope so." Carma sat at the dining room table.

Ryan offered the blessing on dinner. When he finished, everyone stood and walked to the kitchen island to serve themselves. After her exchange with Andrea, Natalie looked forward to a simple family meal.

"That's sure a lot of spaghetti, Ryan," Carma said.

"I get hungry after practice." He piled on another helping.

"Is it soccer you're playing?"

He nodded. "Yeah."

"How is it going?" Carma seemed genuinely interested.

With a surly expression, he said, "Bad. My coach wants me to play in some tournaments, but I can't."

"Why not?" Carma tilted her head, her gaze fixed on Ryan.

"Because they're on Sunday. I want to get as much playing time as possible before I try out for the high school team. The other guys are playing a lot more than me, so they'll make the team." He gave a half-shrug. "I probably won't."

Natalie's face warmed. Exactly the ammo her mother needed.

"Oh, no. We can't let that happen." Carma turned to Natalie and frowned.

As calmly as she could, Natalie said, "Mom, we've already discussed this with Ryan. He understands why he can't play with the tournament team."

"Obviously, he doesn't. You don't want to ruin his chances to make the high school team, do you?"

Typical Carmanipulation.

"Of course not," Natalie said, knowing that was exactly what her mother wanted her to say but having no other answer.

"Then why not let him play in the tournaments?"

"I—"

Carma suddenly let out a scream.

"What is it?" Spence asked.

Carma jumped to her feet, screeching as if her life were in jeopardy.

"Mom, what's wrong?"

"It's a . . . a . . ." she screamed, shaking her hands and hopping from one foot to the other.

"What?" Natalie asked with a loud voice.

Justin leaned over from his chair. "Uh-oh."

"Don't even say it." Natalie brought her hand to her forehead.

"I thought I shut the top," Justin said meekly.

"A lizard?" Spence asked.

Justin shook his head. "The snake."

"A snake was trying to . . . Natalie, don't you have enough children without adding animals to the mix?" Carma shrieked, on the verge of hysteria.

"Mom, calm down." She craned her neck, trying to catch a glimpse of the reptile.

"Calm down? You didn't have a snake trying to crawl up your leg. Where is it now?" Carma backed away from the table.

Natalie bent down to look under the table and saw the snake slithering under one of the chairs on the other side. "There it is, under Mariah's chair," she said, pointing to the brown-patterned two-foot-long bull snake.

Justin scurried on his hands and knees toward the snake and extended his hand to grab it behind its head. "I've got it." He stood with the snake wrapped around his hand. "Sorry, Grandma."

"I might have had a heart attack." She fanned herself with her hand. "A snake? In the house?" She threw a sharp look at Natalie. "I didn't teach you that."

Natalie tried to console her mother, but the harder she tried the funnier it seemed. Of all people to cozy up with, the snake had chosen her mother. As she envisioned the snake making its way up her mother's leg, a case of the giggles engulfed her. She quickly covered her face, attempting to stifle the chuckles escaping her lips.

"Mom?" Laura said.

Natalie didn't reply.

"Why are you shaking like that?" Ryan said.

"She's laughing," Andrea said in a disgusted tone.

"Laughing?" Carma said. "I've been mauled by a snake, and you're laughing?"

Natalie tried to think sad thoughts or angry thoughts or even serious thoughts, but the harder she tried the less control she had. After the confrontation with Andrea and with her mother, the emotional release was cathartic. Finally, she left the kitchen to gain control of her laughter.

Spence followed her. "Are you all right?"

"I'm sorry. It's been such a stressful day, and the snake finding my mom hit me as funny."

"Shame on you for laughing at your poor mom's predicament."

Natalie looked at Spence, and they both started laughing.

Chapter
TWENTY

$\mathcal{A}$ few days later, Natalie loaded the kids into the van and drove the twenty minutes into Farmington for her prenatal appointment. She waited in the van for several minutes in the parking lot, hoping Spence had solved the server problem at work and would make it for the appointment. She tried his cell phone, but it went directly to voice mail, so she figured he was still working on the computer problem.

Disappointed, she unbuckled both kids from their car seats and proceeded into the doctor's office. She wrestled with Mariah and Bradley in the waiting area for almost thirty minutes before a Native American nurse called her name and escorted her to an examination room.

After the nurse left, she crossed her fingers that Mariah and Bradley would behave during the appointment. Several minutes later, Dr. Thomas walked into the room. "The hospital sent over the results from your ultrasound." He had a file in his hand. "The technician said the baby wouldn't cooperate, so we don't know if it's a boy or a girl."

Natalie turned to Mariah. "Please, don't get into that drawer."

"It looks great," he said.

"The ultrasound is normal? Nothing alarming?"

He sat on a stool, looking over her file. "Not that I can see. The baby looks healthy."

"That's good news," she said with relief.

"Of course, since you've had other children, you're aware of the testing we can do to be certain there are no chromosomal abnormalities."

"You mean an amnio?" The thought of having a large needle inserted into her belly made her shudder.

He nodded.

"Do you think that's necessary?" Natalie stood and grabbed Bradley before he climbed up on the exam table.

"I don't see anything in the ultrasound, but you are an older mother," he said with a smile.

"Gee, thanks." She grabbed Mariah and sat her on the floor.

"Medically speaking, you are at a higher risk for certain fetal abnormalities because of your age, so the recommendation is for further testing. However, it's your decision. We'll want to do another ultrasound about a month before delivery to make sure we're on target with the date."

He stood. "If you'll get up on the table and lay back, I'll get some measurements." The doctor measured her abdomen and then placed a monitor on it to hear the heartbeat.

"What's that, Mommy?" Mariah grabbed Natalie's purse.

"It's the baby's heartbeat. Please, put my purse down."

Mariah cocked her head. "Sounds like a choo-choo train."

"Are you having a baby sister or a baby brother?" the doctor asked Mariah.

"A baby sister. Definitely."

"Are you sure?" the doctor said.

"I already got a baby brother." She pointed at Bradley, who was wearing a big grin. "I don't want another one."

Natalie and the doctor laughed.

Mariah picked her nose and wiped it on Bradley, who let out a scream.

"Bradley, Mariah." She wasn't sure whom to scold. She gave a weak smile and thanked the doctor as he exited the room.

Natalie left the doctor's office exasperated by her youngest children's antics. She called Spence on his cell phone to tell him about the results of the ultrasound. He apologized for missing the appointment, and they decided to meet at Fuddruckers for lunch. At the restaurant, Spence apologized again. They sat in a booth at the back of the restaurant surrounded by photos of a young Elvis Presley.

After the waitress served them their meals, Natalie said, "I'm so relieved that the ultrasound is normal. You know me—I'm always so paranoid when I'm pregnant that there'll be something wrong with the baby, but every time I've prayed about this one, I've felt like everything will be fine. I have this peaceful feeling, so I'm sure we don't need to worry." She patted her tummy. "If only we didn't have to worry about Andrea."

"Something happen?" Spence took a bite of his bacon cheeseburger.

"I'm still worried about finding that card from Zales." The sinking feeling returned.

"She said it was a joke, right?" He wiped his mouth with a napkin.

"That's what she said, but I don't believe her." Natalie sipped her water.

"Why not?" Spence peered at her.

"Something about the way she looked. I think she likes him a lot more than she's letting on, but she doesn't want us to know because he isn't LDS."

"Bradley took my fries," Mariah interrupted. She made a pouty face.

"Eat your own lunch," Natalie said to Bradley. She handed him his burger. "No touching Mariah's."

Natalie leaned in closer to Spence and lowered her voice. "I'm worried they'll start dating exclusively, if they haven't already." Angst weighed heavy on her.

"We need to sit down and have a serious talk with her about the specific consequences of dating him."

"It's happened so fast. I hope it's not too late."

On the drive home, Mariah sang out, "I spy with my little eye something that is blue."

"The sky?" Natalie asked.

"Nope." Mariah giggled.

Natalie searched the road ahead. "That sign?"

"Wrong," Mariah said with another giggle.

"That house over there." Natalie pointed to a mobile home on the east side of the highway.

"Yep. You guessed it. Now, it's your turn."

Natalie continued to play the game with Mariah the rest of the way home while Bradley napped in his car seat. She fantasized about taking a nap herself.

When she arrived home, she unbuckled the kids and lugged Bradley into the house. She saw the answering machine flashing. She turned to Mariah. "Take Bradley and play in the family room while I listen to the messages."

Natalie played the first message. "Sister Drake, please call me. This is Susannah."

The next message said, "Sister Drake, where are you? Please call me. This is Susannah again."

The third message, "I need you to call me, Sister Drake. It's Susannah."

The last message was a hang up. Worry penetrated her heart.

"Can we watch a movie and have popcorn?" Mariah tugged on Natalie's shirt.

"Can you play with Bradley? I need to make a phone call."

"To who?"

"A new lady in our ward. I think there's an emergency." Stress sat squarely on her shoulders.

Mariah trotted out of the room.

Natalie attempted to call Susannah but got a busy signal. A few minutes later, she tried again only to get another busy signal. She called a few more times but still couldn't get through. Her worry turned to desperation as several scenarios played in her head.

"Mariah?" she yelled in the direction of the family room.

Mariah ran into the kitchen.

"Bring me Bradley. I need to drive over to someone's house and check on her. I think she's having a serious problem."

During the drive to Susannah's house, Natalie prayed that Susannah hadn't suffered a tragedy. The voice on the machine seemed so distressed. Susannah and her husband, Sean, had recently moved into the ward. They had a young son named Jack, and she was expecting a baby in less than two months. Sean had a job with one of the gas well companies, and Susannah stayed home to tend Jack. Natalie considered many scenarios, including a complication with the pregnancy or an injury to Jack.

She pulled into the driveway, her heartbeat racing. "Please, stay in the car a minute while I check and see what's going on," Natalie said to Mariah. "Give Bradley his little car to play with, okay?"

Mariah nodded.

Natalie hurried to the front door of the small white stucco home and rang the doorbell. She stood on the porch for a minute, concern eating her nerves, before Susannah opened the door wearing plenty of makeup and a salmon-colored maternity shirt. "Sister Drake. Come in. Where have you been? I've been calling you all day." She flipped her chocolate brown hair behind her shoulders.

"I'm sorry, Susannah. What's wrong? I'm here to help you in any way I can." Natalie braced herself for the news as she stepped inside the furniture-heavy house.

Tears fell from Susannah's eyes. "I . . . need . . . dinners."

Natalie jerked her head back. "Huh?"

"I'm completely overwhelmed with Jack. He's so hard all the time, and today he's gotten into everything. I know he's only two, but I can't take it. My baby is due in seven weeks, and I'm tired. I need the sisters in the ward to make dinners and bring them to me until after the baby is born."

Natalie struggled to bite the words that wanted to pop out of her mouth. *Susannah was overwhelmed? She left desperate messages because she wanted dinners?* Natalie searched her mind for something to say that wouldn't sound like chastisement.

"Sister Drake, I need help. Do you think you could ask some sisters to come clean my house every week? No, I think it needs it twice a week. Oh, and laundry."

In a slow and deliberate voice, Natalie said, "Susannah, I'm sure you feel a little overworked right now, but I believe you can best help your situation by serving your family."

Susannah ran her manicured nails through her hair. "But that's all I ever do. I only get together with my girlfriends a few times a week, and I only get my hair done every other week. My husband doesn't understand how important it is to have some time for me. That's why I need the sisters to take care of these things, so I can focus on taking better care of myself."

Susannah's whiney voice made Natalie's nerves stand on edge. "Um . . ."

"Oprah had a show all about this today. I know I was inspired to watch it because this is what I need."

"Oprah said so?"

"Oh, yes. And she had experts."

Natalie swallowed back the less-than-kind response that wanted to escape and said, "I see."

"I know it's too late for tonight, but could you please start the assignments for dinner tomorrow?" She played with the diamond ring on her pinky finger.

Natalie silently prayed for inspiration. Finally, she said, "Susannah, there are a lot of things going on in the ward right now, and I don't think I can ask the sisters to take on this kind of commitment."

Susannah furrowed her brows and then turned to Natalie. "Then can you do it?"

Natalie reached down and rubbed her own belly. "Actually, I'm going to have a baby too."

"You are?"

"Yes. So I'm a little—"

"But you have a lot of kids. I'm sure you're used to being pregnant and doing everything. Your family always looks so good on Sundays, and you never seem overwhelmed at all. Could you start by bringing me a dinner tomorrow night?"

Natalie fought the impulse to vocalize her first thought. She wanted to tell Susannah that she was only thinking of herself and that she was an able-bodied young woman who could easily take care of her family. "Susannah, I've found that when life feels overwhelming, the best thing to do is to serve someone else."

"What?" She crinkled her nose.

"When we lose ourselves in the service of others, we tend to forget about our own problems. I'd like you to think of someone in the ward that you can serve. When you do, you'll feel much better."

"But—"

"I'm sure the Lord will bless you as you seek to help others around you." Natalie stepped over to the door.

"I don't know very many people in the ward."

"Why don't you pray about it? I'm confident the Lord will guide you."

Natalie opened the door.

"But, Sister Drake . . ."

Natalie patted her on the arm. "Everything will be fine. Good-bye, Susannah."

While Natalie drove home, she contemplated this unusual encounter. Though she'd felt inspired to ask Susannah to serve someone else, she second-guessed herself all the way home. She still didn't feel confident in her calling and hoped she'd done the right thing.

❧

That evening after dinner, Natalie and Spence invited a reluctant Andrea up to their bedroom for a private discussion. Andrea perched on the edge of the bed with a stubborn look on her face.

"We want to talk about Tristan," Spence said in his gentle way.

"Dad, there's nothing to say." She gazed up at the ceiling.

"I think there is," Natalie said.

"Is this about the Zales card? I told you that was a joke." Andrea glanced between her parents.

"Are you, or are you not, dating Tristan?" Spence asked, his gaze fixed on Andrea.

"We want to know how you feel about him."

Andrea let out a long sigh. "We have fun together. No big deal."

Spence rubbed his chin. "Your mom and I are concerned that you're—"

Andrea cut in. "I don't know why this is such a big deal."

"Because, if you fall in love with him, he can't take you to the temple," Natalie said.

"Seriously? I don't want to get married. I'm too young. Zale's was a joke, remember?"

Natalie looked at Andrea. "Love can change your mind. It's better that—"

"I don't see him?" Andrea's face radiated attitude.

"That would be safest," Spence said. "The prophet has counseled youth to date, and marry, those who are temple-worthy. You can't treat this lightly, Andrea, for many reasons. Even if you only date him, he may expect you to do things—"

"Dad, he's not like that. I wouldn't spend time with him if all he wanted was that."

Spence rested his hand on her shoulder. "But you're old enough to fall in love, so you need to be careful about who you date."

Andrea shook her head. "I like hanging out with him. No plans to do anything else."

A few heavy minutes passed while Natalie silently prayed for inspiration. Her voice trembled as she said, "Our family is the most important thing to me. I don't want anyone to be left out—"

"No one is going to be left out. I promise, I won't fall in love with Tristan and want to marry him. He's a cool guy. We have fun. That's it."

"We want you to understand the consequences," Spence said in a sober voice.

"I do." Andrea checked her watch. "I have a big project I need to work on. Are we done?"

Spence glanced at Natalie and then looked back at Andrea. "It's our job as your parents to warn you of the danger we see ahead. Please, be careful."

"I will."

"I love you." Spence gave Andrea a hug.

Natalie also embraced Andrea. "I love you, Andrea."

"I love you, too," Andrea said, and she left the room.

"Do you think we got through to her?" Natalie feared that Andrea had let the discussion go in one ear and out the other.

"I hope so." Spence pulled Natalie into a bear hug.

Chapter
TWENTY-ONE

A few weeks later, the mid-May sun still hung high in the sky as the stadium filled with family and friends of the Farmington High School graduates. Natalie waddled up the stairs of the bleachers at Ricketts Park while holding Mariah by the hand. She recognized parents from school functions and waved to several of them. Spence, Carma, and the other kids filed in behind her.

"I think this is a good place to sit. I want to get pictures of Andrea and her friends after graduation." Natalie reached into her bag and pulled out the Olympus camera. Even though she and Andrea had argued quite a bit lately over chores, getting ready for graduation, and college plans, she looked forward to watching her first child graduate and then celebrating by spending some time together.

The audience stood when the graduates entered and walked along the field to their seats. The ceremony included songs by the choir and speeches by the class valedictorian and the principal.

When the president of the school board announced Andrea's name, the whole family cheered. Natalie tried to jump to her feet with everyone else, but her large girth prevented her, so she handed the camera to Spence and settled for screaming Andrea's name.

At the conclusion of the graduation, Natalie finally found the strength to stand. She watched Andrea exit the field as a new high school graduate. Gratitude and pride wrapped around her. A twinge of sadness settled at the edge of her happiness as she realized how quickly time had elapsed between Andrea's birth and her graduation. Vivid memories waltzed across her mind, and a tear escaped her eye. Life with Andrea had been much simpler back when her biggest problem was which Barbie she wanted for Christmas.

The family moved out of the bleachers toward the front of the stadium. An ocean of green and white robes spanned out ahead of them.

"Can you see Andrea?" Natalie said to Spence.

"Not yet."

"I think she's over there by the Rec Center," Laura pointed to a large building with a crowd of graduates congregated next to it.

"I see her by the corner," Ryan said.

Natalie looked in the direction of the building and searched for Andrea. Finally, she caught a glimpse of her. She stood next to a tall young man with dark, wavy hair. He had his arm around her shoulder. A troubled feeling emanated from the pit of Natalie's stomach. *Must be Tristan.* From the looks of it, things had progressed past "hanging out."

They eventually made their way toward Andrea, and when she saw them, she stepped away from Tristan.

"Dad." She gave her father a hug.

Natalie reached over to hug Andrea. "Congratulations."

"Thanks."

"It was a nice ceremony. Colby Jackson did a great job on his speech. I remember when he was in elementary school with you. Seems like only yesterday," Natalie eked out.

Carma hugged Andrea. "I can't believe my granddaughter is now a graduate. How exciting to go on to college and use your knowledge for a successful career." She shot a maybe-my-granddaughter-won't-be-a-disappointment look at Natalie.

"Thanks, Grandma," Andrea said.

The rest of the family proceeded to give Andrea hugs. Natalie noticed that Tristan hung back from the group but didn't leave.

"Let's go to Fuddruckers and get some shakes to celebrate," Spence said with enthusiasm.

Andrea hesitated.

"You don't graduate from high school every day. We need to—"

"I have plans, Dad." Andrea glanced in Tristan's direction.

"Like what?" he asked.

"Plans."

"With a group of friends?" he probed.

Andrea cleared her throat. "We have the after graduation party at the Royal Spa. We can swim, play games, eat. Stuff like that."

"Is that where you're going?" Natalie said, trying to pinpoint Andrea's plans.

Andrea's gaze darted between her parents. She looked past them and gave a nod. Tristan walked over. "I want you to meet—"

"Tristan, is it?" Natalie said. He was dressed in a button-down, blue-striped shirt; jeans; and cowboy boots.

He grinned, exposing straight, bright white teeth. "Nice to meet you."

Carma stepped forward. "My, you are a handsome young man, aren't you? What dreamy green eyes. And your smile takes my breath away."

A flash of discomfort crossed Tristan's face.

"Oh, Andrea, you better hang onto this one. He's definitely a winner." Carma reached out and patted Andrea on the arm. "Don't let him get away."

Natalie grabbed her mother's arm and pulled her to the side. Through clenched teeth she said, "You're embarrassing everyone."

"Nonsense, Natalie. I want Andrea to know what a catch he is."

"Mother, please don't say any more," Natalie whispered.

"Fine," Carma said with contempt.

Andrea tugged at Tristan's hand. "Tristan and I want to go out and—"

"What about the after graduation party?" Spence said.

"We want a quiet celebration." The way she smiled at Tristan made Natalie want to scream.

Andrea was willing to forgo celebrating with her classmates, some she'd known since she was in kindergarten, to spend the evening with Tristan. Obviously, their relationship had become serious. In fact, they seemed to be a couple in love, exactly what Andrea had promised wouldn't happen.

"What's that supposed to mean?" Natalie asked.

Andrea turned to Tristan and said, "Why don't you wait for me in the car?"

"Uh, nice to meet all of you," Tristan said as he backed away.

"What are you doing?" Natalie stepped closer to Andrea.

"What?"

"You've been lying to us." A heaviness dropped to the bottom of her stomach.

"No, I haven't."

"Looks like you're pretty involved with Tristan."

"Well . . ."

"You promised us it wouldn't go anywhere, telling us you were only hanging out, that you had no intention of seriously dating him." Natalie tried to control her fury-induced shaking.

"That was a long time ago." Andrea stepped back from her mother.

"It was last month."

"Mom, I don't want to talk about this right now."

"You've been keeping things from us and—"

"I'm an adult, and I decide who I date." Andrea's face contorted in anger. "You can't tell me what to do."

"Let's calm down," Spence said. "We need to talk about this."

"I love Tristan and . . ."

"You *love* him?" Natalie wanted to grab Andrea and shake some sense into her.

"Yes and . . ."

"What?" Natalie braced herself for the one thing she did not want to hear.

Andrea took a breath and then squared her shoulders. "I might want to marry him."

"You can't mean that. You promised—"

"I know, but—"

"Can we discuss this somewhere else?" Spence attempted to hush their heated argument.

"I'm hungry," Mariah said as she yanked on Natalie's arm.

Breaking into the conversation, Ryan said, "I can't find Bradley."

"What?" Natalie turned to Ryan.

"He was right here a second ago." Ryan started to search.

"Spread out and look for Bradley," Spence said to the other kids.

"I think I see him over there," Justin pointed to an entrance gate.

"I'll go get him," Ryan said. Spence followed him.

Crowds of people pushed past Natalie as she considered what to say to Andrea. She begged Heavenly Father through a silent prayer to bless her with the right words. "Please, don't make any rash decisions. Come with us to celebrate your graduation and we'll talk about this whole thing."

"No, Mom. I know how you and Dad feel. You've already told me."

"Andrea . . ." She reached out to grab Andrea's hand, but Andrea turned and walked away. Natalie's heart shattered.

"You didn't handle that very well," Carma said with condescension.

Natalie clenched her teeth. She had no desire to discuss the situation with her mother.

"He's a handsome young man." Carma's voice had the familiar you're-being-too-narrow-minded ring to it.

Natalie shook her head and simply said, "You don't understand."

"Of course I do." She paused to look directly at Natalie. "He isn't Mormon, is he?"

Natalie didn't reply.

"You know," she pointed her finger at Natalie, "that doesn't mean he can't be a good person."

Natalie's neck muscles tensed. "I never said that. You always put words in my mouth." She pulled Mariah toward the street to meet up with Spence and the other kids. She was relieved to see Bradley in Spence's arms.

"You're going to drive her away if you insist on the Mormon thing."

Incensed, Natalie said, "You don't get it."

"You're right. I don't." Carma walked ahead.

Later that night in bed, Natalie said, "This is exactly what I've been worried about." She paused, trying to control the raw emotion in her voice. "What did I do wrong?"

"You didn't do anything wrong." Spence laid his hand on hers.

"I've spent the last eighteen years raising her, teaching her the gospel, and encouraging her to find her own testimony. I've lived my life as best I can so she'd know how important temple marriage is. Now, she's going to throw all of that away for him. I've failed."

"You haven't failed."

"Yes, I have." She flicked a tear from under her eye. "All I've ever wanted is for my children to live the gospel and get married in the temple. I can't even think of her not going to the temple." A physical pain shot through her chest.

"I don't understand this, either. But, unfortunately, it's her choice to make." His voice cracked.

"But it's the wrong choice."

"You and I both know that." Spence squeezed her hand.

"When I first held her in my arms, I imagined so much for her. She's always had this rebellious streak, but I thought underneath it all, she had a testimony and wanted to be married in the temple."

"I think we need to show her an increase of love and kindness."

Natalie startled. "Are you saying I've been unloving toward her?"

"Not at all. I think she knows this is upsetting us, and she may feel we'll abandon her because she's making a choice we don't agree with."

"We'd never abandon her. She's our daughter, and we'll love her no matter what she does." In a soft, quivering voice, she added, "I only wish she wouldn't do this. I wish she'd stop and think about the implications."

"Me too."

Spence squeezed Natalie's hand and then said good night. Natalie rolled to her side, trying to find a comfortable position in which to sleep, but sleep didn't come. Her thoughts tumbled around in her mind. She must've failed somehow with Andrea even though she'd worked so hard to be a good mother and had spent almost half of her life dedicated to raising a righteous family. She'd tried to warn Andrea, but Andrea didn't want to hear it because she thought she knew better. All the prayers Natalie had uttered over the years to help her children gain their own testimonies—were they in vain? Had Heavenly Father heard her?

Chapter

TWENTY-TWO

The next morning, Natalie's stomach grumbled as she followed the kids into the dining room. "I made pancakes for us this morning," Spence said.

"With chocolate chips?" Mariah asked, rubbing her eyes.

"Yes." Spence reached down and gave Mariah a hug.

"I think we'll all go up to the mountains today and spend some time together as a family," Spence said.

"Can we go fishing?" Justin asked, his brown hair mussed.

"Maybe," Spence said.

Laura scrunched up her nose. "Will we have to eat the fish?"

"Absolutely. What's the point of catching the fish if we don't eat them?" Spence smiled.

"Can Grandma come?" Mariah asked.

"Hmmm. Fishing and your grandma? Now that's something I'd like to see." Natalie chuckled as she pictured her mother touching worms and trying to bait a hook.

She hugged Spence and whispered, "What about Andrea? She won't want to get up right now since she came home so late, and we certainly can't leave her here alone."

"I'll go wake her if you'll finish these last pancakes." Spence gave her a reassuring look.

Natalie flipped the pancakes from the griddle to a plate and placed them on the table. After a few minutes, Spence came up the stairs followed by Andrea, who still wore her makeup from the night before. Seeing Andrea made Natalie's heart hurt.

"What did you do last night?" Laura asked. She poured syrup on her pancakes, and Natalie listened for Andrea's answer.

"We hung out with some friends." Andrea sat at the table and reached for some orange juice. Her arm hit Justin's cup, and juice ran across the table. Natalie jumped up, grabbed a dish towel, and mopped up the juice.

"Because what?" Laura said to the kids.

In unison they sang out, "We can't have a meal without someone spilling something."

"Well, it's true," Natalie said in response.

"Andrea, will you offer the prayer?" Spence said.

Andrea said a short blessing on the food.

"Let's finish breakfast, and then we'll head up to the La Platas," Spence said.

"I told Tristan I'd go out with him this afternoon."

"Andrea—" Natalie started.

"Invite him to come along," Spence said.

"Seriously?" A puzzled expression flashed across her face.

Natalie tensed. Inviting Tristan to a family outing would make it look like they accepted him with open arms.

Natalie rummaged through her closet trying to find something to wear. She pulled out a pair of maternity jeans and then threw them to the ground in a crumbled heap. She yanked on another pair of super-sized black paneled pants and then tossed them on the floor, her clothes suffering the brunt of her anger.

"How could you invite him?" she said to Spence when he entered the bedroom.

"Don't you think we need to spend some time with Tristan?"

"I'd rather spend the day with my mom listening to her nit-picking than with this Tristan kid." She tried on a tent-looking T-shirt but took it off.

"If Andrea feels this strongly about him," he said, stepping closer to her, "I think we need to get to know him."

Natalie shook her head, frustration pricking her. "This Tristan thing makes me ill."

"I feel the same way."

Natalie picked through more shirts and finally settled on a gray one. She held it up and said, "Matches my mood."

"We both want Andrea to go to the temple. But she'll never come around if we treat her, or Tristan, badly. We need to show her that we love her."

"But if we welcome him with open arms, it'll be like we approve of it." Natalie held her hand up. "I can't do that."

"No. It will be like we love our daughter, and though we don't think this choice will make her happy, we still love her. We need to separate her from her choice."

Natalie sat on the bed with a sigh.

Spence sat next to her. He took her hand in his. "We can't give up. We have to keep praying, and we shouldn't distance ourselves from her, especially if she hasn't settled on marrying him yet." He rubbed her hand. "This decision is too crucial, and if we can have any influence on her to make a better choice, we'll have to do it through love."

Natalie's eyes stung, and she laid her hand over her chest. "My heart feels like it's being crushed." She buried her head in Spence's neck.

While Natalie loaded kids into the van, Tristan drove up in his black truck. She struggled to swallow her disappointment and sadness. She said a quick prayer for strength to be around the young man that may keep her daughter from the temple and prevent them from being an eternal family. With as much courage as she could muster, she turned and said, "Hello, Tristan," when he exited his truck.

"Hi, Mrs. Drake. Thank you for inviting me along." He wore a cheerful expression.

At least he was well-mannered. Natalie gave a slight smile and nodded. "Andrea will be out in a minute."

During the hour or so drive to the mountains, Natalie gazed out the window, watching the mountain range grow in size as they approached it. Snow still adorned the highest peaks as it would for the next month or so until the summer heat finally melted all of it. Bare trunks of aspens were interspersed among the evergreens.

Several conversations going on at the same time made it impossible for Natalie to talk to Spence. She noticed that Andrea and Tristan seemed to be involved in their own discussion, making her edgy.

When they arrived, they parked the van at the edge of a stand of pine trees and walked along the brimming river. Justin and Ryan picked up rocks and threw them into the rushing water. Natalie grabbed Bradley's hand to keep him as far from the river as possible so he wouldn't take a swim.

"How long will we be here?" Laura asked Natalie.

"I don't know. A few hours."

Laura gave a sigh while she adjusted her baseball cap.

"Why?"

Laura glanced up at the cloudless sky and said, "I wanted to hang out with Chelsea and Alana today."

Natalie looked at her self-centered daughter. "Can we enjoy some family time?"

"I guess." Laura shrugged.

They walked about a mile or so before leg spasms prohibited Natalie from moving any farther. "Can we stop and rest a minute?"

Spence took Ryan, Justin, and Bradley up the river a bit while Laura, Andrea, Tristan, and Mariah stood by the edge, about forty feet away from Natalie.

Natalie found a soft spot next to a tree and sat down. She watched Andrea and Tristan interact with each other. Their ease with one another made Natalie uncomfortable. She saw the smile that enveloped Andrea's face when she looked at Tristan. When he reciprocated with a wide grin and a playful grab around Andrea's waist, Natalie's heartbeat increased. She watched for a few more moments until Mariah caught her attention. "Be sure to keep an eye on Mariah," she yelled out.

"We will," Laura shouted back.

Natalie closed her eyes and let the soft late-spring rays bathe her face. She had to admit that Tristan seemed like a decent kid, and she could understand why Andrea was attracted to him with his wavy dark hair, green eyes, and tall, lean frame. He was polite and seemed to treat her well. All good things, but if they were going to pursue a serious relationship, the fact that he wasn't a member of the Church was a huge obstacle.

Unfortunately, Andrea was too intoxicated with him, and it colored her ability to see five or ten years down the road. Natalie pondered on how she could make Andrea understand the gravity of the situation and the long-term implications of this decision without alienating her.

Suddenly, Natalie heard a scream. Her eyelids flew open, and she scrambled to stand. She rushed to the kids in time to see Mariah floating down the river, face down. "Spence," she hollered as loudly as she could, but he was too far away. Panic rushed through her veins, leaving a tingling in her hands and feet. As if time slowed, she watched Tristan take a few steps, jump into the river, and make his way down the river after Mariah.

Natalie ran along the bank, pleading with Heavenly Father to help Tristan reach Mariah in time. With the recent rains and melting snowpack, the river was swollen and moved quickly. Natalie clutched at her chest.

Tristan finally reached Mariah and yanked her out of the river. Though it seemed like hours, only a minute had passed. Natalie rushed over to them. Fear held her in its grip.

Mariah's dark hair was a wet, tangled mess across her face, but Natalie could see Mariah's closed eyes. She was so still, lifeless, and Natalie's legs felt like they might buckle any moment. She knelt down next to Mariah, unsure what to do except to pray that Mariah would take a breath.

Mariah suddenly coughed, and her eyelids flew open with a look of terror in her eyes. She coughed again and then started to cry. Natalie picked her up, examining her, and found that aside from being scared and dripping with algae-smelling river water Mariah appeared to be okay.

"I tried to swim, but it was too big," Mariah said through her sobs.

"It's okay. You're with me, and you'll be fine." Natalie, filled with gratitude, cradled Mariah to her chest and rested her face against Mariah's head.

Spence rounded the bend back toward Natalie, and she called out, "Hurry, Spence. It's Mariah."

Spence broke into a sprint and the other kids followed behind him. "What happened?" he asked when he reached them, panting from the run.

"She fell into the river." The possibility of a tragic outcome smacked Natalie with tangible force. Tears welled in her eyes.

Spence examined Mariah. "How are you feeling?" he asked in a tender voice.

"Better," Mariah said with a trembling lip.

"She seems to be all right," Spence said, his hand on Mariah's head.

"More scared than anything, I think," Natalie said.

Andrea bent down, wiping at her eyes. "I only turned to Tristan for a second and then . . . I'm sorry, Mariah, I didn't—"

"One small decision can have a domino effect," Natalie blurted out.

"I didn't mean for her to fall into the river." Andrea was on the defensive. Again.

"I know." Natalie could only focus on Mariah at the moment.

"I've had first aid training. Is there something I can do to help?" Tristan knelt down next to Natalie and Mariah, compassion evident in his eyes.

Natalie grabbed his hand. "You saved her life. Thank you." She gave it a squeeze. "I'm so thankful you came with us." Surprisingly, she meant it.

"That's probably enough excitement for today. I think we should head home." Spence took Mariah from Natalie's arms and carried her to the van.

The kids didn't say much on the drive back home, allowing Natalie to decompress from Mariah's fall into the water. She said several silent prayers of gratitude.

When they arrived home, Spence, with Bradley in his arms, escorted Natalie and Mariah into the house while Ryan and Justin attended to animals, Laura went to her room to change her clothes, and Andrea walked Tristan to his truck.

"Do you want to rest on the couch?" Natalie caressed Mariah's head.

Mariah squeezed her arms around Natalie's neck even tighter. "I want to stay with you."

"Okay. I'll sit with you and read you some books."

Mariah managed a smile.

"I'll put Bradley down for a nap." Spence carted Bradley up the stairs.

After rocking Mariah for ten minutes or so, Natalie gathered up some of Mariah's favorite books, including one about cats getting into jam. Then she read some Dr. Seuss favorites and a book of poems by Shel Silverstein.

Spence returned to the family room. "Bradley is down, and Ryan's going to help me change the oil in the van. Do you need anything?"

"I think I'll keep reading with Mariah, and then I'll figure out what we can eat for an early dinner." Ideas of possible dinners floated around her mind, and she decided she'd make pizza, and then they could all enjoy a family movie night together. "Maybe you can find out what Andrea's plans are. Laura wants to meet her friends in town, and I don't want to drive her to Farmington."

Spence left the room but returned soon after. "There's several hang ups and a message on the machine from Susannah." His eyes looked worried.

"Again?"

"She seemed upset." He wrinkled his forehead.

"She always seems upset. I'll call her back later when I have some time."

"Okay. Andrea agreed to drive Laura to town." Spence walked out of the room.

Natalie picked up *Old Hat, New Hat* by Dr. Seuss, but her mind wandered back to Susannah. Natalie didn't consider Susannah's calls the emergencies that Susannah did. Susannah seemed to live on the edge of catastrophe, or at least that's what *she* thought, and she still hadn't taken Natalie's advice and found someone to serve, which frustrated Natalie.

Susannah refused to work through her visiting teachers. She called Natalie for every little thing. Natalie had not only assigned sisters to bring in meals for over a week after Susannah gave birth to her baby girl about ten days earlier, but she had also gone over herself and cleaned Susannah's house, done several loads of laundry, and tended Jack on two different occasions so Susannah could rest. Susannah could wait while Natalie focused on her own daughter for a while.

About twenty minutes later, Spence walked into the house with Bishop Franken behind him. Natalie lay the book down that she was reading to Mariah. "Hello, Bishop."

Spence scooped up Mariah in his arms, and they left so Natalie could speak to the bishop privately.

Natalie stood to face the bishop.

"Sister Drake, I'm sorry to barge in. I tried calling earlier but no one was home. I tried your cell phone."

"I haven't been able to find my cell phone today. Sorry about that." She reminded herself to look for it again.

"I thought I'd stop by on my way down to Farmington to see if I could catch you." The grim expression on his face made her stiffen, anxiety rising.

"What's wrong?" she asked.

"It's Susannah Littleton."

"Oh." Did she actually call the bishop to tattle on Natalie for not bowing to her every whim?

"Her baby is in the hospital. She's critical."

It felt as though an invisible force made contact with her chest.

Chapter
TWENTY-THREE

Bishop Franken cleared his throat. "The baby seemed warm so Susannah took her temperature, and the baby had a fever. But Susannah decided to wait until this morning to see if it went down, hoping to avoid a doctor visit. She took the baby to the doctor, who immediately sent her to the ER."

Worried thoughts circled Natalie's mind as she envisioned the tiny newborn in the ER.

"They think it's spinal meningitis."

"Oh no." Natalie's stomach started to ache. She recalled her friend Janelle's son, who'd had meningitis when he was only a few months old. The doctors had told Janelle that her little boy might die or have brain damage. Thankfully, he'd recovered, but he lost his hearing as a result. "It can be very serious."

"They've been running tests. But,"—he paused for a moment—"they think there's already brain damage." Natalie felt as though the wind had been knocked out of her.

"What should I do?"

"We need to attend to the immediate needs, like childcare for her son. He's with a neighbor right now. We'll then assess the other needs. Her husband was out of town, but he cut his trip short and is now at the hospital. I'm on my way over there."

"I need to make sure I have a sitter, but I'll be down there as soon as I can," she said. Since the older girls were already gone and Ryan planned to go to Ben's house, Natalie decided to call her mother to watch the younger kids.

After the bishop left, Natalie fell into the loves seat in the living room. Fear and guilt covered her like a heavy wool blanket.

Spence walked into the room, and Natalie explained the situation. She added, "The worst part is that I didn't even respond to her call. I figured she wanted to whine. She needed me to fulfill my calling, and I blew her off."

"You didn't know."

"But I should have. Isn't that my calling? To know when people need me." Her shoulders slumped forward while an intense sadness encompassed her.

Spence placed his hand on her back.

"I can't imagine what's going through her mind having a child so ill. I need to go see her and offer whatever help I can."

"I'll drive you," Spence said in a soft voice.

After her mother arrived, they drove twenty-five minutes to the San Juan Regional Hospital and found their way up to the ICU floor, the smell of disinfectant filtering through the air. A feeling of weakness overcame Natalie, and she had to stop for a moment. She spotted the waiting room with a crowd of people, including the bishop, who was speaking to a hospital worker.

Natalie saw Susannah sitting in a chair in the waiting room. Next to Susannah sat an older woman with dyed black hair and a thick waist, who Natalie assumed was Susannah's mother. Natalie moved as quickly as she could over to the women. She introduced herself to the older lady and then placed her arm around Susannah. "How's little Lindsay?"

Susannah said nothing, a vacant expression on her face. Susannah's mother leaned forward and in a barely audible whisper said, "We lost the baby."

Natalie couldn't make her tongue form any words. Grief swelled in her throat.

"They tried everything, but it was too late to save her." Tears leaked out of the woman's puffy eyes.

Natalie turned to Susannah, unsure of what to say to comfort her. She embraced Susannah and caressed her head.

Natalie pulled back, but Susannah still said nothing. Her husband sat at the end of a row of chairs, his shoulders shaking, while an unfamiliar older woman stroked his back. The depth of sorrow hung heavy over the waiting room.

Natalie saw Spence talking to the bishop. She rose and walked over to them.

The bishop turned to Natalie and said, "I'll ask about the arrangements."

Natalie nodded, grateful the bishop was willing to take charge of such a painful duty.

Spence reached over and grabbed her hand. She looked at him with tears in her eyes. Natalie noticed Susannah's mother step out into the hallway, so she followed her. Natalie whispered, "What can I do to help?"

"Nothing right now." She blew her nose. "My daughter is in shock. She blames herself for not knowing how sick the baby was." A sob escaped her lips. With a quivering voice, she continued, "She thought the baby was a little sleepy and not too hungry, but how could she have known it was," she paused, "meningitis?" She wiped at her bloodshot eyes.

Natalie remained silent but reached her arms around Susannah's mother and allowed her to cry for a few moments.

Susannah's mom pulled away and said, "I'm sorry. I didn't mean to break down."

Natalie squeezed the mother's hand and said, "No need for an apology."

"Thank you for your kindness. Susannah speaks so highly of you. I know she appreciates you being here," Susannah's mother said, trying to muster a smile.

Natalie felt like she might collapse under the weight of her guilt for ignoring Susannah's call and relegating it to not-important status. Though she'd experienced her own trauma earlier with Mariah, it certainly didn't compare to Susannah's.

After an hour with the family, Natalie and Spence left for home. As they drove out of Farmington, Natalie said, "I need to make some phone calls." A lump grew in her throat.

After several silent miles, Natalie voiced her thoughts. "I don't understand why a sweet new baby had to die." A single tear traveled down her face. "Heavenly Father has the power to heal anyone. Why wouldn't He heal a newborn with so much life ahead of her? Especially when her death is going to cause so much grief and guilt."

Spence laid his hand on her leg, and she watched a tear roll down his cheek. He cleared his throat and said, "My heart hurts."

"It doesn't make sense. Her death seems so pointless."

Natalie turned to look out her window and watched the sagebrush-dotted landscape pass by the car. She couldn't shake the guilt and shame she felt for ignoring Susannah's call. Feeling like she should've been inspired to know that Susannah needed help, she wondered why she didn't have a prompting.

The answer was simple.

She wasn't cut out to be Relief Society president because if she were, she would never have blown off Susannah's call. She would've known.

When they arrived home, Carma met them at the door. "What happened?" Carma asked, concern in her voice.

"The baby didn't make it." Natalie walked through the house and into the kitchen, sadness weighing her down.

"I'll check on the kids," Spence said. He disappeared up the stairs.

"What a tragedy to lose a new baby and never see it again. Heartbreaking." Carma handed Natalie a glass of water.

Natalie couldn't respond. The grief seemed to smother her. Of course, she knew the plan of salvation, but spending so many months in anticipation of a new baby and imagining that child as part of the family, only to lose it after a few days of life would leave anyone with a shattered heart.

"If there's truly a God, why would He let an innocent baby die like this?" Carma asked. "In my opinion, there can't be a God."

Natalie took a sip of water. "Mom, we don't understand everything that happens. We need to have faith."

Carma waved her hand. "I think that's an excuse. People don't want to consider these hard questions because there are no answers." She leaned against the counter.

"I don't have all the answers—"

"You don't think about why God would let these horrible things happen? Why do criminals continue to hurt others? Why doesn't God strike down men before they can molest children?" Carma's gaze hardened.

"Sometimes, I wish He would interfere, but we all have our agency."

"I still don't see how there can be a God when so many bad things happen in the world."

Natalie rubbed her eyes. "I can only tell you that I know He exists and that He's real."

"How?" Carma almost sounded interested, but Natalie wasn't about to be blindsided.

"I've seen His hand in my life." A few experiences flashed across her mind.

"For example?" Carma crossed her arms in front of her chest.

"I don't have the energy to argue with you about religion today, Mom."

"I'm not trying to start an argument. I want to know why you believe in God." She uncrossed her arms.

"You do?" Natalie blinked in shock.

Carma looked at her. "Is that so hard to believe?"

"Based on my experiences?" Natalie tilted her head. "Yes." She refilled her glass with water.

"I might have been quick to judge in the past."

Natalie glanced at her mother, stunned at her admission.

Carma shifted her weight. "Now that I'm living near you and will be spending so much time here, perhaps I need to . . ."

Natalie studied her mother to make sure she wasn't hallucinating. A gentle warmth filled Natalie's heart. She contemplated sharing a spiritual experience with her mother. After a few moments, she decided to reveal something close to her heart.

With a thick voice, she said, "The night I found out that Daddy had died, I was devastated. I loved him so much, and I felt so sad. I sat on the couch and stared into the darkness for a long time, praying. Then I thought I felt Daddy's hand on my shoulder, and he whispered, 'I'm okay.'" The memory of that night sent shivers across her shoulders, reminding her of the tender testimony she received of life after death.

"Really?" Carma's eyes expressed surprise.

Natalie nodded, engulfed in the Spirit. Even still, reliving that experience filled her with immense love and gratitude for both her mortal dad and her Heavenly Father.

Carma wiped her eyes, and Natalie hoped her mom could feel the presence of the Holy Ghost.

The day of the baby's funeral was solemn. Even the younger kids were more subdued than usual, as if they understood the sorrow. Natalie dressed the kids and instructed the younger ones to be respectful during the service at the church. She mentally psyched herself up to withstand the outpouring of grief she was sure she'd encounter. She wanted to be strong for Susannah and the other sisters in the ward.

Natalie followed Spence in a separate car over to the church on Apache Street. She was thankful the bishop had volunteered to help with the funeral arrangements and allowed her to deal only with the meal for the family after the service. She appreciated his sensitivity to her delicate emotions surrounding her own pregnancy.

Natalie, Spence, and the children entered the chapel. A tiny casket, adorned with pink roses and white carnations, rested at the front. The scent of cut flowers permeated the room while faint organ music played in the background. Natalie studied the stained glass window at the front of the chapel with its vibrant reds, deep blues, and shimmering golds. She focused on the statement under the picture depicting the Savior in the Garden of Gethsemane. It read, "Not my will, but thine be done." The words she'd read so often while sitting in sacrament meeting suddenly had a powerful impact on her fragile heart. Though it seemed senseless to her mortal mind, this was Heavenly Father's will. She needed to trust in His will, even when she didn't understand it.

The service began with a prayer and then some of the Primary children stood to sing, "Families Can Be Together Forever." The message of the song hit Natalie on many levels. She thought about Susannah's family. Then her thoughts turned to Andrea and what a heartbreak it would be if she actually married Tristan. Her hand then rested on her belly as she thought about the new life inside her.

After the service and internment, she and several other sisters served lunch to the family and then cleaned up afterward. Spence had already taken the children home, so Natalie could stay until the last few people left.

"Sister Drake." Natalie turned to see Susannah standing in the doorway, her eyes still swollen.

"Yes?"

"Thank you," she eked out, her voice shaking.

"I'm so sorry, Susannah." Natalie gave her a hug.

"I have to have faith it will all work out and I'll see my little Lindsay again." She flicked a tear away. "But it's hard. If only I had taken her to the hospital right away or known she had meningitis." She held her hands out. "Or woke her up to feed her and noticed she didn't want to eat." She shook her head. "I'll wonder for the rest of my life."

"You can't second-guess yourself. This isn't your fault." She gazed deeply into Susannah's troubled eyes.

Susannah's lips quivered. "I sure feel like it is."

Natalie rubbed Susannah's arm, hoping to communicate her love and concern.

"Why didn't God tell me through the Holy Ghost that my baby was so sick?" A tear trickled down her cheek.

"I don't know." She desperately wanted to find the right words to comfort Susannah, but no words came.

In the car on her way home, Natalie turned off the radio so she could process the last few days' events. As she drove, her arms felt heavy and her head ached. When she'd accepted her call to serve as Relief Society president, she hadn't realized how spiritually painful it would be.

Feeling emotionally exhausted, she uttered a prayer. "Heavenly Father, I have a testimony of Thy restored gospel, but I am struggling to understand Thy will in Lindsay's death. I feel so sad that she died, and I worry about her parents. Please comfort them, and please help me to accept and trust in Thy will and have faith in Thy plan." She reached up and wiped the tears from the corners of her eyes. She concluded the prayer, thankful for the peace that encompassed her.

Chapter
TWENTY-FOUR

After dinner, a few days later, Natalie found Andrea in her bedroom painting her fingernails. Natalie asked, "Mind if I come in?"

Andrea shrugged.

Natalie stepped over clothes, magazines, and several pairs of shoes. She scooted a pile of shirts to the side, so she could sit on the bed. The smell of dirty clothes laced through the stale air. "I like that color." She pointed to Andrea's purple fingernails.

Andrea didn't say anything.

Natalie chewed on her lip, wondering how to break down the glacier that separated them. Several minutes passed. Natalie cleared her throat and said, "I know we're not on the greatest terms right now, and I don't like it. I feel sad that we've been arguing about Tristan."

Andrea kept her gaze on her hands.

"I want you to be happy."

With a quiet voice Andrea said, "I am."

"Are you still thinking about marrying him?" Knots formed in Natalie's stomach.

Andrea glanced up. "Maybe."

"Maybe?" Natalie studied her daughter. "What does that mean?"

"It means we're not engaged or anything right now." Andrea tightened the cap on the nail polish bottle and blew on her fingernails.

"Have you talked about getting married?" Natalie asked with a shimmer of hope that they hadn't yet discussed marriage.

"Not really. We're both young, and we still have college ahead of us." Andrea stood and walked over to her closet. She rummaged through her clothes and grabbed a few shirts.

"I think you're being wise." Natalie didn't want to show her excitement so she kept her face emotionless. "No need to rush into anything."

"Yeah."

Inside her head, Natalie was doing cartwheels. Maybe marriage wasn't a done deal with Tristan. Maybe . . .

Andrea turned and faced Natalie. "But I do love him, and I think we'll get married eventually."

The cartwheels stopped while Natalie considered her next question. "What about the temple?"

"Mom, Tristan is a good person."

"I agree." Natalie nodded. After a few moments, she said, "But what about the temple?" She knew she was pushing the line.

Andrea held a black shirt up to her chest and gazed at herself in the mirror. "Tristan said he's interested in learning more about the Church."

An idea formed. "We should invite him over to hear the missionary lessons. You should see when he's free," Natalie said, feeling a bit of hope return.

"I don't want to pressure him." Andrea pulled a pair of jeans off her shelf. "There's plenty of time for that."

Natalie shook her head, dismayed at Andrea's casual attitude.

"What?"

"You can't treat this lightly. It's too important."

Andrea glanced up at the ceiling. "I know, Mom, but you can't force Tristan to be Mormon just because you want him to be."

"Don't you want that?" Natalie stood. "Don't you want to be married in the temple?" Her face warmed.

"Yes, but I'm not worried about it right now." She picked out a pair of black high heels.

"You should be—"

Andrea cut her mother off. "You're getting all upset again. That's why I don't want to talk to you about this."

"We need to talk about it." She moved toward Andrea.

Andrea stepped around her mother. She tossed her jeans on the bed and placed the shoes next to them. "No. I'm going upstairs to take a shower." She grabbed her lime green robe and left the bedroom.

Natalie sat on the bed, amazed at the speed in which their conversation turned south. One minute, she thought they were communicating, that there was still hope Andrea wouldn't marry Tristan, or at least she'd take time and allow him to investigate the Church, and the next minute—crash and burn. Every time she tried to talk to Andrea, it ended in disaster. *How would she ever convince her to make the right choice?*

A couple of weeks later, Natalie visited her obstetrician. "Since I'll be going out of town, we'll set the induction at the hospital for July 12," Dr. Thomas said. He made some notes on Natalie's file folder.

"I hope I can go into natural labor before then. The induction with Bradley was so much more painful than my natural ones." Natalie avoided thinking about the impending pain.

"Any questions?" Dr. Thomas leaned against the wall.

"Did you get the results from my last ultrasound?" She'd wanted to ask the technician about the results, but it was against hospital policy, so she'd had to wait until her doctor's appointment. She was eager to find out. She'd been praying every morning and night that the baby would be healthy.

"Yes." He scanned a paper in her file. "Completely normal. Baby looks to be a good size, but we still couldn't determine the sex."

"Probably wants to keep it a secret to be obstinate. Sounds like he, or she, will fit right into my family." Natalie laughed.

He removed his glasses and said, "Try to get some rest, and I'll see you next week."

"Thanks." Relief washed over her knowing that her last ultrasound was normal. She was grateful for an answer to her prayers. Although she wasn't excited for the pain of labor and delivery, she couldn't wait to hold the baby in her arms and bring it home to the family. Bonding with a new baby was a period of time she anticipated with joy.

That night at dinner, Natalie looked forward to a calm evening without commitments or appointments. She related the news from the doctor to the family. "Dr. Thomas says everything looks good, so in a few weeks we'll have a snuggly new baby."

"I'm so excited. I can't wait," Spence said.

"Can we name her Rose Magic Carpet?" Mariah asked.

"What?"

"Rose Magic Carpet." Mariah emphasized each word.

"Where did you get a name like that?" Natalie tried to squash the laugh building in her mouth.

"I was watching *Aladdin* and Magic Carpet is sad at the end. If we name the baby after it, then it can be happy. And I like Rose," Mariah said matter-of-factly.

"Does that make sense to anyone?" Laura asked.

"Does Mariah ever make sense?" Ryan added. He shoved some mashed potatoes into his mouth.

"I want Rose Magic Carpet." Mariah stomped her foot.

"We'll see, okay?" Natalie said, trying to avert a Mariah meltdown.

After gulping down his milk, Justin asked, "What are we naming the baby for real?"

Natalie looked at Spence. She cut up a banana and placed it on Bradley's plate.

"We'll wait and see when the baby is born. If it's a girl and she looks like a Rose Magic Carpet that's what we'll name her." Spence winked at Natalie.

Before Natalie could respond, the house phone rang, and she left the dinner table to answer it. "Hello?"

"Sister Drake?"

"Hi, Susannah."

"Can you come over?" Desperation laced Susannah's voice.

Natalie's heartbeat increased. "What's wrong?"

"Sean is so upset. He's blaming God for Lindsay's death." She paused for a moment. "I—I don't know what to do."

"I'll call the bishop, and then I'll be right over."

Natalie hung up the phone, called the bishop, and then explained to Spence that she needed to leave to be with Susannah.

While she drove the ten minutes over to Susannah's house, she prayed for guidance on what she could say, or do, to help. She entered the house and could immediately feel a sense of darkness. A pungent smell of dirty diapers combined with rotting food stung her nose.

Clothes were strewn about the room and trash littered the floor. She walked over to Susannah, whose bloodshot eyes only slightly registered her presence.

"He's so angry." Susannah wiped her nose with her sleeve. "He's locked himself in the bathroom. He said he's done with God and with our family. I know he blames me."

The doorbell rang. Bishop Franken walked into the house. Natalie spoke to him quietly to apprise him of the situation. The bishop left to talk to Sean while Natalie remained with Susannah, attempting to console her.

"I don't know what to do. Everything is falling apart." She gasped for air between sobs. "I called my mom, but she can't be here until tomorrow. I'm afraid." Susannah covered her eyes. "I can't lose Sean too."

Natalie embraced Susannah, allowing Susannah to weep on her shoulder.

Susannah pulled away. "He keeps saying that God can't be real and let a little baby die. He keeps asking me why I waited so long to take her in." She cradled her head in her hands. "I feel so empty inside. Why did this happen?"

Natalie quietly listened, hoping Susannah could release her feelings.

"Maybe Sean's right. Maybe . . . I'm not sure I believe in God anymore."

"What?"

"I prayed so hard for Lindsay. I had faith. I believed she'd recover. But exactly the opposite happened."

Natalie stroked Susannah's hair. "You've had a traumatic experience. You aren't thinking straight."

"If God answers prayers, why didn't He answer mine? Why did Lindsay die?"

Natalie drew in a deep breath. She could give her the standard answers she'd taught in her Young Women and Primary lessons over the years, but somehow that seemed hollow. She searched her mind for something deeper, something that would satisfy Susannah's plea. She silently prayed for inspiration. "Sometimes it's difficult to understand Heavenly Father's ways. We think something should turn out a certain way and when it doesn't, we think He doesn't hear our prayers. We don't know or understand everything like He does, and we don't see things the way He does." She rubbed Susannah's back. "We can only see mortality, and He sees eternity. Maybe we aren't meant to understand some things until after mortality." The words still sounded too superficial, but they seemed to soothe Susannah as she sobbed in Natalie's arms.

After several minutes, Natalie said, "Please, turn to God and let Him heal you. He can make it better. He can help you find joy again. He can take away the pain because the Atonement isn't only for our sins, it's also for all the sorrow and pain we feel, even when our pain comes from not understanding His will." Appreciation for the Lord's tender mercies encircled Natalie as she realized He'd spoken through her.

Chapter
TWENTY-FIVE

Natalie drove home with mixed emotions—sadness, grief, fear, confusion, hope. She felt gratitude that her own family was healthy. She uttered a prayer of thankfulness and, once again, petitioned Heavenly Father to bless her growing baby with protection, safety, and health.

She stepped into the house wanting to rest and recover from her emotionally draining visit with Susannah. Spence met her in the entryway. "How did it go?"

"They're so sad, and I feel sad for them. I understand the plan of salvation, but thinking about losing one of my kids makes me sick to my stomach. I can't even imagine the pain they are feeling." She laid her hand across her stomach. "I worry about our baby. What if—"

Spence cut in. "Don't spend time worrying. Go upstairs and lie down. I'll take care of everything with the kids." He gave her a kiss and then gently guided her to the stairs.

Natalie only had her eyes closed for a few minutes, or so it seemed, when Mariah startled her. "Mommy, I want to give you a makeover to help you feel better."

"Not now, honey. I'm so exhausted. I need to take a rest." She yawned.

"Please, Mommy. I have pretty makeup," Mariah pleaded.

Though Natalie had no desire to play this game, the thought of Mariah not being around prompted her to allow it. "Okay. I'd love a makeover."

"Close your eyes. I have lotion and makeup."

Natalie closed her eyes.

Mariah rubbed lotion on Natalie's face for several minutes. "I think that's enough. In fact, I think it's too much, and it's stinging. Let's wipe some off." Natalie reached her hand out, hoping for a tissue.

Mariah jumped off the bed and scampered into the bathroom. She returned and used a towel to wipe the excess lotion off Natalie's face. "Uh-oh."

"Did you make a mess?" Natalie visualized lotion smeared all over her bed.

"Nope."

"Did you spill something?"

"No."

"What is it?"

"You look weird."

"Why?"

"Your eyebrows are all gone."

"What do you mean?" Natalie rose up on the bed and grabbed for the hand mirror Mariah had brought into the bedroom. Sure enough, her eyebrows had vanished.

"How? What?" She grabbed the lotion bottle. "Where did you get this?" she said, pointing to the bottle.

"In the bathroom. Laura and Andrea use it."

Natalie gasped. Through clenched teeth she said, "It's Nair."

Mariah's eyes grew large. "Is that bad?"

"You removed my eyebrows, and now I look—"

"Weird?"

Taking a few deep breaths, Natalie said, "Mariah, go to your room and don't come out until I tell you."

"But I want to do a makeover on you," Mariah whined.

Natalie couldn't control the rising anger in her voice. She yelled, "You already have."

Mariah rushed out of the room, crying.

Natalie resisted the urge to go after her and instead walked to the bathroom to wash the excess Nair from her face. She gazed at herself in the mirror for almost a minute. Then she slid to the ground, laughing. She was eyebrowless, and all she could do was laugh because if she didn't, she'd cry. Of all things for Mariah to use on her face, it had to be hair remover.

Spence found her laughing. "What's going on?"

Natalie looked up at him, and his eyes widened. She said, "Important safety tip, Egon. Never allow your five-year-old daughter to use Nair as face lotion."

"Oh no." He tried to conceal a smile.

Natalie nodded. "Yep, not a hair left."

"What can we do?"

"I suppose I'll learn how to use an eyebrow pencil. My grandma used to draw on her eyebrows." She paused. "In light of what's happened with Susannah, losing my eyebrows seems pretty insignificant."

Spence wrapped his arms around her. "I'm sorry Mariah did that."

Natalie rested her head on Spence's shoulder, recalling her harsh tone with her daughter. "I need to talk to Maraih because I hurt her feelings."

Spence gave her a gentle kiss on her cheek. "I'll finish dinner. Come down when you're ready." He left the room.

Natalie found Mariah still crying on her bed.

"I'm sorry, Mommy," she sniffled.

Natalie opened her arms wide, and Mariah ran to her. "I know."

"I love you."

"I love you too. Next time, I need to check the items for the makeover." She inhaled the strawberry scent of Mariah's hair and rocked back and forth with Mariah in her arms. She wasn't thrilled to have a bald face, but she was thankful that her little Mariah was alive and well.

With Mariah's hand in hers, she descended the stairs and mustered enough courage to face the family. No one said a word until Justin blurted out, "Your eyebrows are—"

"Gone," Ryan finished.

"Mariah gave me a makeover with some Nair," Natalie said as upbeat as possible.

Laura covered her mouth.

Ryan and Justin broke out in loud laughter.

Natalie sprawled out on the couch in the family room, contemplating an eyebrowless life for the next few months, while she listened to Mariah sing.

"For the temple is the house of God, a place for Sleeping Beauty. I'll repair myself . . ."

Natalie chuckled to herself and didn't correct the mistaken words from the familiar Primary song.

The doorbell rang.

"Who could that be?" Natalie rested her hand across her forehead and hoped it was for anyone but her.

"I'll get it," Laura said, jumping to her feet.

A few moments later, Natalie spied her mother walking into the room. "Mom." Natalie's muscles tensed.

"I came to check on you to see how you're doing." Jasmine perfume filled the room.

While looking down, Natalie sat up and brushed at her maternity shirt. "I'm fine. How about you?" Natalie could feel her mother's searing gaze, but she refused to meet it.

"What's wrong?" Carma stepped closer.

"Nothing."

"Why won't you look at me?"

Natalie knew that her mother would flip out once she saw the absent eyebrows.

"Natalie?" Her mother sat on the couch. It was useless to hide her face any longer.

She gazed at her mom.

Carma shrieked. "What on earth happened to your face? Your eyebrows!"

Natalie related the events with the lotion and Nair mix-up. Her mother responded with plenty of clucks of her tongue and shaking of her head, as Natalie expected.

"That makes it easy," her mother said.

"What?"

"My decision."

"You've lost me."

"You're obviously overwhelmed with so much to do." She patted Natalie on the arm.

"I can handle it." Maybe not well, but she could still handle it. *Sort of.*

"You look awful."

"Thanks." She gave her mom a big smile. "I'm sure my eyebrows will grow back. Eventually."

"No, I mean you look run down and exhausted. I knew this pregnancy would be too much for you." She wagged her finger at Natalie. "I've decided to move in until the baby is born."

"You're what?" She couldn't possibly have heard right. Her stomach churned as she waited for the answer.

"Moving in." Carma smiled with satisfaction. "I'll cook, clean, and take care of things for you. It'll give me a chance to get to know the kids better too."

"That doesn't make much sense. You only live twenty miles away." Reason was always a good tool with her mom.

"Yes, I know. But that's too far for me to be much help. I've already got my things packed. I'll go get my bags."

Natalie tried to talk, but words wouldn't form. All she could muster were a few squeaks.

Carma stood and marched out the door to retrieve her things. Natalie lay back on the couch, wishing it would swallow her. She reached up and massaged her temples to ward off the headache destined to stay until after the baby's birth.

Chapter
TWENTY-SIX

While her mom was busy taking over Andrea's bedroom, Natalie flopped on her own bed upstairs. Several minutes later, Spence entered the room with his usual cheerful expression.

"You'll survive your mom," Spence said.

"No, I won't." She held her hands up in the air. "Why would she come to stay here? She lives in Farmington. Isn't that punishment enough?"

"She wants to help." He sat next to her.

"No. She wants to butt in and tell me what to do."

"I think you need to give her a chance."

"Are we talking about the same woman? Short dark hair, lots of makeup, bossy, nitpicky, rude. Oh, and the look that says, 'No matter what you do, you'll never live up to my expectations.' That woman? Is that who we're discussing?" She ran her fingers through her hair.

"You're pregnant—"

"I am? Really?" She gave Spence an exaggerated look. "Is that why there's this enormous bulge in the front of my body? Because I'm pregnant?"

"You always get—"

She squinted her eyes. "Don't even go there. I am not cranky. I am not unreasonable. I am not overly emotional. My mother is the enemy."

Spence reached over and kneaded the knot in Natalie's neck. "You're all tense."

"Of course I am. Momzilla is living in my house."

"She wants to serve you."

Natalie shot him an incredulous look.

"It might do both of you some good."

Natalie tapped her ear. "I don't think I heard you right."

"You're due in two weeks."

"Might as well be a thousand," she muttered under her breath.

"Why don't I put your mom to work making dinner, so she'll feel useful and you can read a book or something?"

Natalie eyed *Alma the Younger*, a historical novel she'd purchased a few weeks ago, still on her nightstand. She liked the idea of reading for pleasure for a little while. "That sounds nice."

Spence stood and left the room.

"Do you think you'll have the baby today?" Carma asked as she placed a glass of orange juice in front of Natalie.

"You've asked me that every single day for over a week and the answer is still, I don't know." The sound of her mom's voice grated on her nerves.

"I'm anxious to see it, that's all. Are you having any of those false labor pains?"

"Braxton-Hicks."

Carma gave her a puzzled look.

"The false labor pains are called Braxton-Hicks. And, yes, I've been having those for about a month. In fact," she placed her hand on her hardened belly, "I'm having one right now."

"Maybe today is the day." Her mom's face brightened.

"We'll see." After having six children, Natalie knew Braxton-Hicks were nothing to get excited about.

"Why didn't you find out if it's a boy or a girl?" Carma sat at the dining table across from Natalie.

"When I had the ultrasounds, the baby was turned so the technician couldn't tell. I'm glad because I want to be surprised."

Carma sipped some orange juice and puckered her lips. "Remind me to buy the more expensive juice when I do the shopping. This tastes bitter."

Natalie ignored the jab about her beverage choice. "I don't care what sex it is. All I want is a healthy baby that I can bring home and snuggle with. Having the baby on the outside, instead of the inside, will be a big bonus."

"Boy or girl, I guess it doesn't matter. Have you chosen a name?"

Natalie hesitated. Her mother's strong opinions about names always brought contention. She had reacted rudely to Natalie's choice of names for Andrea, Mariah, and Bradley. "We're going to wait and see what the baby looks like before we decide." *Sounded reasonable.*

"I've always liked the name Stanley."

Natalie laughed.

Carma tilted her head. "What?"

"Reminds me of a cartoon."

"I knew quite a handsome young man. In fact, if I hadn't married your father . . ."

"Stanley?"

"Yes, it's distinguished." Carma stood and grabbed a dishcloth from the drawer. She ran water over it.

Choking back another laugh, Natalie said, "You haven't ever mentioned that name."

"I haven't spent this much time with you before the birth of a baby. I feel more connected." Carma wiped down the counter.

"I'm glad." Natalie wasn't sure who was more surprised to hear those words come out of her mouth.

Carma turned and looked at her with a bewildered expression. "You are?"

"Yes."

Carma smiled. "I can't wait to see the baby."

A few days later, after a visit to her obstetrician, Natalie dialed Spence's cell number while she sat in the van with the air conditioner blowing on her in the parking lot.

"Hey, honey buns," he said when he answered.

"Hi. I'm about to leave Farmington."

"How was your appointment?"

"We're still planning on the induction for the twelfth, unless the baby decides to come on its own." Natalie hoped for the latter.

"Everything went well?"

"Heartbeat was 155 and my stomach measured normally for 39 weeks. I'm dilated to 2 centimeters, which is better than nothing. And the best news? I've gained another two pounds since last week. Woo-hoo."

"Now, honey, you're beautiful whether you're pregnant or not."

"Thanks." She smiled. "I finished the shopping."

"I wish you'd let me do the grocery shopping. You're—"

"Big as a barn?" She rubbed her protruding belly.

"No, doing too much. You should be taking it easy."

"I know. But since I had the doctor appointment I figured I might as well shop."

"Where are the kids?"

"With my mom. I put Bradley down for his nap, so she only has to watch Mariah and Justin." Visions of Mariah's past escapades floated through her mind.

"I hope—"

"Mariah doesn't drive her over the edge? Oooo, maybe then she'd go back to her own house."

"I thought things were better with your mom."

"They are, I guess. She's actually been helpful and she's not as impatient with Bradley or Mariah. But I'd still rather have her living in her own house. Anyway, do I need to pick up anything else?" She lifted her hair off the nape of her neck.

"Not that I can think of."

"I decided to get some take-out Chinese for dinner because I don't feel like cooking, and I'm pretty sure my mom will be worn out from chasing kids."

"See you at home then."

"I love you."

"I love you too."

Natalie left the parking lot and drove back across town toward the La Plata Highway. After stopping at Arches restaurant for the Chinese food, she got back into the oven disguised as her van. She blasted the air conditioner to compensate for the near one-hundred-degree temperature outside and cranked up the tunes on her favorite country station as she drove home.

When she arrived home, she took a few bags of groceries into the house. She wiped at the perspiration on her face.

"How did everything go?" Her mother unpacked the bags. Carma's usually perfect appearance was a bit bedraggled, and she seemed tired.

"Fine, but I'm bushed. I brought some Chinese food home for dinner." Her mouth watered at the thought of sweet and sour pork, sesame chicken, and fried rice.

"That sounds delicious." Carma smacked her lips.

"It's still in the car."

"I'll get it for you, Mom," Justin said.

"Okay. Thank you." She turned to her mom. "How were things here? Any catastrophes?"

"No. Bradley is still sleeping. Justin worked on some kind of fort by the big tree while Mariah and I read books, played hide and seek, planned a wedding for Barbie and Ken, and watched *The Little Mermaid*."

"Sounds like you had a busy afternoon." Natalie let out a laugh.

Justin ran into the house, shouting, "Mom! Mom!"

Natalie circled around. "What? What's wrong?"

"Come outside right now," he said between breaths.

Natalie waddled as quickly as possible outside.

"In here." Justin pointed to the van.

Natalie rushed over and immediately saw the cause of his alarm. Between the two van seats sat what was supposed to be dinner. Contents of the take-home cartons lay scattered across the floor. Natalie gritted her teeth. "I'm going to kill that dog with my own bare hands."

"No, Mom, he didn't mean to do it. I'll take him to the backyard." Justin scurried away calling the dog's name.

Natalie, with her shirt sticking to her back, grabbed what was left of dinner and trudged toward the house muttering threats against the dog.

"What's wrong?" her mother asked.

Natalie held up the mess in her hands. "This was dinner." She lobbed it into the trash can.

"What happened to it?"

"The dog."

Carma arched her eyebrow. "Why did you let the dog eat it?"

The absurdity of her question hit Natalie, and she broke into hysterical laughter. She struggled to breathe. Tears poured down her cheeks.

Her mom approached her and put her arm around Natalie's shoulders. "This is worse than I thought. You're beyond exhaustion. I'll take care of dinner."

"Why did I let the dog eat dinner?" She barely eked it out between laughs. She wiped at her eyes.

"Go upstairs and splash some cold water on your face." Her mother pushed her toward the stairs.

As Natalie ascended the stairs, she said to herself, "She thinks I've lost my mind. She could be right."

Later that night, after the kids and Carma were in bed, Andrea wandered into the house wearing a silly grin. One look at her and Natalie knew. Her stomach twisted.

"You seem happy tonight," Spence said.

Andrea hardly registered the comment. "Oh, hi, Dad."

"Something you want to tell us?" Natalie said, fearing the answer.

"Tristan . . . asked me . . . to marry him."

The knots turned to cramps that caused a cold sweat to form on Natalie's neck.

"You're engaged?" Spence said, alarm apparent in his voice.

"Uh-huh. I know what you're going to say, but I don't want you to ruin this for me." Andrea held her hands up.

"You said you hadn't talked about marriage. You said you were young and that you planned to go to college." A queasy feeling overtook Natalie.

Andrea shrugged. "That was then."

"Less than two weeks ago?" Natalie said. "You've changed your mind that fast?"

"Uh-huh."

"I can't believe this," Natalie blurted out, disappointment warming her cheeks. "How can you turn your back on the temple? On God? You know better."

Andrea rolled her eyes. "You've already said all of this, but I'm

171

going to marry him whether you like it or not." Her words were like daggers.

Spence stepped closer to Andrea. He reached his arm around her and said softly, "Can we talk about this?"

"No, Daddy. I want to marry him. He said he'd listen to the missionaries after we're married. We'll end up going to the temple. I'm sure of it."

"That's a huge risk to take," Spence said.

"But it's my risk, Daddy, and I think it's the right decision."

Natalie rubbed her forehead. Anger, frustration, and sadness melded together to wallop Natalie in the chest. "This is such a mistake."

Andrea's face hardened, and her eyes grew cold. "You're right. It was a mistake to tell you."

"Andrea, this isn't a game. This is real life, and we're talking about eternity. You're willing to abandon all you've been taught?" she pleaded.

"Mom, you're making a way bigger deal out of this than it needs to be."

"Because I want our family to be eternal?" The idea of losing Andrea pierced her heart.

"You should be happy for me." Andrea stomped down the stairs.

Natalie turned to Spence. "I can't believe she's going to marry him. We should've intervened. We should've forbidden her from dating him in the first place." Anguish enveloped her. "How can we stop this?"

Spence blew out some air. With a grim expression, he said, "We can't. It's her choice to make."

"But it's wrong." She buried her face in Spence's neck, and he reached up to stroke her hair.

"Yes, it is."

"Why do children have agency? Why can't we choose for them?"

"That's not part of the plan."

Natalie pulled away and swept a tear from her eye. "I don't like this part of the plan at all."

"She's so young. Maybe we can talk to her and convince her to at least wait—"

"She's already made up her mind. You know how stubborn she is. Why can't she be stubborn about doing the right thing?" She wrapped her arms around herself. "I should be thrilled she announced her engagement." She drew in a deep breath. "I imagined a temple wedding, the luncheon, the reception . . ."

"I did too. In my mind, I've always seen Andrea kneeling across the altar from a worthy young man." He pursed his trembling lips.

"I feel like there's a knife twisting in my heart." Natalie clutched her chest, tears forming in her eyes. "Do you think she doesn't believe in the gospel anymore?" Uttering the words brought feelings of despair.

Spence's voice quivered as he said, "I think she fell in love."

"We tried to warn her over and over and over again."

Spence nodded. "Yes, we did."

Several tense moments hung over them. "I can't support it." She couldn't even entertain thoughts of watching Andrea marry outside the temple because it hurt so much. Andrea's decision would break the sealing of their family, something that Natalie had worked her entire marriage to secure.

Spence cleared his throat. "We need to make sure that she understands we still love her—"

"I don't think . . ." She felt a gush. "Uh-oh."

"What?"

"My water just broke."

Chapter
TWENTY-SEVEN

On the way to the hospital, Natalie listened to the hum of the engine, a million thoughts jostling in her head. She visualized arriving at the hospital to deliver her baby and then holding it in her arms for the first time. She didn't want to focus on the impending labor pain or the anguish associated with Andrea's announcement. Watching the moonlight bounce between the sagebrush plants, she was jerked out of her thoughts when the car began making a strange fwmp . . . fwmp . . . fwmp sound. "What is that?"

"I think we have a flat tire," Spence said.

"You've got to be kidding."

Spence pulled the car onto the shoulder and went outside to check it. He leaned back in and said, "Definitely a flat tire."

Natalie bit at her thumbnail. *What were the odds they'd have a flat tire on the way to the hospital?* She did *not* want to give birth behind a clump of sagebrush. At least she wasn't in active labor, for the moment.

Spence lifted the trunk open and then returned. "I think Justin used the flashlight and didn't put it back."

"We have no flashlight?" She leaned her head back against the seat.

"Maybe there will be enough moonlight."

Natalie's nerves frayed while she waited for Spence to change the tire. She prayed that he'd be able to use the Braille method to change it.

After twenty minutes or so, Spence entered the car, concern etched on his face. Beads of sweat collected at his hairline. "All done. Are you okay?"

"Other than totally stressed, yeah, I'm fine. No contractions yet, thankfully." She patted her stomach.

The rest of the drive was uneventful. They arrived at the hospital, and a tall, dark-haired nurse approached them after they'd checked in. "Is this your first baby?" She directed Natalie to a wheelchair.

"No."

"Second?" Her voice was upbeat, even in the middle of the night.

"Seventh."

"You have six kids?" She leaned down and gazed at Natalie.

"Yes."

"Wow. Your house must be full of energy." She pushed Natalie in the wheelchair.

"It is."

"Good for you. Very few people have large families these days." Natalie was surprised at the nurse's positive reaction—certainly not the norm.

The nurse assigned Natalie to a birthing room she'd had before.

"Go ahead and change into the gown, and I'll be back to check on you in a bit," the nurse said with a cheery smile.

Natalie shuffled into the small, brightly lit bathroom, changed into her hospital-issued gown, and folded her street clothes. She looked at herself in the mirror, suddenly struck with intense fear of the foreboding pain she knew she'd experience. She shook her head and exited the bathroom.

Spence escorted her to the bed.

"You'd think after six kids, I wouldn't feel so apprehensive, but I do."

Spence rubbed her shoulders.

"Even though I'd rather be anywhere but here, I'm excited to have a newborn that I can bring home and hold for hours on end. Makes it all worth it." She sat on the edge of the bed. "Do you still think it's a boy?"

"Yeah."

"I don't care. I just want to be on the other side of this pregnancy and have a healthy baby with its newborn smell." She smiled. "And the little noises. There's nothing like a newborn baby. We're so lucky." She squeezed Spence's hand while gratitude coursed through her.

"You're right. We've been blessed with another wonderful baby." A smile exploded across his face. He leaned over Natalie's belly, put his face up against her stomach, and said, "Hello, this is your daddy." The vibrations tickled Natalie's tummy. "Come on out."

"No matter how many babies I've had, I still can't believe there's a little person inside of me. It's such a miracle."

A knock sounded at the door.

"Come in," Natalie said.

"I need to check your dilation," the same nurse said. She grabbed a pair of latex gloves.

"Lovely." Natalie knew she'd retain no dignity in the upcoming hours.

The nurse concluded her examination and said, "About 3 centimeters. Are you having any contractions?"

"No."

The nurse hooked her up to the familiar machine. "We'll monitor you for a little while and if nothing changes, we'll call Dr. Thomas to see if he'd like us to begin an induction."

"I want to go natural." The thought of Pitocin running through her body like an army set to attack her uterus made her shudder. The memory of Bradley's induction still haunted her.

"We can wait for a few hours. Why don't you try to get some rest?" The nurse patted Natalie's shoulder.

After the nurse left, Spence and Natalie attempted to sleep. A few hours later, Natalie got up to use the restroom. When she returned, Spence was surfing through the television channels. "Hey, look, it's *A Baby Story* on TLC. Do you want to watch it?"

"I think I'll pass since I'll be having my own story today."

They decided to walk around the maternity floor. Natalie hoped it would engage labor, but they returned to her room without any contractions.

Another nurse, with a long red braid and freckles across her nose, entered the room and took Natalie's blood pressure. "Dr. Thomas would like to start the induction."

Natalie gave a disappointed sigh. She felt the stab when the nurse inserted the IV to administer the Pitocin needed for the induction.

Natalie and Spence settled on an episode of *The Brady Bunch* as they waited for the doctor.

After a couple of back-to-back episodes and the nurse checking on her a few times, Dr. Thomas walked into the room wearing green scrubs. He shook Spence's hand and then turned to Natalie. "How are you doing?"

"Eager for this baby, but not looking forward to the labor."

"As fast as you deliver, the induction probably won't take too long, especially since your water broke on its own." He checked her chart and then bid them good-bye.

After another hour or so, Natalie shifted her weight in the bed. "I can feel the contractions. They're finally getting stronger but not too painful yet. I'll be so relieved when it's over. I can't wait to hold our baby and take it home."

"Me too." Spence leaned over and kissed Natalie on the forehead.

About fifteen minutes later, Natalie turned on her side. The pain centered in her back and radiated through her legs, each contraction more painful than the last. She began moaning.

"Should I check her?" the dark-haired nurse said.

"No, please don't check me again," Natalie said between groans.

"But we need to know how far along you are," the nurse said.

"I need to push," Natalie said, the uncontrollable urge overtaking her.

"Huh?" the nurse said.

Natalie turned to her back. "I need to push." She panted in an effort to delay her body's natural reaction to the final stage of labor.

"Let me call the doctor," the nurse said.

Natalie shook her head. "No time," she whispered. The urge to push enveloped her.

"I've delivered plenty of babies. Let me at least get my gloves." The nurse grabbed a pair of gloves and took her place at the end of the bed.

With the force of a hurricane, Natalie pushed the baby down the birth canal.

"I can see the head," the nurse said.

"The baby has lots of hair," Spence said.

Natalie used all of her strength to push the baby's head out.

"Don't push. I need to suction the baby's mouth. Use your breathing," the nurse said firmly.

Natalie gripped the handles by the sides of the bed and concentrated on not pushing. She panted.

"Baby is suctioned out," the nurse said.

Dr. Thomas entered the room and replaced the nurse. "A gentle push. Here are the shoulders. Another push."

With a gush, the rest of the baby was out, and the ecstasy of relief flooded her body.

"Congratulations, you have a baby girl." The doctor placed the baby on Natalie's now flatter belly. The nurse toweled off the baby.

Natalie touched her new daughter. "She doesn't look like any of our kids."

Spence's eyes leaked tears. "You're right. I can't tell who she looks like."

"I need to take your daughter for a moment and get her cleaned up," the nurse said.

Natalie laid her head back and gave a long sigh. "I'm so glad that's over."

Dr. Thomas finished caring for Natalie, congratulated her again, and left the room.

"Your baby girl is eight pounds and seven ounces," the nurse said.

Natalie raised her head and gazed at her new baby. Her swollen face appeared different somehow, but Natalie attributed it to the quick delivery.

After a few minutes, the nurse placed the swaddled baby in Natalie's arms. Natalie kissed her daughter and held her close, feeling the warmth of her newborn against her skin. She couldn't wait to take her new daughter home to the rest of the family.

Not more than ten minutes had passed when the door opened and Dr. Thomas entered the room. He wore a distressed expression.

He took the baby from Natalie and studied her. "The nurse remarked that your baby has a few characteristics of Down syndrome." He turned the baby over and examined her back. "You might want to have her tested to see if she has the extra chromosome."

His words slammed Natalie like the aftershock of an explosion. Down syndrome? Her baby?

"She has a flat nose bridge and the distinctive folds on her eyelids." He pointed both of these things out to Natalie and Spence. "She also has narrow shoulders." His voice sounded far away. Garbled. Natalie's heartbeat pounded in her ears.

"What do we need to do to have her tested?" Spence said.

"I'll make sure someone comes in to speak with you about it. Since you chose not to have an amniocentesis during the pregnancy and by the time you came in it was too late to administer the usual screenings. There was no way to know for sure."

"It won't make a bit of difference one way or the other," Spence said.

Spence and Dr. Thomas continued their conversation, but Natalie could hear very little. She knew that Down syndrome was always a possibility, as was any other abnormality, but she never felt like it was something that one of her children would have. Why would Heavenly Father send her a baby with something wrong with it? Especially since she'd felt like the baby was healthy and fine. *This doesn't make sense.*

She pulled her daughter close.

A short Native American nurse entered the room. "I need to take your baby to the nursery. I'll bring her back in a while after I've bathed her."

"How long will it take?"

"About forty-five minutes."

Natalie handed the baby to the nurse and watched them leave the room. After Dr. Thomas left, she turned to Spence. "Down syndrome?" Saying it aloud made her stiffen.

"We need to find out for sure before we get all worked up." He pushed her damp hair away from her face.

"But my ultrasounds were all normal. No signs or markers for Down syndrome. I don't understand. It must be a mistake."

Spence caressed her cheek. "Maybe the ultrasound couldn't detect it. Whatever the outcome, we'll be okay."

Natalie closed her eyes. She tried to keep the tears from overflowing, but she couldn't.

She opened her eyes when the same Native American nurse entered the room after only fifteen minutes. The nurse sat on the bed and rested her hand on Natalie's leg. "I was bathing your little girl, and her lips turned blue."

"What does that mean?"

"She needs oxygen."

Natalie's chest tightened, and her eyes felt like they were on fire. "Oxygen?"

"Yes," the nurse said.

"Can I see her?" Natalie said.

The nurse nodded. "I'll get you a wheelchair." She stood and left the room.

"I can't believe this," Natalie said. "I haven't even digested the fact she might have . . . and now she's on oxygen?" The muscles constricted in her neck and shoulders, while fear crept up her spine.

The nurse pushed the wheelchair into the room, and Natalie moved over to it. They made their way down the long corridor that led to the nursery. Natalie could hear other babies in their mothers' rooms. A new daddy wheeled his baby by in the hospital bassinet. Natalie closed her eyes, trying to shut out the sights and sounds of what she didn't have—her baby in her arms.

"Here we are," the nurse said.

Natalie opened her eyes, and her gaze settled on a small bed where several nurses were gathered. Between the bodies, she could see her baby's legs. She moved closer to the bed.

"We've got her on 100 percent oxygen right now, and we've called your family doctor's office, so he can come and evaluate her," a tall nurse said.

"Her color is good now and her heartbeat is steady," a nurse with brown hair and glasses added.

Natalie nodded. The swelling in her throat prohibited her from saying anything.

"When will the doctor be here?" Spence said.

"The answering service didn't say," the tall nurse said.

After fifteen minutes, the baby was steady, and only one nurse remained to keep an eye on the vital signs.

"Maybe it's good news that most of the nurses have left," Natalie whispered, her arms aching to hold her newborn.

"I think so," Spence said.

"I want to take her home."

Spence leaned in close. "Me too."

"The kids will be here any minute to see her. They'll want to hold her, but they can't," Natalie said, her disappointment multiplied six times.

"I'll go out to the lobby and wait for them to let them know what's going on." Spence left the nursery.

Natalie stared at her daughter through the oxygen tent. She had blonde hair, chubby arms, ten fingers, and ten toes. Natalie inhaled deeply. She was supposed to have a healthy baby like the rest of her children, bring it home right away, and enjoy bonding time with the family. It wasn't supposed to be like this.

Spence walked back into the nursery and pointed to a window. "The kids are right outside. They want to see the baby." He paused. "Andrea brought Tristan with her."

Natalie straightened in the chair. All she needed was Tristan staring at her while she processed all that was happening with the baby.

"Excuse me, could we open the blinds on that window? Our kids are here," Spence said to a nurse who was attending to another baby.

The nurse walked over to the window and opened the blinds. The kids all stood at the window oohing and aahing. Mariah pressed her nose against the glass, and Bradley, held up by Ryan, started tapping the window.

Spence shook his head, and Bradley stopped. All the kids smiled and waved. Natalie spotted her mother standing to the side. Tears filled Natalie's eyes, and she attempted to blink them away, but they spilled down her cheeks. She feared her mother's reaction to the possibility that the baby might not be perfect, afraid of the accusation that she'd already had so many children that something like this was bound to happen, especially at her age.

Spence turned to Natalie and said, "Let's go back to the room and talk with the kids."

Spence wheeled Natalie back to her room, and she focused on controlling her fears and emotions. The kids came into the room smiling.

"What's her name?" Mariah asked.

Natalie and Spence exchanged looks.

"Rose Magic Carpet?" Mariah asked.

"That's the silliest name I've ever heard," Justin said.

"Is not." Mariah stuck out her tongue.

"Is too." Justin thumped her on the head.

"You two stop it." Laura picked up Mariah.

"Congratulations, Mrs. Drake," Tristan said.

"Thank you." Natalie tried to disguise the disapproval in her voice.

They all visited for a few more minutes. "We better get going," Andrea said.

"Don't worry about a thing. I've got it all taken care of." Carma ushered the kids out of the room.

"Thank you, Mom," Natalie called after her.

Carma stepped back into the room. "She's a beautiful baby, and you're a wonderful mother."

Natalie jerked her head back.

"You have a large family, but you do it well."

"I do?" Natalie wasn't prepared for her mother's words and the emotions that welled up inside because of them.

"Don't act so surprised."

"I . . ." Natalie tried to clear the thickness from her throat and stop the tears that built behind her eyes.

"Will you be home tomorrow?"

Natalie nonchalantly wiped at her eyes. "Uh, we don't know yet. The baby needs some oxygen, so we'll wait to hear from the doctor."

"Oxygen?" Carma furrowed her eyebrows. "Why?"

Natalie answered quickly. "We don't know yet. We'll call you when we hear from the doctor. Thanks for everything, Mom."

Carma smiled and exited the room.

After everyone left, Natalie said, "I can't believe she brought Tristan, knowing how we feel." Flashes of Andrea with Tristan darted back and forth across her mind. "I'm sure my mother had something to do with it. She keeps encouraging them."

"Andrea wants to marry him, and it doesn't matter what we say. In her eyes, he's already part of the family." Spence sat on the edge of Natalie's bed.

"I can't deal with it right now." She needed to put thoughts of Andrea aside so she could focus on her new baby. "We need a name for the baby." She drew in a breath. "How about Gabrielle Rose?"

"That will make Mariah happy."

Natalie placed her hair behind her ears. "Does she look like a Gabrielle?"

"Let's go see."

Spence pushed Natalie in the wheelchair down the hall. They approached the nursery and could see a man with a bushy gray moustache examining the baby.

"Hello," Spence said.

"Hi. I'm Dr. Ward covering for Dr. Sanderson this weekend." He shook Spence's hand.

"How is she?" Spence leaned over the large, hooded bassinet and caressed the baby's chubby arm.

"Seems to be doing well, except for the oxygen. I've turned it down, but it's still high. I've left a message for the on-call pediatrician. We should hear from her soon." His gaze darted between the two of them. "Have the nurses mentioned anything about testing your baby for Trisomy 21?"

"Do you mean Down syndrome?" Spence asked.

"Yes."

"Is it possible that she has some of the characteristics, but doesn't actually have it?" Natalie hoped he'd answer affirmatively.

He nodded. "These characteristics are all common in the population, but when a few or more appear in one person, it may indicate a genetic abnormality."

"I've seen kids with flat noses and eye folds," Natalie said, trying to convince the doctor that her daughter didn't need to be tested.

He picked up the baby's tiny hand. "She doesn't have the single line across her palm, which is common in Down syndrome."

"But these could be normal for her and don't necessarily mean she has Down syndrome, right?" Natalie said, emphasizing her words.

"Exactly. That's why it's important to do the karyotype test and find out the chromosome count."

"How long will she be on oxygen?" Spence rubbed the baby's leg.

The doctor turned to Spence. "I don't know yet. We'll see how she does tonight."

"When the oxygen level in her blood is normal, will we be able to take her home?" Natalie asked.

"Yes. I'm still waiting to confer with the pediatrician, but taking her home shouldn't be a problem." His voice sounded reassuring and Natalie was comforted by that fact.

Chapter

TWENTY-NINE

About an hour later, the doctor walked into the nursery wearing a solemn expression. He approached Natalie and Spence. "I've spoken with the on-call pediatrician. She's prepping for surgery right now so she can't come down to the nursery, but," he paused, "she feels it is best to life flight your baby to UNM in Albuquerque."

Natalie's eyes fluttered. "What?" Her heartbeat drummed in her ears.

"Albuquerque? That's over 150 miles from here," Spence said.

"She feels that since your daughter may have Trisomy 21, her low oxygen level may be due to a common heart defect. If she crashed, we don't have the capability to deal with that in this nursery. We don't want to transport a critically ill newborn." He stepped closer to the baby's bassinet.

"Transport?" Natalie eked out through the waves of nausea assailing her.

"The life flight team will arrive here in the next hour." The tone of his voice punctuated the gravity of the situation.

"Don't we have any say?" Spence asked, raising his eyebrows. His forehead wrinkled the way it always did when he wanted clarification.

"I'm afraid not. The pediatrician, Dr. Susan Keyes, made the decision." Dr. Ward rested his hand on the side of the bassinet.

"How can she make a decision to fly the baby to Albuquerque without even examining her?" Spence said, his voice rising.

"It's in the best interest of the baby. We don't want to lose her."

"I can't believe this. It keeps getting worse," Natalie choked out. She hugged herself and rocked back and forth.

"The team will need to speak with you once they arrive. Until then, you are free to spend the time with your baby." He peered at Natalie. "I hope we're only being overcautious and your daughter will be fine," the doctor said with sincerity. He left the room.

Natalie cradled her face in her hands. She felt like a semitruck had hit her.

"I want to give her a blessing," Spence said.

Natalie wiped at her eyes. "That's a good idea."

In the relative quiet of the nursery, Spence laid his hands on Gabrielle's head and proceeded to give her a blessing of comfort and safety. He also blessed her that Heavenly Father would watch over her.

Natalie rested her hand on Gabrielle's tummy and caressed it. "I didn't even get to hold her for very long, and now they're going to rip her away from me. What if there's something wrong with her heart?" She swiped the back of her hand across her nose.

"Heavenly Father will watch over her," Spence said.

"This isn't how I planned it. I thought I'd come in, have a baby, and bring it home. Never in my wildest imagination . . ." She couldn't finish her sentence.

Spence and Natalie sat next to the bed and watched the nurse take Gabrielle's vitals. Natalie noticed her daughter's sweet face and heart-shaped lips. She wanted to pick her up and hold her tight, but for the moment, all she could do was stare at her, trying to memorize every detail of her face.

"I want to go with her," Natalie said. "I don't want her to go to Albuquerque without me."

"You still need to recover from the birth. We don't want to put your health at risk." Spence placed his hand on hers.

"I'm not worried about me."

"I am." He gazed at her with a concerned expression.

"You should go with her, then." She felt torn between wanting Spence to be with Gabrielle or stay with her.

Spence shook his head. "I'm going to stay here with you. As soon as the doctor releases you, we'll drive down to UNM. Okay?"

A hefty woman entered the nursery. "Excuse me. I'm Darla, a nurse with the flight team. We need to prepare the baby for transport. Can we ask you to wait in your room?" she said with a slight southern accent.

Natalie nodded numbly, still trying to make sense of all that was happening.

"We'll come talk to you before takeoff," Darla said.

Two men and a woman all dressed in the same type of navy blue uniform rolled in a stretcher with a glass-enclosed incubator that resembled a coffin. Natalie squeezed her eyes shut as Spence wheeled her out of the nursery.

⁓⁓⁓

The door opened, and the flight nurse walked into Natalie's hospital room with a folder of papers. "We need some signatures so we can fly your baby to UNM."

"Her name is Gabrielle," Natalie said with authority.

"It's possible she may need to be resuscitated during the flight. If she does, we need your consent to perform a tracheotomy. You need to understand that it may cause permanent damage or long-term effects," Darla said in a clinical tone. She pushed a paper toward Natalie and Spence.

Spence picked up the paper and read it over while Natalie seethed at the nurse's callous treatment of the situation.

"Will they be able to tell us in Albuquerque why she needs oxygen?" Spence asked.

"Yes. I've been a neonatal nurse for more than twenty years, and my guess is that your baby has Trisomy 21 and has the heart defect. They will perform an echocardiogram on her in the Neonatal Intensive Care Unit at UNM to determine the extent of the defect."

Natalie fought the desire to slap the nurse. She didn't know what was wrong with Gabrielle. She wasn't a doctor, and she had no business making such a diagnosis.

Darla added, "It's also possible we may not be able to revive your baby. You need to be aware of that. We'll try to resuscitate her should the need arise, but we don't have all the capabilities of a hospital on the helicopter." She handed Spence another form to sign. "She'll be in the NICU within an hour." She glanced between Natalie and Spence. "I know this is hard."

Really? Natalie didn't need any platitudes from someone who'd already condemned her baby to a life-long condition or possibly death.

Darla collected all of the papers and stood. "We'll be on our way then."

"I want to see Gabrielle before you leave," Natalie insisted.

Darla hesitated and then said, "For only a moment. We need to get her to UNM as soon as possible." Darla opened the door. On the stretcher, inside the incubator, Gabrielle lay still.

Natalie covered her mouth, trying to stifle her sobs. A cold sweat broke out across the back of her neck.

Spence walked to the stretcher. "Your mommy and daddy both love you very much. We'll see you soon." He placed his hand on the incubator.

Gabrielle didn't stir. Natalie watched them wheel her baby down the hall and out the door. She collapsed into Spence's arms.

An hour later, Natalie stared at the ceiling trying to fall asleep but knew it wouldn't come easily. Her baby was over a hundred miles away, and she wasn't sure when, or if, she'd ever see her alive again. Natalie rubbed her stomach. Twenty-four hours earlier, Gabrielle was still safely ensconced in her belly and Natalie had blissfully thought she'd have a healthy baby and a normal birth experience. Now, she had no idea what lay ahead in the immediate, or distant, future.

After a fitful night of little sleep, the early morning light sifted through the blinds in Natalie's room. She focused her eyes and saw it was almost 7:00 a.m. She watched Spence as he slept in a small chair and wondered if he'd ever be able to use his neck again. It seemed ridiculous that birthing rooms didn't have comfortable chairs for the new dads. Of course, everything seemed ridiculous now.

A new nurse with thick glasses entered the room. "Hi, we've spoken to Dr. Thomas, and he's agreed to let you leave this morning. Here's your paperwork. You can sign them and leave them here for me. There's also the birth certificate if you want to fill that out. Congratulations." She left the room.

Natalie nodded as she fought tears. She rose from the bed.

Spence stirred. He opened his eyes and looked over at her.

"The doctor has released me." She walked to the small closet to retrieve her belongings. "I want to leave for Albuquerque as soon as possible."

"I'll call the kids and let them know." He massaged his neck.

Natalie eyed Spence. "Let's not mention anything about . . . the Down syndrome." The words still stuttered on her tongue. "I don't want to . . . we don't even know that she has it." She held onto the hope that Gabrielle didn't have the extra chromosome.

Spence nodded. "I'll see if the girls can pack a suitcase for us."

The ride home seemed especially long. Natalie laid her head back, contemplating what to tell the kids, but never quite found adequate explanation. Eventually, they drove down the lane to their home.

Spence helped Natalie out of the car and into the house.

"Natalie, how's the baby?" Carma said as soon as they stepped inside the house.

Natalie's insides twisted.

"Why is she at UNM? Laura said something about her breathing."

Natalie moved slowly to the family room. "She's had some difficulty getting enough oxygen into her blood so they decided to send her to UNM." Natalie sat down to ward off the lightheadedness.

"It must be serious. What else is going on?" Carma gazed at Natalie.

Natalie shifted her weight and cleared her throat. "Nothing we know of." *It was the truth.*

"Why couldn't she stay at the hospital in Farmington?"

Natalie steadied herself. "We had no control over the decision. They called for the helicopter, and it came and got her. That was it."

Carma's brows knit together. "But why? It seems odd to me that they'd send her all the way to Albuquerque."

"We need to get down there so we can get some answers," Natalie said, hoping to divert her mother's line of questioning.

"How about some breakfast?" Carma rummaged through the pantry. "I'll organize this while you're gone. No sense in you coming home to such disarray."

Though the comment stung, Natalie didn't have the strength to respond.

"What did you name her?" Carma said over her shoulder.

"Gabrielle Rose," Spence said.

"Oh," Carma said.

"You don't like the name?" Natalie stiffened.

"It's a fine name." Carma reached into the refrigerator and pulled out some eggs. "Will you call her Gabby?"

"I don't know. For now, I only want to bring her home." Thoughts of Gabrielle safely tucked into her arms brought Natalie some solace.

"Of course," Carma said. "That's the most important thing right now."

After breakfast, Spence finished loading the car. "Thank you for packing the suitcase, girls," he said as they stood on the porch saying their good-byes.

"You're welcome, Dad," Andrea said. "We're all pulling together for Gabrielle."

"Is Gabrielle going to be okay?" Laura asked.

"Yes," Spence said.

Natalie's heart ached. She didn't know the answer to Laura's question. She didn't even know if she'd ever bring her baby home.

Chapter
THIRTY

As they headed toward Albuquerque, miles of nothingness stretched out before them. In any direction, the desolate desert met the azure sky at the horizon with only clumps of grass or saltbush to break up the monotony of the dry, dusty ground.

Natalie, still sore from the delivery and with a headache descending upon her, struggled to make sense of the situation. "When I prayed, I felt like everything was fine." Warm tears slid down her cheeks. "That I didn't need to worry about any abnormalities." She caught a breath and then continued in a trembling voice. "I specifically prayed that this baby would not have Down syndrome. What if she has a major heart defect? How . . . ?" Her sentence trailed off into the damp tissue she held against her face.

"Don't get all worked up about something we don't even know is true."

"But there's something wrong." She wiped at her eyes while her stomach churned. "Why else would they have flown her to UNM?"

"I think we need to get to the hospital, see Gabrielle, and talk to the doctors. Maybe they'll know more about her oxygen level, and we can go from there."

"I feel so overwhelmed."

Spence rubbed her hand. "It's going to be okay."

"How do you know that? We might get down there, and she'll be . . ." She couldn't bring herself to say it. Images of the tiny coffin holding Susannah's baby shot through her memory. She reached for another tissue and wiped her eyes.

Spence squeezed her hand. "We still have about two hours. Why don't you try to get some rest?"

Natalie nodded. She drew in a deep breath and leaned back. She said a silent prayer pleading with Heavenly Father to bless Gabrielle with a healthy heart and a normal chromosome count. Once she finished her prayer, she allowed sleep to overtake her.

⸎

When Natalie awoke, she noticed the sharp peaks of the Sandia Mountains on her left. Cars whizzed past them while they drove along I-25. She yawned. "Are we almost there?"

"Yes. Look for the Lomas turnoff," Spence said.

A few minutes later, Natalie pointed to the large green sign. "There it is."

Spence changed lanes and exited the freeway.

They circled around the hospital parking garage, level after level, trying to find a spot to park.

"Must be a busy place," Spence said.

"These people need to move out of my way so I can get to my baby." Natalie finger-combed her hair. She didn't need to look in the mirror to know her eyes were still puffy.

"There's one." Spence pulled the car in. He walked around the car and opened the door for Natalie, who stepped out of the car and stretched her arms. Spence reached his arms around her and hugged her for a moment. They maneuvered around the parked cars and climbed the stairs that led to the bridge connecting the parking garage to the hospital entrance. They passed by a woman with gray hair who was crying, a Native American family with two small children, and a portly security guard.

They entered through sliding glass doors, and a hospital employee directed them to the entrance of the Neonatal Intensive Care Unit where they waited at a glass-enclosed desk.

Spence leaned forward and spoke through the mouthpiece in the glass. "Our baby was admitted here earlier this morning."

"Name?" the woman wearing brightly colored scrubs said.

"Gabrielle Drake."

"Can I see your wrist bands?"

Spence and Natalie each showed the woman their wrists, and she matched the numbers on the bands they'd received in Farmington to the one listed on her paperwork. She nodded, and a buzzer sounded, which opened the door to the NICU.

A nurse with a long, black braid instructed them on proper hand washing and then led them to a pile of yellow smocks, asking them to each wear one every time they entered the NICU.

It seemed like it was taking hours to get from the parking garage to Gabrielle's bedside.

Natalie worked at scrubbing her hands and arms. Spence helped her with her gown and tied it in the back.

She glanced at Spence and said, "You look like Big Bird." A stress-relieving laugh escaped her lips.

Spence smiled and gave her a soft kiss on her cheek.

They walked through a large room filled with incubators housing babies hooked to tubes and monitors. Natalie's gaze darted between all of the beds, searching for Gabrielle. Each heartbeat constricted her blood flow until she felt faint. She stopped for a moment and breathed in and out several times.

"Are you okay?" Spence supported her with his arms.

She nodded. "Worried about what we'll find." She uttered a quick, silent prayer for her newborn.

A nurse in blue scrubs approached them and directed them to a bed on the left side at the end of the long, sterile room.

Natalie spotted a sleeping Gabrielle. Realizing that her baby could be much worse off, Natalie gave a quick prayer of thanks and unclenched her fists. Gabrielle wore a blue and pink striped hat, and a plain white blanket swaddled her small body. An oxygen mask lay next to her while a machine monitored her vitals.

"Are you the parents?" a nurse asked.

Natalie nodded. She reached out and touched her daughter.

"She's doing well. The pediatric cardiologist has seen her. She had an echocardiogram right after she arrived." She thumbed through some papers.

Natalie's heartbeat quickened while she waited for the results. "And?"

"The echo came back normal. The cardiologist didn't find anything wrong with her heart."

Natalie let out a long breath of relief. A heaviness lifted from her shoulders while she uttered a prayer of thanks.

"She's had an X-ray of her lungs to see what might be there, and we should have the results shortly. Until then we'll be administering antibiotics to treat her for newborn pneumonia." The nurse laid the papers on the table next to the bed.

Pneumonia? Though she didn't like the idea of Gabrielle having pneumonia, she could deal with it, especially after worrying about a heart defect.

"How would she have contracted pneumonia?" Spence asked.

"Some babies are born with pneumonia, and we don't know why. We treat them with IV antibiotics."

Natalie gazed at the nurse. "May I touch her?"

The nurse nodded.

Natalie stroked Gabrielle's head. Gabrielle stirred and opened one eye. "Hi, beautiful girl." The yearning to hold her baby overpowered her.

"Daddy's here too," Spence said in a soft voice.

"I plan to breastfeed, so I need to know when I can feed her." Maybe she could finally enjoy some normalcy of life with a newborn.

"The notes on her chart indicate she needs a karyotype to determine her chromosome count."

Natalie glanced up at the nurse. "Yes, I know. For some reason they seem to think she has Down syndrome."

"If that's the case, she may not have the strength to breastfeed," the nurse said.

Natalie blinked several times.

"Babies with Trisomy 21 have weakened muscles in their mouths that make it difficult to breastfeed."

"Can I try?" Natalie said, undeterred in her resolve to nurse Gabrielle.

"Sure. We'll need to monitor her feeding. I'll help you keep track. Do you have any other questions?"

"Do you know when they'll test her for Down syndrome?" Spence asked.

"A geneticist is scheduled to evaluate your baby on Monday, and she'll arrange the test." She checked the monitor.

"Can I hold her now?" Natalie said, anxious to bond with Gabrielle.

"Yes. She'll need this cannula so she can get the oxygen she needs while you hold her." The nurse put a tube around Gabrielle's face under her nose and adjusted it for a snug fit. She picked up Gabrielle and placed her in Natalie's arms. The tiny bundle not only warmed Natalie's arms, but also sent a tingling sensation that traveled through her entire body. Natalie bent down to rest her cheek against Gabrielle's and breathe in her newborn scent. She let Gabrielle melt into her grasp. Finally, Natalie could hold her baby and actually imagine bringing her home.

Refusing to give up, Natalie worked for over an hour to nurse Gabrielle. After a few successful sucks, Gabrielle fell asleep. Natalie wrapped her with the hospital's receiving blanket, convinced the doctors and nurses were all wrong. Gabrielle was a perfectly normal baby, and she couldn't wait to escape the hospital and never have to think about Down syndrome again.

"You need some food. It's almost time for the nurses to change shifts. Let's get something to eat," Spence said, interrupting her visions of a normal life with Gabrielle.

"I hate leaving her here alone. Without me."

"She'll be okay. And we'll come back so you can feed her again and tell her good night."

Natalie agreed with reluctance.

"Maybe I should take you to a hotel so you can rest, and I'll bring in some dinner?"

She scrunched up her nose. "No, thanks."

"You look exhausted." He brushed a lock of hair away from her face.

"I don't want to be alone. I'd rather stay with you."

After a short drive, Spence and Natalie found a nearby restaurant. Natalie surveyed the menu, but nothing looked appetizing. The mixed smells of cooked broccoli, spaghetti sauce, and frying meat made her queasy.

"What would you like to eat?" Spence asked while he looked over the menu.

Natalie shrugged.

He looked at her, concern filling his eyes. "You have to eat so you can recover from giving birth and so you can feed Gabrielle."

"I want to call her Gabby. It makes me think of her chatting away with her friends."

Spence nodded. "I like it."

"I think we'll find out she doesn't even have the extra chromosome." She sipped her water as she recalled her prayers in Gabby's behalf. She'd been praying fervently that Gabby would have a normal chromosome count. Even if Gabby had been born with an extra chromosome, Natalie was confident she could pray it away because if she had enough faith, she could pray away anything, even Down syndrome.

Natalie awoke to the shrill ring of her cell phone. "Who'd be calling us?"

"Maybe it's the hospital."

Natalie's heart pumped hard as she fumbled for the phone on the nightstand. She recognized the number on the caller ID but decided to answer it anyway. "Hi, Mom." She laid her hand over her chest and let out a breath.

"How's the baby?"

"We don't know much yet." She didn't want to discuss anything with her mother.

"Spencer hasn't given us much information."

"That's because there isn't much to give. Gabby's still on oxygen. Her echocardiogram came back normal, so it's not her heart." Natalie rose from the bed.

"Why did they think she had a heart problem?" her mother said in her detective-like tone.

Natalie cleared her throat. "Low oxygen levels can mean there's a problem with the heart."

"I don't understand all of this."

"I don't either, Mom." Changing the subject, she asked, "How are the kids?"

"They're all fine. Don't worry about them."

"I appreciate you watching them." She meant it.

"I'm glad to do it." She paused for a moment. "It's nice that you need me."

"What?" Her mother's statement confused her.

"Oh, nothing. Are you getting some rest and enough to eat?"

"Yes. Spence is making sure of that." She glanced over at her groggy husband.

"Will you call when you have more information?" Her mother sounded sincere.

"Yes."

"I'll talk to you later, then. Good-bye."

Natalie tossed the cell phone on the bed. "I'm sure you figured out that was my mother."

Spence nodded.

"She said everything's okay at home. She was fishing for information."

Spence sat up in bed. "She wants to know because she cares about Gabby. And about you."

Natalie stared at the ceiling. "I don't want to raise her suspicions and have her grill me about Gabby when there's no proof that Gabby is anything but completely normal."

After showers and the hotel's continental breakfast, which consisted of a piece of toast and some diluted orange juice, they headed to the hospital.

"Maybe they'll know more today since she's already been in the hospital for over twenty-four hours," Spence said.

"I hope so. More than that, I hope we can take her home soon." She'd never wanted anything more in her life than to bring her baby girl home and forget this nightmare.

Looking like Big Bird's cousins, they walked through the NICU.

"I don't see Gabby. Where is she?" Natalie said, anxiety gripping her chest.

A nurse with short blonde hair met them and said, "Your baby has been moved to the Intensive Care Nursery. It's a step down from the NICU, which is good news. She doesn't need the care we provide in here." The nurse's pleasant expression gave Natalie more hope than she'd felt since their arrival.

"She's doing better?"

"Yes. I'll take you to her."

They followed the nurse through some double doors and into another room filled with bassinets and minimal equipment. The sunlit room was brighter, and the atmosphere less daunting.

"Here she is," the nurse said.

Gabby was sleeping on her left side, her tiny head barely visible above the blanket. "Can I hold her?" Natalie said.

"Of course."

Natalie picked up her daughter and held her close. She sat in a rocking chair and closed her eyes while she nuzzled Gabby, allowing Gabby's baby-soft hair to tickle her nose. She imagined being in her recliner at home, watching Mariah and Bradley spin in the center of the family room while Spence stood at the stove preparing one of his special breakfasts. She could almost smell the sizzling bacon on the griddle while she waited for the other kids to join her for a big family breakfast to welcome the newest Drake. Tranquility enveloped her. The hospital experience would soon only be a distant memory.

"Honey?" Spence's voice jolted her from her self-induced dream state.

"Huh?"

"What're you thinking about so hard?" Spence sat in a chair next to Natalie.

"Being at home with Gabby and the kids."

An older woman approached Spence and Natalie. In a gentle voice, she said, "Hello. I'm Dr. Grayson. I'm a geneticist. I understand you'd like me to examine and test your baby."

Reality stung Natalie. "Ah, yes."

"They have talked to you about how your baby has some characteristics of Trisomy 21." Natalie looked forward to never hearing that sentence again. Now that an expert was here, she could put to rest any suspicions about Gabby, especially when her physical examination proved no further testing was necessary.

"What's involved in diagnosing it?" Natalie asked.

"I'll do a physical examination, and then we'll draw some blood to have it analyzed for the chromosome count."

"We want to know one way or the other," Natalie said, sure her prayers would be answered and her daughter would not have the extra chromosome. Then no one would *ever* mention it again.

Dr. Grayson handed Spence a pamphlet and some other papers. "Trisomy 21 is the most common genetic abnormality. Those who have this genetic condition do live quality lives. We have programs, such as early intervention, to help with some of the difficulties that babies born with Trisomy 21 may encounter."

Natalie rocked Gabrielle. This was a waste of time. Gabrielle didn't have a genetic abnormality because Natalie had prayed, long before the birth, that the baby would not have Down syndrome or any other malady. But she was willing to appease the doctor if it meant she could leave the hospital earlier.

"May I examine the baby?"

"Yes." Natalie placed Gabby in the bassinet and removed the hospital-issued gown.

Dr. Grayson began at the top of Gabby's head. "She does have a long soft spot that runs the length of her head and ends with another soft spot back here." She pointed it out to Natalie and Spence. Natalie ran her fingers along Gabby's head.

After mentioning the flat nose bridge and eye folds, Dr. Grayson used a small flashlight and shone it into Gabby's eyes. "I saw a reflection of red which means she doesn't have cataracts."

Dr. Grayson continued her evaluation. She examined Gabby's ears and pulled out a small ruler to measure them. "Her ears measure within normal limits. Commonly, people with Trisomy 21 have smaller ears."

"So her ears are a normal size?" Natalie asked, emphasizing *normal*.

"Yes."

Natalie smiled.

The doctor ran her hands down Gabby's arms. "Her palms show two fold lines indicating normal hand movement in utero."

Natalie studied her own hand noting the creases.

Dr. Grayson checked Gabby's hips and legs. "Her skeletal structure is intact and her feet are typical: no extra space between the large toe and the rest of the toes." She listened to Gabby's chest. "Heartbeat sounds good, and I understand the echo was normal."

So far, the scale weighed heavily on the *normal* side. Natalie waited for the doctor to dismiss all doubts about Gabby's genetics.

Dr. Grayson removed her stethoscope. "She does have a few characteristics of Down syndrome, and I would advise that you test her."

Her words sliced into Natalie. "But . . ." Her disappointment prevented her from saying anything else.

"We'll draw her blood. It will take a couple of days for the results. If you've left the hospital, we can contact you at home."

"If she does have the extra chromosome, how will she do?" Spence said.

"We can't predict how she'll do or how she'll be affected. I can tell you, with all of my experience, that people with Down syndrome lead happy, fulfilling lives. Your daughter will have a bright outlook and will live a valuable life."

"*If* she has Down syndrome," Natalie said, coming out of her stupor.

"I will schedule the test for today, so you can know as soon as possible," Dr. Grayson said.

"Thank you," Spence said.

"Your daughter is beautiful. It was a pleasure to meet you."

Natalie watched Dr. Grayson leave the room, glad to see her go. "I keep looking at Gabby, and I can't see it. She looks like a regular baby to me. I think the doctors and nurses are all nuts."

"That's why it'll be good to get this test, and then we'll know for sure one way or the other," Spence said, reaching over and squeezing Natalie's hand.

❧

A few hours later, Spence and Natalie sat in chairs next to Gabby's bedside. A skinny woman dressed in green scrubs approached them. "I'm going to draw some blood for the karyotype."

"Okay," Spence said.

"I prefer that you wait in the hall outside those double doors until I'm done. It shouldn't be but a few minutes," she said in a nasal voice. "I'll call you back in when I'm finished."

Natalie didn't want to leave her baby, but she wanted to get the test over with once and for all, so she trudged out of the room. Spence followed her into the hall, where she sat in a padded chair against the wall and bowed her head.

She pleaded with Heavenly Father to bless Gabrielle that she wouldn't have the extra chromosome. She thanked Him for Gabby, and she begged Him to bless her baby girl to be normal in every way.

Natalie's ear picked up some crying. "That's Gabby."

"I know," Spence said.

"I hope she finishes soon." Natalie rubbed her chin, her nerves on edge.

Several minutes passed as Natalie listened to the torturous screams of her three-day-old baby. "How much longer?"

"They should be done any minute."

Natalie arose and walked to the double doors. She couldn't see Gabby through the windows but could hear her cries of pain. "I can't stand this." She chewed on her lip and squeezed her eyes shut.

Ten more minutes passed and still Gabby screamed.

Natalie paced the floor. Her heart thudded. Her nerves were on fire. She wanted to burst through the doors and rescue her baby. "What on earth is taking so long?"

"I don't know. Why don't you sit down? You look pale," Spence said. Though he attempted to hide his anxiety, Natalie knew him well enough to sense it.

Natalie sat next to Spence. She let her head hang low and placed her hands over her ears. Again, she prayed that the blood draw would conclude soon, that Gabby would be okay, and that the chromosome test results would be normal.

Another fifteen minutes, and Gabby continued to cry. Perspiration collected at the back of Natalie's neck while her heartbeat raced. Anxiety rushed through her veins. "This is unbearable. I want the nurse to stop," Natalie said with tear-filled eyes.

"I'm sure she's doing the best she can." Spence reached for her hand, and Natalie could see the strain on his face.

Natalie stood, her fingers jittery. "Is this the first time she's ever drawn blood from a baby?" Her anger, mixed with anguish, roiled inside her.

Gabby's cries echoed in the hallway. With each scream, Natalie's heartbeat throbbed in her cheeks. "We should have never agreed to the test. I didn't know it would be like this."

Spence placed his hand on her shoulder. "Getting the test is the right thing to do, so we'll know. I didn't think it'd be like this, either. I can't imagine why it's taking so long." His eyes reflected worry, exhaustion, and distress.

The nurse emerged. "We're done."

Natalie rushed to Gabby's bedside. She reached for her, but the skinny nurse said, "I'm sorry, we're not going to handle the baby for a while since this was so traumatic."

Traumatic couldn't begin to describe it. "I can't hold her?" Surely, the nurse would let Natalie comfort Gabby.

"Not right now. It took much longer than we anticipated to draw the blood, and she was quite upset."

"I know. I could hear her the whole time," Natalie said, not hiding her contempt.

"It's difficult to find a vein in newborns. The best thing to do now is to let her rest."

Though Natalie was fuming at the nurse's incompetence, she wanted to do what was best for Gabby, so she agreed.

Chapter
THIRTY-ONE

"I can't believe how long it took that inept nurse to find a vein," Natalie said when they got into the car. She bit at her thumbnail.

"I'm sure they were trying their best, but it was very hard to sit out there and do nothing while she cried. It made me hurt all over."

"I'm getting tired of all of this. I want to take her home. Is that so wrong?"

Spence touched her face, and she leaned into his hand.

They drove along a road by the hospital. The heat rose in waves from the asphalt as they searched for a restaurant. "Where do you want to eat?" Spence said.

"I'm not hungry. I'd love to go back to the hotel and take a nap."

"Sounds like a good idea."

As they walked into the now familiar hallway of the musty hotel, Spence put his arm around Natalie. "I love you. I know this is hard."

Natalie nodded, barely containing her emotions. They entered the room, and before Natalie knew it, she was asleep.

"What time is it?" Natalie sat straight up in bed.

"Four o'clock."

"Oh, no. Let's go. I didn't mean to sleep that long." She stood. "Why didn't you wake me?"

"You needed the rest."

"But Gabby may be awake and want to nurse." She envisioned her tiny baby crying out for her, and it made her heart ache. "No matter what, I'm going to breastfeed her like all the other kids."

While they drove to the hospital, Natalie silently chastised herself for sleeping instead of attending to Gabby's needs. Once they arrived, they made their way through all the critical babies back to the doors of the ICN.

An older nurse with a grave expression met them at the door. "I need to tell you what happened to your baby."

Fear thrust its fingers into Natalie's chest and squeezed her heart until she thought it would burst. Through trembling lips she uttered, "Is Gabby dead?"

The nurse shook her head. "No, no. Was I too serious?"

Natalie worked to contain her breathing so she didn't hyperventilate.

"I'm sorry. Your baby is all right, but when the nurse attempted to draw blood earlier, the IV in your baby's scalp worked loose. We had to start another IV for her antibiotics."

"Okay," Natalie said, not comprehending the importance of the news.

"It took us about an hour to find an acceptable vein. The baby was so upset that she then refused to take a bottle, so we had to insert a feeding tube."

Natalie heaved in a breath, imagining Gabby's pained cries.

"She's exhausted from being handled so much." She looked at Natalie. "We need to leave her alone until later this evening."

"So I can't nurse her. Again." Frustration needled her.

"Can we see her?" Spence asked.

The nurse seemed to have an internal argument but finally agreed.

Natalie and Spence followed the nurse to Gabby's bedside. Gabby rested, swaddled in a blanket. Natalie reached out and caressed her daughter's head. Gabby breathed a bit differently, seeming to acknowledge her mother's touch.

Natalie spun around and exited the nursery. Spence was right behind her.

"I can't take this. I'm not sure they're even helping Gabby." Anger burned inside her. "How much more does she have to endure?"

After the usual nighttime visit to the hospital, Natalie fell into bed in the stale hotel room. Shadows danced across the walls and ceiling as cars passed by the aging hotel.

Pain hammered inside Natalie's head. It seemed as though they were wasting time. No one knew for sure why Gabby needed oxygen. Instead of getting answers, more questions volleyed in her mind. Thoughts about Down syndrome seeped in, but Natalie thrust them out. Instead, she silently prayed for her baby's release. She prayed for the strength to endure the time at the hospital. And she once again prayed for a miracle—that despite some characteristics, Gabby would not be cursed with an extra chromosome. She prayed as hard as she'd ever prayed and implored Heavenly Father to bless Gabby to be fine, just as she'd felt she was during the pregnancy.

Natalie awoke to the hissing of the shower. It was almost time for the morning feeding, and she wanted to get to the hospital before the nurses gave Gabby a bottle, or worse, tried to force-feed her through a tube again. Her irritation flared.

She rolled out of bed and found her maternity pants and a big T-shirt. She pulled her hair back into a short ponytail and washed her face with some water. Maybe today would bring good news and an end to this nightmare.

When they entered the ICN, a tall, older man with silver hair was examining Gabby. "Hello, I'm Dr. Hill. I'm the neonatologist here."

"Hi," Spence said.

"I've visited with the radiologist and we re-examined your daughter's X-rays. We've both concluded that she doesn't have pneumonia. I'm not sure why they diagnosed her with pneumonia in the first place."

"Then why does she need oxygen?" Spence stepped closer to the bassinet.

"Sometimes, when babies are born, it takes a little longer for their lungs to get used to the pressure outside the womb. I think that's what happened here. Most babies adjust at birth while some it takes a few hours up to a few days."

"Will she have any long-term effects?" Spence said.

"I don't think so." He pushed up his wire-rimmed glasses. "I don't see any reason why she can't go home."

"Really?" Natalie said, happiness and gratitude showering her.

"We'll keep her on oxygen, but we can send you home with a temporary unit and get you set up at home until your family doctor decides to remove it."

"Can we take her home today?" Spence said.

"Probably tomorrow. We need to put in an order for oxygen and fill out all the paperwork. I've already stopped the order for antibiotics. I'll sign the order for release."

The doctor left to examine other babies.

Spence gave Natalie a hug.

A nurse approached them and said, "We had a baby in here last year with Down syndrome who couldn't swallow, so we had to insert a feeding tube. He had a reaction to the tube and ended up staying in here for over three months. You're very lucky that your baby is doing so well."

Natalie forced a smile, but she was sick and tired of the assumption that Gabby had Down syndrome. The test results had not come back yet. Besides, being able to take Gabby home tomorrow was a direct answer to her prayers, and she was sure Heavenly Father would bless Gabby once again and the karyotype would come back with the normal forty-six chromosome count. The doctors and nurses could guess all they wanted, but she had a secret weapon—prayer.

After a restless night at the hotel and traveling back to the hospital for two successful feedings, Natalie and Spence were ready to take Gabby home.

"Is Gabby ready?" Spence asked an unfamiliar nurse.

The young nurse gave him a quizzical look.

"We're ready to go home. *Now*," Natalie said.

"I don't think this baby is scheduled to leave today."

"Excuse me?" Natalie said. This was not up for debate.

"I don't see any release orders." She thumbed through papers on a clipboard.

Spence calmly said, "Yesterday the doctor told us she'd be able to go home today."

The nurse gave them a condescending look, but she said, "I'll check again." She walked over to a desk in the room.

Natalie sat in the rocker next to Gabby's bed and bowed her head. She uttered a prayer asking Heavenly Father to allow them to take Gabby home.

The nurse returned and said, "I'm sorry, but it looks like she won't be ready to be discharged today."

Natalie's face flushed, but before she could say anything, Spence said, "Could you please go check again. I'm sure the doctor said she could leave today."

"I already checked, but I'll call the doctor if you'd like," the nurse said with a flippant tone.

Several long minutes passed and the nurse returned. "I spoke to Dr. Hill and he did write the discharge orders. We have a new nurse on staff, and she might have put them somewhere else. But everything is in order. As soon as the oxygen tank arrives, you'll be set to leave," she said in a contrite voice.

"When will that be?" Spence asked.

"I—" started the nurse.

A young man with a large tattoo on his forearm walked over to the bed carrying a small oxygen tank. "Drake?"

The nurse nodded.

The young man left, and Spence said to the nurse, "Anything else?"

Natalie began dressing Gabby in a pink polka-dot outfit that drowned her. She smiled to herself, recognizing the Lord's hand and knowing that He made it possible for them to leave so fast.

Spence finished signing the paperwork, and they loaded Gabby into her car seat.

"Quick, let's get out of here before they change their minds." Spence grabbed the car seat with one hand and Natalie's hand with his other.

Giddiness encircled her as they rushed out of the hospital toward their freedom.

About an hour into the drive home, Gabby fussed a bit. They pulled over and Natalie cradled Gabby to her chest and nursed her. She latched on and fed for a few minutes. Further proof that Gabby was an ordinary baby.

"As far as I can tell, she's a typical newborn," Natalie said while caressing Gabby's head and feeling the warmth of her body.

"Everything will work out fine." Spence reached out and touched Gabby's arm.

"Yes, it will," Natalie added, knowing that she'd prayed the extra chromosome away.

∽⧂⧄∾

After driving two more hours through the same barren desert toward La Plata, they pulled into their driveway.

"Home has never looked so good," Natalie said, stress from the last several days slowly dissolving.

Spence let out a long breath. "I can't wait to show Gabby to her brothers and sisters. What a great family reunion." His grin stretched across his face.

They stopped the car not far from the house and got out of it. The front door swung open, and they could see Mariah hopping up and down. "They're home," she yelled out.

Natalie grabbed Gabby and the car seat from the car while Spence carried the suitcase. As soon as they walked into the house, everyone swarmed them.

"Can I hold her?" Mariah asked.

"Me first," Laura said.

"I want to hold her," Justin said, pushing Laura out of the way.

"Everyone calm down," Spence said.

Natalie stepped over to her mother. "Would you like to hold your newest granddaughter?"

Carma looked at Gabby and cocked her head. "She looks—"

"Tired, I know. We're all exhausted." Natalie pulled Gabby from her car seat and placed her in Carma's arms. "Isn't she adorable, Mom?"

Carma nodded.

"My turn." Mariah pawed at Carma.

"Everyone will have a chance to hold her," Natalie said, overcome with joy and gratitude.

After each family member held her, Natalie took Gabby upstairs. "You are my beautiful girl, and you're perfect."

That night, Gabby slept without stirring while Natalie monitored her oxygen. Even though she awoke frequently, Natalie felt more relaxed and rested than she had in almost a week.

As the early morning sun peeked over the horizon, Natalie held her new daughter in her arms, imagining her life ahead of her. Tubes, tests, and suggestions of Down syndrome floated away.

Natalie and the kids spent the morning in her bedroom, taking turns holding Gabby, reading books, and enjoying time together.

"I'm so glad to be home." Relief draped around Natalie like a favorite blanket. She'd never been so grateful to be home, surrounded by her family.

"I missed you," Mariah said.

"Miss you," Bradley added.

"I missed all of you too. But now we're home and everything will be great." Nothing could ruin her perfect family life.

"Can we call her Rose?" Mariah patted Gabby's cheek.

"That's her middle name, but I think we'll stick with Gabby."

The kids left, so Natalie placed Gabby in the bassinet by her bed and then stepped into a long, hot shower. The water filtered through her hair and slid down her back. The delivery hadn't gone as planned, but now she had her baby home and nothing could dampen her spirits. All the heartache she'd endured the previous week slipped into the drain with the water. Life was good and would only get better.

Natalie spent the next day holding and nursing Gabby, reading books to Mariah and Bradley, listening to Justin's stories, and talking to her older kids. Andrea seemed to enjoy the day with the family, and the subject of her upcoming nuptials never crossed her lips. Natalie hoped that Andrea had reconsidered her decision.

The summer sun shone on the rural landscape while birds chirped upbeat melodies in the branches of the trees outside her family room window. She watched the kids play together and even had a decent conversation with her mother. The scent of hamburgers cooking outside on the grill wafted through the open windows, and Natalie finally had her blissful life with Gabby.

When she laid Gabby in the small crib that night, she stood over her for several minutes, filled with a depth of gratitude and love she'd not experienced before. Heavenly Father had truly answered her prayers and blessed Gabby—she was fine, just like Natalie had felt during the pregnancy. Joy washed over her.

Though she awoke a few times to check on Gabby, she felt rested and buoyant the next morning. She held Gabby in the chair next to her bed and gazed at her petite face. Gabby opened her eyes and made soft cooing noises before drifting back to sleep. Another perfect day with her perfect baby.

Spence entered the room and closed the door behind him. "How are my two girls?"

Natalie smiled at her handsome husband. "Wonderful."

Spence stroked Gabby's head. "I'm always surprised at how much love I feel when our babies are born."

"Me too." A warm sensation swallowed her.

"The doctor called."

"To check on Gabby?" Natalie studied the tiny features of her baby girl and grinned. She kissed her forehead.

"No."

Natalie looked at Spence. "Why then?"

"With the test results."

Immersing herself in her home, encircled by love and safety, she'd almost forgotten about the chromosome test. "Oh, what did she say?"

Spence paused. He placed his hand on hers and said, "It was positive for Trisomy 21."

A sudden shot of adrenaline burst through Natalie's chest, and she felt as if she were pinned to the chair underneath the weight of a piano. "What?" Her voice quivered.

"She definitely has Down syndrome."

Natalie's heart thudded in her ears. "No." She shook her head. "The test has to be wrong."

"I don't think it is." He traced a pattern on Gabby's cheek.

Natalie stood and handed Gabby to Spence. "But I prayed."

Spence gave her a questioning look. "We all prayed for Gabby."

"No, you don't understand." Her face heated.

Spence wrinkled his eyebrows. "What are you talking about?"

"I prayed it away." Her words hung over her, taunting her.

"What?"

Natalie's eyes stung. Her head throbbed. "I prayed that extra chromosome away. I prayed for Gabby to have a normal chromosome count."

Spence didn't say anything.

She ran her fingers through her hair. "I don't get it." She covered her face with her hands and then drew them back, lacing her fingers behind her neck. "It doesn't make sense."

"What do you mean?"

Natalie glanced at Spence. Perceiving his inability to comprehend what she was trying to explain, she kept the rest of her thoughts to herself. She didn't want to vocalize the doubts spinning out of control in her mind.

"Let's talk about this." He placed Gabby in her bassinet and stepped closer to Natalie. He reached his hand out for her.

Natalie turned away. "I'm tired. I'm not thinking right. I need a nap." She hoped he'd leave her alone.

"I'll nap with you." His face reflected his concern.

"I'd prefer to nap alone."

"But—"

"Please. Go check on the kids or something." Her icy tone surprised her, but she needed solitude to sort through her thoughts.

"I'm worried—"

"Don't be. I'm tired and need to rest. That's all. I'll be fine," she lied. She wanted Spence to leave so he didn't hover over her while she processed the test result and what it meant to Gabby and to her.

"I'll be downstairs if you need me." He kissed her on the cheek and left the room.

Natalie fell on the bed in a heap. Heavy tears slipped down her face and soaked into the comforter. Thoughts twisted around in her mind. She'd prayed for Gabby to be normal. She'd felt like Gabby was fine, yet she wasn't normal and she wasn't fine. Why didn't Heavenly Father answer the most important prayers she'd ever uttered? Why would He mislead her to feel that Gabby was fine, when she wasn't?

Through tear-filled eyes, she watched Gabby sleeping in her bed. Why would God send her a child with such a devastating condition when she had so many other kids to raise? What could be the purpose?

Maybe she'd been kidding herself all these years. Maybe it was only coincidences that *seemed* like answers to prayers. Maybe her mother had been right all along. Maybe there wasn't a.... She pushed that thought from her mind, not wanting to think it through. After all, her entire life hinged on her belief in God. If He wasn't real, the foundation of her life would crumble, leaving her with nothing.

Chapter
THIRTY-TWO

The next several days were much of the same. Gabby started to eat more but still slept most of the time while Natalie went through the robotic motions of mothering. She tried to keep up pretenses of adjusting to a new baby as normally as possible, but serious doubts gnawed at her while she fought the demons in her mind.

It was Saturday morning, the usual time the family sat together for a big breakfast prepared by Spence. Natalie numbly took her place at the table.

"How are my beautiful wife and my new gorgeous daughter?"

"Good, I guess." Natalie attempted to sound pleasant, so she wouldn't expose the tug-of-war going on in her mind.

"What's wrong, Mom?" Laura asked.

"Nothing." Natalie poured herself a glass of apple juice, avoiding eye contact with everyone.

After a breakfast of crepes smothered in strawberries, Spence grabbed Natalie by the hand and led her back up to their bedroom.

"You've not said much for the past few days. You've avoided me and the kids. I'm worried about you." His eyes clouded with distress.

She sat on the bed, different images colliding in her mind—Susannah's face with deep lines of grief etched across it, Lindsay's tiny coffin covered in flowers, and the little girl with Down syndrome she'd seen so many months ago at the restaurant. She recalled the nasty things the father had said to his daughter, things she knew people would say to Gabby. Somehow, life seemed much crueler now. It wasn't the same anymore, and the more she thought, the more it seemed that the God she'd believed in didn't actually exist—something with which her mother would agree.

"Honey?" Spence's voice broke through her mind haze.

"Yes?"

"What's going on with you? You're so . . . distant."

She nodded.

He rubbed her hand. "Please, tell me what you're thinking."

Natalie wasn't sure she could share the dark thoughts swirling around her brain. He'd be so disappointed in her if she voiced her doubts. He was so solid.

Immovable.

Steadfast.

Like a rock.

But she wasn't. She'd been knocked flat, and she didn't know if she'd be able to get up again. All she wanted to do was stay in bed, pull the covers over her head, and forget about all the pain. Where would that leave him?

"Please talk to me. I love you, and I feel like you're slipping away from me." She could feel the gentle pressure of his hand.

Silence hung over them. She didn't know what to say because she didn't want to share the words that floated through her.

He massaged her shoulders. "You can tell me anything. You know that."

How would he react to her questioning God's existence?

He turned to her, placed her face between his hands, and gazed into her eyes. "Please, talk to me."

She couldn't take his intense look, so she pulled away. After several minutes, tears welled up and fell down her cheeks.

He caressed her face, his eyes pleading with her.

She heaved out a breath. "When I prayed about her, I felt like she was fine."

Spence seemed bewildered. "Why isn't she?"

Natalie jerked her head back. "Because she has Down syndrome."

"Maybe you need to reconsider what 'fine' means."

"Well, I know it doesn't mean Down syndrome."

"Why not?" He wasn't grasping the implications of Gabby's condition.

"She's going to have life-long problems."

"We don't know that."

"We don't?" She stared at Spence, wondering why he didn't understand. "That's what the doctors say. The web pages. The experts. I've read all about it over the last few days. You should see the long list of medical problems I found on the Internet."

"All we know is that she's healthy right now, and she needs us. That makes her the same as any of our other children."

Exasperated at Spence's inability to comprehend the situation, Natalie said, "But she isn't like the other kids."

"Because she has an extra chromosome?"

"Exactly." Finally, he understood.

"What difference does that make? Especially in the eternal sense."

Natalie rubbed her temples. "I don't understand why Heavenly Father wouldn't answer my prayers about her." Unless, of course, she'd been pleading with a nonexistent being.

He reached up and touched her face. "His will isn't always the same as ours."

"It's not like I asked that she have super powers or something. I only asked that she be healthy."

"Isn't she?"

Natalie inhaled deeply and then exhaled slowly, trying to process his words. Perhaps, he was right. Or, perhaps, the whole "His will isn't the same as ours" was only a cop-out. She rested her head in her hands.

"We do need to tell the kids."

She whipped her head up. "Why? Why do they have to know?"

"You're acting as if this is some curse or something to be ashamed of," he said in a firm voice.

If she vocalized Gabby's condition, she'd not only have to deal with people's pity, she'd have to determine the answers to her questions. "I . . . I don't want to talk about it anymore. Please, leave me alone." It was useless trying to get Spence to understand.

Despite Spence's protests, Natalie insisted on her privacy.

After he left the bedroom, Natalie pulled Gabby close to her and stared at her angelic face while she slept. After several minutes passed, someone knocked at the door.

"Please, leave me alone." She couldn't explain her feelings to Spence anymore. It was a mistake to try in the first place.

The door creaked open, and Carma stood in the doorway. "Can I come in?"

Natalie's heartbeat quickened. The last person she wanted to see was her mother. She definitely didn't want her mom to know about Gabby's condition because she couldn't deal with Carma's negative reaction. In fact, she planned to keep the information from her mother for as long as possible. "Looks like you're already in."

Carma studied a sleeping Gabby. "What a doll." She cupped her hand around Gabby's head. "I brought you something."

"What?" Natalie wiped at the corners of her eyes.

Carma laid out a tiny white dress with rows of lace at the bottom. "What's this?"

"I bought it for Gabrielle. You do blessings at your church, right?"

"Yes, but you didn't—"

"Do it for any of the other kids. Yes, I know. I can't explain it, but something about Gabrielle has . . ." She reached out and brushed her fingers across Gabby's face.

Natalie stared at her mother and watched as Carma's eyes glistened. Natalie didn't know how to react to her mother's uncharacteristic show of positive emotion.

"There's something I can't explain about her, almost like she's an . . . angel." She cleared her throat. "If I believed in such things. But there's something." She leaned down toward Gabby. "I feel drawn to her. She's so peaceful. So perfect."

Before she could stop herself, Natalie blurted out, "She's not perfect. She has Down syndrome." She waited for her mother's bad reaction, the first of many she knew she'd experience.

Carma knit her brows together. "She's a mongoloid?"

Natalie tensed. "They don't use that word anymore, Mom."

Carma glanced at Gabby. "What does it mean? Is she retarded?"

"She has an extra chromosome that may interfere with some of her development. I'm not sure at this point."

"Hmmm." Carma bent down and studied Gabby, tilting her head to the right.

With her cheeks blazing, Natalie said, "I'm sorry she isn't perfect."

Her mother stood abruptly. "Natalie—"

"You don't need to give me your all-too-familiar disappointed look. She has something wrong with her. Deal with it."

Carma took a step back, her mouth falling open. In a higher-pitched tone she said, "But—"

Natalie held up her hands. "And don't lecture me about already having too many kids and being too old and that's why I gave birth to a child with a genetic abnormality. I don't want to hear it."

Carma shook her head. "I wasn't—"

"I'm tired. Can you please go away?" She didn't want to be in the same room as her mother any longer.

"Calm down, Natalie. You're not giving me a chance to say anything."

"You're right. I already know what you're thinking. I could hear it screaming in my ears the moment we found out. I've never lived up to your expectations. How could she?" She pursed her trembling lips.

"You aren't being fair." Carma's voice quivered.

"Have you been? All my life you've compared me to others. You're never satisfied with me or my life. You nitpick at everything," Natalie shouted, tears running down her face.

"That isn't true." Carma brought her shaking hands to her cheeks.

"Yes, it is." Natalie narrowed her eyes. "Now you have a grand-daughter that everyone will point fingers at, and you won't be able to take it. Your moving here was a mistake."

Carma gasped.

Natalie pointed her finger at her mother. "All you've ever done is criticize me. I won't let you do that to Gabby."

Carma wiped at her eyes. "You think I can't love Gabby because—"

"She has Down syndrome." With ice in her voice, Natalie confirmed, "Yes, I do."

Blinking several times, Carma eked out, "I had no idea you thought this of me. Maybe I *should* reconsider living near you."

Natalie said nothing.

Carma turned and left the room.

Natalie squelched the guilt that attempted to surface. She'd used her mother to unleash her pent-up feelings. Maybe it wasn't fair, but after all the years of enduring her mother's biting remarks, she found it difficult to summon up more than a pinch of remorse.

That night as they lay in bed, Spence said, "What happened with your mom today?"

"The usual. She'll never accept Gabby."

"Are you sure?"

The exchange with her mother had freed her. Not only had she expressed long-suppressed feelings about her mom, she'd also spoken with confidence about the reality of Gabby's condition. "Yes. I know my mother better than anyone else—even you. Everything and everyone has to be perfect, otherwise she can't deal with it." She rolled to her side.

"She was very upset when she left, and she hasn't been back or called."

"Good."

"You don't mean that."

"Yes, I do." She paused. "I don't want her around Gabby."

"Why not?"

She took a few moments to put her thoughts into words. "Because she'll only criticize her and remind me that it's my fault."

"Your fault?" He sounded surprised.

"If I'd had more faith, she wouldn't have Down syndrome." *Wasn't that obvious?*

"What?" He rose up behind her.

"It's true."

"No, it isn't." He pulled at her shoulder.

"Well, then the only other explanation is that there's no God." It was out and she couldn't call it back.

The hot, heavy air weighed down on her, threatening to crush her. "Take your pick. Either I didn't have enough faith or there's no God." A deep sorrow encased her.

Spence cleared his throat, but his voice was still thick. "Neither of those options is true. Gabby having Down syndrome isn't a punishment."

"Isn't it?"

"Of course not."

"She'll spend her life being mocked and ridiculed. She'll never date or marry or have children. She'll struggle in school, have health problems, and never be able to do anything with her life. I'm being realistic." The inferno behind her eyes intensified.

In a soft voice, Spence said, "Have you ever considered that Heavenly Father sent her to us as a reward?"

"A *reward*? How could a child with Down syndrome be a reward?" Spence was crazy.

"She won't have to experience the same tests as our other kids, and she'll return to the celestial kingdom."

Natalie shrugged. She tried to swallow the emotion in her throat.

"Gabby is a blessing to us."

She stared at the ceiling and in a trembling voice said, "If I had the power to take her extra chromosome away, I'd do it in a heartbeat."

"You would?"

"Yes. But, obviously, prayer doesn't work, or she'd have a normal chromosome count." The acid in her words burned as they exited her mouth.

Spence shook his head. "I don't understand why you feel this way."

"You don't need to. It is what it is."

"Natalie, there's a reason God sent Gabby to us with Down syndrome. It's all part of the plan, and she's exactly the way she's meant to be." Spence reached out to touch Natalie's face, but she turned to her side, away from him. Natalie said nothing else, forcing her eyes shut and willing herself to sleep.

The next day she stayed home with Gabby while the family attended church. She was glad that she could use the excuse to stay home and care for Gabby because, truthfully, she didn't want to see anyone. She wasn't sure she ever wanted to see anyone again. Keeping Gabby protected in her bedroom, away from prying eyes and cruel judgments, was the only thing that appealed to her.

In the back of her mind, she remembered her calling and felt a twinge of guilt at passing off her responsibilities to her counselors.

But she couldn't think about that right now. She couldn't think about anyone or anything else but Gabby and shielding her from a world of people like her mother and the man at the fast food restaurant.

She tended to Gabby's needs throughout the day but requested that neither Spence nor the kids bother her. She stayed in her room and sunk deeper into despair.

Late the next morning, Natalie awoke with a yawn. She didn't normally sleep in so late, but Gabby's eating schedule was still erratic. Thankfully, even though the kids usually hounded Natalie on summer mornings, asking to make art projects, go swimming, or play with friends, they'd left her alone. She assumed Spence, who was still taking time off work, had them busy doing chores and other tasks. As long as she didn't have to deal with them, she didn't care what kept them occupied.

She checked on Gabby in the bassinet next to her bed. "It's been over two hours, are you ready to eat again?"

Gabby's eyelids fluttered.

"Wake up, baby. I need to get you ready for your doctor's appointment this afternoon to see if we can get rid of this oxygen."

Gabby yawned and opened one eye.

"Hello, sweet girl. Mommy's here. I'm going to take care of you and protect you no matter what." Her mind flitted back to her conversation with Spence. She was sure he didn't like what she had to say, but her number one priority was Gabby, and she'd do it on her own if she needed to.

After nursing Gabby, Natalie changed her diaper and then dressed her in a lavender-print gown. She placed a matching headband on her head and put white crocheted booties on her feet. She laid her back in the baby bed, locked the bedroom door to protect her from any of the kids handling her, and walked into the bathroom to prepare herself to go to town. After her shower, she blow-dried her hair. She brushed her teeth but avoided her reflection in the mirror. When she returned to the bedroom, she noticed her scriptures on the nightstand by the bed. She stared at them for a moment before picking them up and placing them inside a drawer.

She dressed herself in unflattering but comfortable maternity clothes, and then gathered up Gabby and her light flannel receiving blanket.

❧❦❧

On the way to town, neither Spence nor Natalie said a word. The summer air was blistering, but an arctic breeze blew in the car. They arrived at the doctor's office and waited to be called back to a room. She wanted to focus on removing the oxygen, not on Down syndrome. She'd read enough on the Internet, and she didn't want to dwell on it—it was still too painful.

Dr. Sanderson checked Gabby. Her oxygen stats were normal. "I think we can remove the oxygen now. Are you aware of the early intervention program for children with Down syndrome?"

Natalie's muscles contracted. She tightened her fists.

"No," Spence said.

"The state provides a program to help kids with disabilities. You can enroll Gabrielle, and she will have access to physical therapy, occupational therapy, and speech therapy."

"Do we have to?" Natalie said in a controlled voice.

"No. But it might be a good idea to give her the best available help."

"We'll look into it," Spence said.

Natalie picked at her thumbnail, anxious to leave the office.

"She looks good. I don't have any concerns," Dr. Sanderson said.

Natalie and Spence left the office without saying a word to each other. Spence unlocked the doors and started the engine while Natalie buckled Gabby into her car seat. She entered the car and put her own seat belt in place. She stared out the windshield, the air conditioner blowing on her full blast, and waited for Spence to put the car in gear.

"You haven't said anything all morning," Spence said.

"Nothing to say. I need to care for Gabby the best way I can." She didn't make eye contact.

"You're not alone, you know."

Natalie nodded, but the words didn't sink in.

"Can you look at me?"

Knowing he wouldn't move the car until she complied with his request, Natalie turned and gazed at her husband without seeing him.

"I know this isn't what we expected, but everything will be okay."

Natalie gave a slight nod, hoping he'd accept it, and they could be on their way without further discussion.

He waited for a few moments and then pulled out of the parking lot. After running a few errands and then stopping at the grocery store to pick up some food and more diapers and wipes, they drove home in silence.

It was all too painful—her baby with a birth defect and her failed attempt to put faith in something she wasn't sure she believed anymore. Perhaps if Natalie died, she wouldn't have to face such an agonizing future of watching Gabby struggle to live a life that would only be fraught with heartache, a life that would never be what Natalie had envisioned for her baby. *If I died, it would be so much easier.*

But where would that leave her helpless daughter?

Chapter THIRTY-THREE

When they arrived home, Natalie noticed a black truck in the driveway. She tensed up, assuming she'd see Tristan when she walked into the house. She didn't want to deal with him, and she considered going in through another door but decided to take Gabby through the front door and ignore his presence.

Inside, she found Susannah waiting in the kitchen.

"Sister Drake?"

Natalie gave a tight smile as she set Gabby and her car seat on the floor by the island. Spence excused himself to check on the animals. Natalie mentally rolled her eyes as she waited for Susannah to speak. She didn't want to play the part of Relief Society president and help Susannah solve her problems when her own life was careening out of control.

Susannah pointed to the counter. "Your daughter Andrea said she was babysitting but that it'd be okay for me to wait for you. I brought you some dinner. It's my first time, so I hope it isn't too disgusting. It's spaghetti and rolls. I wanted to bring it and say good-bye."

"Good-bye?" Not what Natalie expected to hear.

Susannah licked her lips. "I'm taking Jack, and we're going to live with my mom for a while. Sean needs some time to think through things. I need some time too." She bent down and reached out to touch Gabby's hand. "You're lucky."

Lucky? Natalie felt anything but lucky.

"I wish I could've brought my baby home from the hospital a second time," Susannah said, her voice shaking. She stood and faced Natalie.

Natalie studied her. Grief radiated through Natalie—grief for the too-short life Lindsay had, grief for the empty life Susannah now had, and grief for the normal life Gabby would never have.

"When they told me Lindsay would have brain damage, I didn't care." Susannah glanced out the window with a faraway look in her eyes. "I just wanted her to be alive. I was willing to do whatever it took to care for her, even if that meant for the rest of my life." She turned to gaze at Natalie, tears sliding down her face. "I guess that wasn't part of the plan."

Natalie searched her mind for something to say to comfort Susannah, but nothing came. How could she offer comfort to someone else when she couldn't even comfort herself?

Susannah attempted to smile through her tears. "I still have faith, though, that I'll see her again. That's the only thing that gets me through the dark nights." She wiped at her quivering lips.

Natalie felt helpless. She had nothing to offer Susannah.

Susannah cleared her throat and brushed the moisture from her cheeks. "Anyway, thank you for all of your help and your soothing words. I kept thinking about what you told me, that I needed to turn to God. You were right." Susannah shrugged. "Somehow, it'll all work out. I know that now."

"Thank you for the dinner." Natalie studied Susannah and wished she could have the same faith she'd once had when she counseled Susannah.

"Your baby is beautiful. I wish . . ." She reached over and gave Natalie a hug.

Natalie returned the hug. "Good luck, Susannah."

Susannah smiled slightly and then left.

Natalie watched her drive away while she considered Susannah's words. Susannah had managed to retain her faith despite losing her baby. Natalie noted the irony.

"Mom?" Andrea interrupted Natalie's thoughts.

"Yes?"

"How's Gabrielle?" She stepped over to Natalie, but Natalie moved in the opposite direction.

"Seems to be doing okay," Natalie said in a monotone voice.

"Good."

Natalie gave a curt nod and ascended the stairs with Gabby in her arms. She sat in the chair in her bedroom and nursed Gabby. Natalie was grateful, at least, that she could breastfeed Gabby, since all the medical professionals had insisted she wouldn't be able to do so. Maybe they didn't know everything. Maybe Gabby's future wouldn't be so bleak. Maybe . . . she pushed the positive thoughts from her mind and chided herself for even allowing them in.

"I want to be the best mother I can to you, but I'm not sure how to do that." She kissed her baby on the forehead and placed her in the bassinet.

"Mom?" Andrea said through the door.

Natalie steeled herself. "Come in."

Andrea tentatively entered the room. "Can we talk?"

"Sure." The last thing she wanted was a conversation with Andrea, but she didn't want a big scene—that'd take too much energy.

Natalie rubbed the center of her forehead, waiting for Andrea to say something.

"I know you aren't happy about Tristan."

Natalie didn't respond.

"I didn't mean to fall in love with him. It just happened." She used her hands to punctuate her last sentence.

Natalie nodded but still said nothing. While she'd heard the words, they failed to arouse any emotion.

"I know you told me this might happen. But I love him, and I want to marry him."

Natalie closed her eyes for a few moments. She opened her eyes and stared out across the room. "I'm tired, Andrea. I need to get some rest. We can talk about this later."

"But I—"

"Please, let me rest."

Andrea stood. Natalie didn't want to look at her, so she kept her gaze on the wall across the room. She couldn't deal with Andrea at the moment, especially since she didn't know what to tell her.

After Andrea left, Natalie pulled her knees to her chest and wrapped her arms around her legs. A month ago, she'd had no idea what lay in wait. She expected a normal baby and birth experience followed by a close bonding time with the family. Instead, she had a baby that wasn't fine, distanced herself from Spence, treated her mother terribly, and cut herself off from the kids. Now she wondered if everything she'd ever believed in was real.

What if God doesn't exist? Her whole life would be a lie. All she'd taught her kids, all she'd done over the years, and all she'd hoped for was for nothing.

She was torn. She had this strong love for and bond to Gabby, yet she couldn't face the future with a child that no one else would love. Worse, she couldn't deal with the idea that God didn't exist. The threads of her life that had once been tightly woven together were now unraveling, and she was powerless to stop them.

Images of her life marched across her mind. Things she'd never questioned before popped out at her, demanding answers. But she had none. Perhaps her mother had been right all of these years. Perhaps she'd been brainwashed into believing in a God that didn't actually exist. Perhaps she wasn't who she thought she was.

She lay down on the bed and closed her eyes, trying to sort through her feelings.

The door opened, awaking Natalie. She noticed it was dusk. Spence whispered, "Natalie? Are you awake?" She didn't want to face him, so she kept silent. He closed the door and stepped over to the bed. He sat next to her and, with his usual kindness, said, "No matter what, I love you and I'm here." She didn't respond because she didn't know what to say.

After several moments, Spence stood and walked out of the room. Sadness and shame settled on her shoulders. Spence didn't deserve this treatment. He deserved the wife he married—strong, dedicated, faithful, and steady.

For the rest of the night, she tossed and turned, in and out of sleep.

When the sun peeked through the window the next day, she sat up in bed, hopeful a new day would bring her some peace. She rolled over to gaze at Gabby. She picked her up and rested her cheek against Gabby's, noticing that Gabby felt warm.

"Did you get hot last night?" She unwrapped the blanket that swaddled Gabby and rocked her for a few minutes, hoping it was only her imagination.

She placed her hand on Gabby's forehead.

A fever.

Stress raced up Natalie's spine while she carried Gabby downstairs to find Spence.

She spotted him sleeping on the couch. She tugged on his arm. "Spence?"

Spence's eyelids fluttered open. In a scratchy voice, he said, "How are you today?"

"Gabby feels hot. What do you think?" She hoped he'd disagree.

He placed his hand on her forehead. "You're right. I'll get a thermometer and see what it says."

Spence returned and measured Gabby's temperature. "It says 102 degrees."

Memories of Susannah's baby shot to the front of Natalie's mind. Suddenly, she couldn't breathe as panic squeezed her lungs.

"Let's take her to the ER," Spence said, sensing Natalie's anxiety.

After they dressed and woke Andrea to babysit the other kids, they drove the twenty minutes or so to the hospital. They parked the car and hurried to the emergency room doors.

"I hope it's nothing. I hope we can take her right back home. I hope . . ." Natalie didn't want to vocalize her fear that Gabby had contracted meningitis like Lindsay.

Memories of the NICU plagued Natalie as they walked through the doors and waited to speak to someone.

"What seems to be the problem?" a nurse with spiked blonde hair asked.

"My baby has a high fever." Fear affected Natalie's voice.

"How old is the baby?"

"Ten days." *The same age as Susannah's baby.*

The nurse wrinkled her eyebrows as concern flashed in her eyes. "Let's bring her back," the nurse said with urgency. Natalie's stomach cramped, and her neck felt clammy.

The nurse took Gabby's temperature. "Looks like it's 102.3." She left for a moment and then returned with a dropper. "We'll give her some Motrin to help combat the fever. I need you to bring her to another room."

Spence and Natalie followed the nurse to a stark room with one bed.

"Could it be a cold?" Spence asked.

"A newborn with a fever needs immediate attention. A doctor will be here soon." Her suntanned face communicated her concern.

After the nurse left, Natalie gazed at Spence, unable to vocalize her fear that Gabby's life might be in jeopardy. Yes, she wanted Gabby to have a normal chromosome count, but if the other alternative was . . . well, she didn't want to lose her baby, no matter what challenges lay ahead.

The nurse returned to the room. "I need to give her an IV."

"Not again," Natalie said under her breath.

The nurse searched for a vein. Numbness enveloped Natalie. It was the NICU all over again. She clutched her head in her hands as the nurse examined Gabby's tiny arm.

Gabby squirmed and then yelped in pain when the nurse inserted the needle. She secured the IV with some tape and a small splint. Shortly afterwards, a young doctor with curly brown hair entered the room.

"Hello, I'm Dr. Johnson."

Spence and Natalie gave him a short welcome. He looked over the paperwork and then said, "I'll need your permission for a spinal tap."

"Why?" Natalie asked, not wanting to hear the answer.

"We need to rule out spinal meningitis as soon as possible because it can be devastating if we don't catch it. In fact, if not treated, it can be fatal." Natalie knew that all too well.

"What's involved?" Spence asked.

"I'll need to insert a needle into your baby's spine and extract fluid to analyze it. Cloudy fluid indicates an infection and will need to be treated. The important thing is to get it treated as soon as possible. We'll start with antibiotics, just in case."

The doctor left the room, and it seemed to shrink around Natalie. Her lips quivered as she tried to control her emotions. Labored breaths pushed through her lips as panic set in. *Was this how it happened with Lindsay?*

Natalie shook her head. She couldn't lose Gabby. She wanted to raise her, Down syndrome and all.

A few moments later, the doctor returned. "I'll need to ask you to leave while I perform the spinal tap."

Out in the waiting room, Natalie paced the floor. She didn't know what to think, and she couldn't bear the idea of burying her baby. All she wanted was for Gabby to be alive. Nothing else mattered.

Spence approached her. "Let's say a prayer."

Natalie agreed to avoid an argument or, worse, Spence delving into her psyche. She hadn't prayed since they'd learned about the test results because, obviously, she wasn't capable of receiving answers to her prayers, for whatever reason.

They found a quiet spot down the hall, and Spence offered the prayer. Natalie felt nothing. No warmth of reassurance. No comfort. No peace. Nothing. Spence studied her. He knew her so well she wondered if he could read her mind. His glistening eyes softened her heart.

After a few minutes, she said, "I feel like I'm drowning, like I've fallen down this deep, dark hole, and I can't find my way out of it." She licked her lips. "I don't even know what I believe anymore."

With a determined look, Spence said, "You can't turn away from God."

"How do I know He's even there? All the prayers I said when she was in the NICU and still, no answers." She searched Spence's eyes for understanding.

"Because He didn't answer the way *you* wanted Him to?"

Feeling like a deflated balloon, she said, "I don't know." The salty taste of her tears edged into her mouth.

Spence reached out to touch her face, but she pulled away and said, "We need to find out the results from the spinal tap."

They walked down the hall and caught sight of the ER doctor. He noticed them and came toward them with a somber expression. "I tried to extract some fluid, but I wasn't successful. It's difficult with a newborn." He glanced between them. "I'm sorry."

"What does that mean?" Spence asked, worry lacing his words.

"We'll keep treating her with antibiotics and if she does test positive for meningitis, she'll have a head start on treatment. We'll start the paperwork to admit her to the hospital. I've left a message for the on-call pediatrician to see if he can come in and do the spinal tap."

"Are they going to send her to UNM?" Natalie asked.

"That depends," the doctor said.

After he left, Natalie fell into the chair. "I can't do this again. What if it's only the beginning, or worse . . . what if it's the end? I don't think I can take it."

Spence knelt down beside her, grasping her hands in his.

"I feel broken." She tried to swallow back the fear. "I don't know where to turn."

"Yes, you do."

She rubbed her eyes. "Your faith is so strong. Mine isn't. It took a beating and didn't survive."

"That's not true." He cupped her chin in his hand. "You still have faith. Use it. Pray for Gabby," he pleaded with her.

"I can't." All of her doubts surfaced. Doubts about her faith, about Gabby, about God.

"You have to get control, Nat. You're letting Satan—"

"No, I'm not." Maybe she wasn't sure about God, but she wasn't entertaining Satan. Of *that* she was certain.

In a harsh voice that took Natalie by surprise, Spence said, "That's exactly what's happening. You're allowing Satan to make you feel afraid and make you feel discouraged. He wants to destroy all we've worked to build, and you're letting him. You know God is real. You've seen too many things to deny it. Stop with the pity party."

Natalie covered her face.

In a commanding voice, he said, "I've let you deal with this in your own way. But enough is enough. Put everything out of your mind but Gabby. She needs you to have faith. She needs her mother to pray for her. Right here. Right now."

Chapter
THIRTY-FOUR

Natalie stood and walked over to the bed. She stroked Gabby's head. "Mommy's here, and she loves you." She stared at her newborn, replaying Spence's words. They'd sliced at her heart, but she couldn't deny them.

Another doctor entered the room. He introduced himself as the on-call pediatrician and asked if he could attempt another spinal tap.

Spence gave him permission, and the doctor said he'd return in a bit.

Several minutes passed while Spence and Natalie waited for the pediatrician to come back. A suffocating silence filled the room. Natalie's heart thumped inside her, sending vibrations throughout her body. Unable to endure it any longer, Natalie walked out of the room and down the hallway to an exit. A wall of hot air hit her as soon as she stepped outside. She sat on the grass under a tree and laid her head on her knees.

Memories of the last twenty years filtered into her consciousness. Visions of faith-promoting experiences took center stage, including the blessing that promised her she'd be a mother. She recalled the tingling sensation when she had found out she was pregnant with Andrea in fulfillment of that blessing. Other memories floated in—times when she'd had no doubt that God not only existed, but He answered prayers; times when she'd seen evidence of His hand in her life; times when she'd felt clothed in the Spirit.

Though she'd tried to deny His existence, too many experiences indicated otherwise. And yet Gabby still had an extra chromosome— something she also couldn't deny.

She felt as though a small figure of her mother stood on her left shoulder shouting at her to use her brain and admit He wasn't real, to give in to her feelings of doubt and ditch the shackles of faith and God.

On her right shoulder stood Spence, asking her to search her soul, to recount the many blessings she'd received, to reach out to God and let Him heal her wounds.

She drew in a deep breath and realized it all hinged on one question. Did God exist? If He didn't, then all of this happened by chance, and there was no sense in anything. If He did exist, then somehow there was a plan orchestrated by Him.

A few more minutes passed while she contemplated the question and searched for an answer. Words she'd said to Susannah resurfaced in her mind. She'd urged Susannah to turn to the Savior, to let Him carry her burden. Could Natalie also put her worries, her fears, at the feet of the Savior and use the Atonement to mend her broken faith and find herself again?

After pondering on the Atonement for several minutes, she decided to check on Gabby and see when the pediatrician would do the next spinal tap. She stood and walked back through the ER doors and into Gabby's room. She found Spence holding Gabby's small hand and, in a soft voice, singing the third verse of "Teach Me to Walk" to her.

When Spence noticed Natalie, he finished the verse and then said with resolution in his eyes, "Before the doctor comes back, we need to say a prayer. Will you say it?"

Natalie considered his request. She'd never felt so defeated, so low.

She gazed at her small, precious baby lying in the bed, helpless and dependent on her to be a mother. Gabby needed her to make a decision—to either give in to her demons or quiet them forever. Could she summon enough courage to voice another prayer in Gabby's behalf? And could she then exhibit faith in His power?

She called on all the courage she had to nod her head. Her heartbeat hammered in her ears. She tried to control the tremors in her hands and the involuntary fluttering of her eyelids while she began to pray. It was rough at first, but the words came, one at a time, to her mind and then tumbled out of her lips.

She prayed, asking that Gabby would be healed and not suffer any ill effects from this fever. Without warning, darkness seized her. She said nothing for a moment, trying to grope around in the blackness, until a brilliant, dazzling light flooded her mind. She struggled to make sense of it when a vision unfolded before her. She could see the image of a child, a girl, with blonde hair and round, blue eyes—the same image she'd seen twenty years earlier. She could see the face with such clarity, it took her breath away—she was looking at . . . Gabby.

Gabby was the baby she'd seen. The one meant for her family. The one who'd been waiting all these years, and, finally, it was her turn, but Natalie had been too blind to see it. She was too consumed with fear and pride. Too caught up in trying to make sense of the situation. Too intent on focusing on Gabby's extra chromosome to notice. It was all part of the plan, organized by Heavenly Father.

Gabby's birth was no accident. Her chromosome count wasn't by chance. Not only was Gabby meant for her family, but she was sent purposely with an extra chromosome.

It was so clear. The plan. God's hand in her life once again. A little girl. Her eternal family. And Satan's attempt to derail all of it.

Spence reached over and squeezed her arm. Gratitude surrounded her. After a few minutes, she concluded the prayer, asking Heavenly Father to bless the doctor to extract enough fluid and, if possible, to bless Gabby that she wouldn't have meningitis. She opened her eyes to see Spence's tear-streaked cheeks.

He cleared his throat and tried to speak but couldn't.

"It's going to be okay." She leaned over and flung her arms around his neck. "Gabby's the one."

"I know."

She sat back to gaze into his eyes. "You know?"

"Yes."

"When?"

"Right after she was born."

Natalie studied him. "Why didn't you say anything?"

He gently placed her hand in his. In a quiet voice, he said, "Gabby is the baby I saw, the baby meant for our family." He paused. "You needed your own witness."

"But I was too upset." She laid her hand across her chest. "I wasn't ready."

Spence nodded.

"Is that why you were so calm?"

"Knowing that she was the baby I saw so many years ago helped me see that this is all part of the plan." Spence rested his hand on her shoulder.

"The second my faith was tested, I caved in to doubt and discouragement. I thought I was so strong." She looked down at her hands. "I thought that through all these years of standing firm, with my mother consistently trying to chip away at my faith, nothing could shake it. I found out . . ."

Spence cupped her chin in his hand and gently tugged it upward. "You're human?"

Natalie shook her head, guilt settling on her. "I shouldn't have doubted. You were right. It was Satan trying to tempt me and destroy everything I've worked so hard to build." Anger and disappointment that she'd been so foolish, that she'd given in to Satan's temptations, rolled around inside her. "It all seems so obvious now, but it wasn't before." She paused for a few moments, contemplating her realization. "Like I was blind, but now I can see." She stood and took Gabby's hand in hers, light and peace replacing the dark and turbulent feelings.

Spence also gazed at Gabby. He caressed Natalie's arm. "You were dealing with some very strong emotions."

For the first time since Gabby's birth, Natalie acknowledged a truth she'd known for so long—Satan had no more power over her than she allowed him to have; it was within her control to deny Satan and his influence. She'd let Satan's loud ranting drown out the quiet whisperings of the Spirit. She'd lost sight of what she knew to be true for only a moment, and that's all Satan needed—a moment.

She felt Spence's hand on her shoulder. She turned to him, unable to stop the tears that flowed down her cheeks. "I thought I was invincible." She wiped her face. "But I'm not. I have to fight to keep my faith strong. If I don't, Satan will sneak in and attack." She shook her head. "I won't be so oblivious in the future."

Spence pulled her into an embrace.

She laid her head on his shoulder and realized that Heavenly

Father had always been there. He hadn't deserted her; she'd deserted Him. In her greatest hour of need, He'd given her what she needed most—a reminder. She needed to bend her will to His, not the other way around. His ways weren't *her* ways, but His ways lead to eternity.

Gabby was a gift, a blessing, a reward. Humility enveloped her. Out of all the mothers in mortality, He'd chosen her to be Gabby's. He'd chosen *her*.

Natalie closed her eyes and reveled in the calm she now felt. She opened her eyes and watched Gabby making some newborn faces. A brief smile crossed Gabby's lips.

"She knows we love her," Spence said.

Natalie nodded, overpowered with love for her daughter. "I don't care that Gabby has Down syndrome. I honestly don't. I only want her to get better, so we can take her home, raise her, and enjoy life with her."

The door opened as the doctor returned to take the sample of Gabby's spinal fluid. Taking a look at the baby, he said, "If we can get enough fluid, we can determine if she has meningitis and go from there."

"We understand," Spence said.

Once again, Spence and Natalie left the room and found two seats in the waiting room. Natalie rested her head against Spence.

While they waited, Natalie silently prayed, trying to express the gratitude she felt for so many blessings. She also prayed that the doctor would be able to extract enough fluid and, if it was God's will, that Gabby might be spared from meningitis.

Natalie looked up to see the doctor approaching them with a smile spread across his face. "Not only could I fill one tube, but three. This is more than enough fluid. We'll get it tested right away."

Natalie recognized the tender reassurance that draped around her.

After a long night in the hospital, Natalie gazed through bleary eyes at the early morning light seeping through the window. She sat up in the hospital bed she used, casting her glance over at Gabby in the hospital bassinet. Gabby's eyes were closed, and Natalie couldn't help but notice the sweet aura surrounding her baby girl.

Spence still slept, restlessly, on the makeshift cot along the wall. Natalie yawned and stretched her arms. She reached back to massage the kink in her neck and heard Spence stirring.

"How'd you sleep?" he asked in a scratchy voice.

"Here and there. You?"

"Looking forward to going home and sleeping in our own bed." Spence rubbed his eyes.

"I hope we'll hear something soon." Natalie stood and walked over to Gabby, admiring her.

Several minutes passed, and then the door opened. The doctor strode in with a pleasant expression and said, "Your daughter does not have meningitis. She still has some sort of infection, but it's not meningitis. We're still conducting tests and may know later today or early tomorrow." His voice was upbeat, and the relief in the room was palpable.

"Thank you, doctor." Spence shook his hand.

After the doctor left, Natalie let out the breath she was holding. The doctor was able to retrieve enough fluid—a direct answer to her prayer. Gabby did not have meningitis. Another direct answer to her prayer. God did hear her.

They spent the remainder of the day in Gabby's room, talking, taking turns holding Gabby, keeping the other kids informed, and waiting for the test results so they'd know what had caused the fever.

A buoyant feeling of gratitude accompanied Natalie throughout the day.

The next day, Spence left the hospital to buy some food for Natalie. She sat in a chair next to the bed, holding Gabby and watching her breathe, mesmerized by the miracle she held in her arms.

About fifteen minutes after he left, a soft knock sounded at the door. It opened, and Carma poked her head inside.

"Hi, Mom," Natalie said.

Carma cautiously entered the room. "How's Gabrielle?"

Natalie smiled. "She doesn't have meningitis, but she has some sort of infection. We're hoping to find out today or tomorrow."

Carma gave a short nod. "Spencer called. I wanted to come by earlier, but I wasn't sure if I . . . I—I'm glad she's doing well." Carma turned to exit the room.

"Mom, wait."

Carma stopped. She kept her head bowed.

"I'm sorry about what I said to you. I was upset, and I lashed out at you." Natalie paused. "It wasn't fair."

"You must have some strong feelings," Carma said without looking up.

Natalie shifted her weight in the chair. "You're right. I guess I do."

Carma glanced at her.

"I feel like no matter what I do, it's never good enough. That somehow, I always fail your expectations." Feelings of inadequacy weighed down on her. "When we found out that Gabby has Down syndrome, I was sure you wouldn't accept her. Or love her." She stroked Gabby's hair.

Her mother pursed her lips for a moment. "Perhaps I've been too rigid, too harsh at times. Maybe I do expect too much." She stepped closer to Natalie. "I only want what's best for you."

Natalie nodded. "I know you do."

Carma reached out and played with Gabby's small hand.

"Mom."

"Yes?"

"I do have what's best for me," Natalie said with conviction.

Carma attempted to speak but had to first clear her throat. "I see that now."

"Really?"

"I can't say that I agree with Mormonism or that I want to live that way, but I can see how it's affected your life in a positive way. The time I spent with the kids allowed me to see it in a different way. You have a wonderful family." She smiled. "What more could I ask for?"

Natalie reached her free arm up for her mother, and they embraced, evoking a closeness Natalie hadn't felt for many years.

After several moments, they pulled away, both with wet eyes.

"Gabby's a lucky girl to be loved so much," Carma said. She dabbed at her eyes.

"I don't know what the future holds for her. But she's part of our family, and we'll work it all out."

"What about Andrea?"

The question caught Natalie off guard. She raised her eyebrows and said, "I don't want her to marry Tristan outside of the temple, but she has to make that choice. I won't stop praying that someday they'll make it to the temple."

"It's that important?"

"Yes." She held her mother's gaze while she said, "I want my family to be eternal. That's what I've always wanted."

Carma smiled. "Then I hope you get it."

Natalie reached up to hug her mother again. Though Carma might not have realized what she'd said, it gave Natalie hope, for the first time, that maybe she'd have more than her children as her eternal family.

Spence walked in the door with a look of surprise on his face.

Carma turned to Spence. "Everything seems to be working out."

Chapter

THIRTY-FIVE

The next afternoon, they left the hospital, able to administer antibiotics by mouth to treat the urinary tract infection Gabby had somehow contracted. After ten days of antibiotics, the doctor expected Gabby to recover and have no ill effects.

Relief washed over Natalie, and though she couldn't predict the future, she hoped this would be the last hospital visit for a long time.

"Things seem to be going well with your mom," Spence said.

"Yeah. Funny how things turn out." She shrugged. "Who'd have thought that Gabby would have such a positive effect on our relationship?" She turned to face Spence. "Thank you for not giving up on me."

"Never." He caressed her shoulder.

"Before Gabby was born, I thought I could pray anything away because my prayers were always answered exactly as I wanted them. I prayed for what I wanted and, boom, that's what happened. I'd never experienced not getting the answer I wanted." She looked over her shoulder at her sleeping baby, admiring her adorable face. "Guess I got a big lesson with Gabby. Probably the first of many."

"I think we'll see a lot of blessings come from having Gabby in our family," Spence said with assurance.

"Knowing that she's the one I saw and that she's been waiting all these years sheds a different light on everything." Natalie's heart felt so full of joy and appreciation she wondered if it might explode.

Spence nodded.

She gazed at Spence, trying to articulate her intense feelings. "Gabby's exactly the way she's meant to be. For whatever reasons, Heavenly Father sent her to us with Down syndrome. I don't need to change that; I need to embrace it and see it as He does."

Again, Spence nodded.

"I do worry about how other people will treat her, especially other kids; how she'll do in school; if she'll ever be able to get married. Whether I'll haul off and slug someone who's mean to her . . ."

Spence gave her a look.

"I'm kidding . . . I think." Natalie laughed.

"As long as she knows how much we love her and she knows that God loves her, she'll do okay."

"You're right. Heavenly Father will bless her. And, somehow, He'll bless me to learn how to help her with whatever she needs," she said with confidence.

"He will."

"I know that now." A tingle edged up her back. "Besides, I'll probably learn more from her than she'll ever learn from me." She looked back over her shoulder at Gabby. "I think she's beautiful."

"I do too."

Natalie watched the desert scenery pass by her window. A few mobile homes dotted the landscape. The light blue sky spanned the horizon while the sun's summer rays shone down on the sandy-colored earth on either side of the highway. "When all is said and done, eternity is what matters, not your chromosome count."

Spence smiled.

"And while we're on the subject of eternity, I guess we'll have to do the same thing for Andrea—make sure she knows we love her and that God loves her."

"Exactly."

"I'm sure that's no guarantee that she'll go to the temple. But I still have my secret weapon."

Spence's forehead wrinkled.

"No, I don't think I can pray away her decision. But I think that through prayer I'll know how to handle it better and, maybe, someday, things will change, and we'll be able to attend the temple with her." She laced her fingers together. "I know that yelling at her about it or getting mad won't solve anything." Peace encircled her.

Spence glanced at her. "She knows what's right, and I think she'll come back to it."

"I hope so. I want to be able to stand in the celestial room with all of our kids. Andrea. Gabby. All of us." She envisioned her family together in the temple and a shiver rushed up the nape of her neck.

They drove down their long driveway. The anticipation of seeing her family was almost too much.

The kids all stood in the front yard. Mariah jumped up and down, clapping her hands and shouting. Bradley spun around in circles, arms outstretched like an airplane, a wide grin across his face.

As soon as they stopped the car and got out, the kids rushed to them.

"Is Gabby okay?" Laura asked.

"Can we play with her now?" Mariah said.

"My mommy!" Bradley screeched. He ran to Natalie and wrapped himself around her leg.

Justin hugged her, and Ryan hugged them both.

Spence retrieved Gabby and her car seat from the back of the van and, as a group, they moved into the house.

Carma served some sandwiches and chips while Andrea and Tristan stood apart from everyone.

Natalie scooped Gabby into her arms and caught a whiff of a soiled diaper. She looked over at Andrea and said, "Could you help me change Gabby's diaper?"

Once upstairs, Natalie began the task of cleaning Gabby while she spoke to Andrea. "I want you to know something."

"What?" Andrea said.

"Our family is the most important thing to me." The emotion rose up in her throat.

"I know."

She turned and faced her first child, hoping to convey her strong feelings without upsetting Andrea. She said a quick, silent prayer. "I want you for eternity. I know you want to marry Tristan, and he seems like a good person, but you won't be part of my eternal family and . . . that makes me sad."

Andrea hung her head low.

"I love you, Andrea. You mean everything to me, and even though I don't want you to marry outside the temple, I will never stop loving you."

Andrea looked at her mom with glistening eyes. "I was afraid you didn't love me anymore."

Natalie pulled Andrea close, not knowing where the road would take them, but certain she wouldn't travel it without prayer or without faith.

EPILOGUE

Natalie opened the front door, and Carma eased into the house. "I have a birthday present for my little angel. I can't believe she's a year old already." She removed her sunglasses and walked toward the kitchen.

"She's in the dining room ready for cake and ice cream." Natalie followed her mother.

The family gathered around the table. They sang, "Happy Birthday" as Gabby watched with her big, sapphire-blue eyes. She grinned and clapped her hands after it was over. Natalie handed her a piece of chocolate cake, and Gabby plunged her fingers into it. She squealed while she attempted to eat it.

"*In* your mouth, Gabby—not on it," Mariah said, shaking her finger.

Laura wiped cake from Gabby's mouth, but Gabby smashed more cake on her face. She turned and threw some cake on the floor. She giggled and clapped her cake-covered hands again.

"Isn't she adorable?" Carma said, pride evident in her smile.

Natalie nodded. "I was so worried about how she'd do, what medical problems she might have, and how I'd take care of her. I thought she'd be a blob in the corner watching life pass her by or, worse, that she'd spend most of the time in the hospital."

"You haven't even been back to the hospital since she had that infection right after she was born. And she's far from a blob. Look at her playing peek-a-boo with Justin."

"Not a blob at all. She interacts with the kids all the time, and now that she's learned how to roll everywhere, I can't keep up with her. She's so much more like my other kids than not." Natalie watched Gabby squeeze cake through her chubby fingers. "Knowing what I know now, I wouldn't have spent even a second worrying about it."

"She's getting so big." Carma waved at Gabby.

Natalie nodded. "She's growing and learning. She's happy. She knows we love her. What else could I want for her?"

The front door opened, and Andrea and Tristan walked in.

"How are the newlyweds?" Carma asked.

Andrea shook her head. "Grandma, you say that every time you see us. We've been married for three months now." Andrea's face radiated the love she felt for Tristan.

"I know, but I like how it sounds." Carma shrugged.

Natalie gave Andrea a hug. Then she turned to Tristan and embraced him. "Welcome to Gabby's party. Let's get you some cake."

After dishing up the cake, Natalie stood back, admiring her family. Spence reached over and grabbed her around the waist, turning her to face him. He planted a kiss on her lips.

"They're at it again. So disgusting," Laura said, gagging.

"You love it," Natalie said.

A piece of cake flew through the air and landed on Carma's head. Natalie gasped.

Carma turned to Bradley, "Did you do that?"

He nodded, bits of chocolate cake between his teeth.

Carma snatched a piece of cake and dumped it on Bradley's head. "How do you like it?" Everyone erupted in laughter, including Carma.

Natalie watched her family with contentment. Maybe things weren't as she'd originally envisioned, but she'd learned over the last year to fully trust in God and in His plan. She'd been able to use that knowledge to better serve in her calling, deal with Andrea's civil marriage, forgive her mother, and embrace Gabby, extra chromosome and all.

Most important, she'd learned that every child is a gift, even if the wrapping is a little different.

Author's
NOTE

Trisomy 21, more commonly known as Down syndrome (named after Dr. John Langdon Down), occurs at fertilization when extra genetic material is present on the twenty-first chromosome resulting in forty-seven chromosomes instead of the normal forty-six chromosomes.

Currently, more than 400,000 Americans of all races and economic levels have been diagnosed with Down syndrome. One in every 733 live births each year in the United States is diagnosed with Trisomy 21. Of all pregnancies diagnosed, 90 percent of those pregnancies are terminated.

Those diagnosed with Down syndrome experience developmental and cognitive delays. There is no cure, but with intervention and loving support, people with Trisomy 21 live quality lives and make valuable contributions to society. Today, with proper medical care, the life span of an individual with Down syndrome has increased to an average of sixty years.

When my son was diagnosed, a few days after his birth, I had no idea what it meant. Though I'd seen people with Down syndrome, I didn't understand it. I was sure my son would never do much and that he would watch life pass him by without participating in it. I've since learned that I was wrong. He interacts with people, plays, laughs, runs, learns, grows, communicates, has likes and dislikes, and gets mad when he doesn't get his way very much like the rest of my children. He is more like my other children than not.

Yes, it takes him longer to do things and he may have more challenges in the future, but doesn't everyone have challenges? In the eternal scheme of things, his challenges will never keep him out of the celestial kingdom while mine will. So, who is truly handicapped?

My son doesn't want people to cure him; he wants them to accept and love him for who he is. It's not a mistake that he came to my family with an extra chromosome. I've learned that I do not need to change him, I need to change me.

It's my hope that we will one day have a world where people will see those with Down syndrome as individuals with talents and dreams, not as chromosome counts.

Rebecca Talley

www.theupsideofdown2.blogspot.com
www.downsyndromeassociation.org

For more information on Down syndrome:
www.ndss.org
www.nads.org
www.ndsccenter.org

Discussion QUESTIONS

1. Does keeping the commandments mean we'll be spared trials?

2. As parents, what can we do when a child decides to stray from our teachings?

3. How can we best teach those who don't understand, or are antagonistic toward, our beliefs?

4. Why was it important for Natalie to see her baby in vision again?

5. How do we exercise our faith in raising our families?

6. Are children born with special needs by accident?

7. Are children with special needs entitled to the same education and treatment as those without special needs?

8. Why do we feel uncomfortable around people who are different?

9. How can we show compassion to those who look or act differently?

10. How can having a child with special needs be a blessing?

ABOUT THE AUTHOR

Rebecca was born and raised in Santa Barbara, California. She spent countless hours swimming in the ocean, collecting shells, and building sand castles.

She graduated from BYU with a bachelor of arts degree in communications. While attending BYU, she met and married her sweetheart, Del. Rebecca now lives in rural Colorado with a spoiled horse, a dog, cats, goats, and a donkey named Starla. She and Del are the proud parents of ten creative and multi-talented children. She is the author of *Heaven Scent* and *Altared Plans*.

Besides writing, Rebecca also enjoys dating her husband, playing with her kids, and dancing to disco music while she cleans the house. She's consumed at least 3,541 pounds of chocolate and even more ice cream.

Visit www.rebeccatalley.com, www.rebeccatalleywrites.blogspot.com, and www.theupsideofdown2.blogspot.com for more information. Rebecca loves to hear from readers at Rebecca@rebeccatalley.com.